PRAISE
BISCUIT BOWL FO

"Here's a recipe for succes
sleuth, determined to achie
objections, and add the complications of murder and kid
ping. Then stir in a large dose of family drama, a dishy
lawyer, a difficult would-be-fiancé, and lots of humor. Season
with murder and kidnapping, then garnish with those sweet
and savory biscuit bowls, and oh my, what a delicious mystery. Fast, fun, and so foodworthy."

—Victoria Abbott, author of the Book Collector Mysteries

"The plot in *Death on Eat Street* is extremely clever and interesting to the reader. Couple that with some unique and fascinating characters, and J. J. Cook has another winner on the market." —Fresh Fiction

"Readers are treated to an eclectic cast of characters and a great new cozy heroine in Zoe Chase. J. J. Cook shows readers how it's done by giving them a well-thought-out mystery that will have them on the edge of their seats . . . A great new book." —Debbie's Book Bag

"I highly recommend this delightful cozy to anyone who enjoys cooking, mystery, and a touch of romance and whimsy . . . I, for one, am looking forward to the next book in the series. Zoe and Crème Brûlée are a hit." —Open Book Society

"Filled with colorful characters . . . The descriptions of the various sweet and savory fillings had my mouth watering."
—Melissa's Mochas, Mysteries & Meows

Berkley Prime Crime titles by J. J. Cook

Sweet Pepper Fire Brigade Mysteries

THAT OLD FLAME OF MINE
PLAYING WITH FIRE
IN HOT WATER

Biscuit Bowl Food Truck Mysteries

DEATH ON EAT STREET
FRY ANOTHER DAY
FAT TUESDAY FRICASSEE

Specials

HERO'S JOURNEY
GATOR BOWL

FAT TUESDAY
Fricassee

J. J. COOK

BERKLEY PRIME CRIME, NEW YORK

An imprint of Penguin Random House LLC
375 Hudson Street, New York, New York 10014

FAT TUESDAY FRICASSEE

A Berkley Prime Crime Book / published by arrangement with the author

ISBN: 978-0-425-26347-1

PUBLISHING HISTORY
Berkley Prime Crime mass-market edition / December 2015

PRINTED IN THE UNITED STATES OF AMERICA

10 9 8 7 6 5 4 3 2 1

Cover illustration by Griesbach & Martucci.
Cover design by Jason Gill.
Interior text design by Laura K. Corless.

Thanks to Susan and Cindy and the other friendly people in Mobile for their help!

ONE

- -

"There you are, Zoe!" My father opened the door to his apartment. "I was beginning to worry."

"Sorry." I put down my cat, Crème Brûléc. He immediately ran to his food bowl. He tends to eat when he's stressed. "It's been a rough day. I was out at six A.M. with the Biscuit Bowl after being up at the other masquerade ball last night until after midnight."

Daddy's critical eyes went over me. "Is there still time to get your hair and nails done? I know you want to look your best tonight."

I slumped in one of his elegant but uncomfortable chairs. "I hope there's time for a nap. I'm so glad this is the last ball. Aren't you exhausted?"

"A nap? With all this excitement?" He dragged me to my feet and danced me around the room.

My father, Ted Chase, and I shared the family legacy of unruly curly black hair. He took care of his by wearing it close-cropped, with a little gray at the temples. His brown eyes were always looking for the next new thing—an investment, a girlfriend, or an adventure.

My hair went its own way, black curls everywhere. I kind of liked it that way, especially since my only other choice seemed to be shaving my head. I'd inherited my mother's blue eyes and her common sense, I hoped.

"You're a very lucky girl to be entering the Mistics of Time masquerade ball on the arm of King Felix."

"Yeah, I know. I felt pretty lucky up until the third ball. Now I just feel tired." I stopped moving. "I can do my own hair and nails. I'm going to sleep for a while. I know you don't want me snoring behind my mask tonight. What would people say?"

"All right. Sleep if you need to." He kissed my forehead. "I'm worried about you, Zoe. You're working too hard. You weren't made for this."

I laughed. "What I wasn't made for was dancing and partying all night. Wake me at six, please."

This was the last formal masked ball that I had to attend with my father before the two weeks of carnival parades leading up to Fat Tuesday, or Mardi Gras.

At least the next day was Saturday, so I didn't have to take my Biscuit Bowl food truck out. I'd been planning to use the weekend to set up for the start of the parades. I was lucky to be chosen as a food truck vendor this year, and I was planning on turning a nice profit, not to mention finding new foodies.

When Daddy had been crowned King Felix—the ruler of this year's carnival—he'd turned to me as his escort. My parents were divorced—not that my mother had ever attended the elaborate pre-Lent parties when they'd been married. She just wasn't the party type, and she disliked Mardi Gras.

I understood that Daddy didn't want to be alone at all the

parties. It was traditional to have a partner. I'd been hoping when I heard about his coronation that he'd have a girlfriend he could invite.

No such luck.

So since last November, every time there was a party, I'd worked all day and then grabbed my cat and my bag to get a taxi to my father's apartment. The party costumes were too elaborate to deal with at the diner where I lived.

I'd been dressing up and going out with him from his place, leaving Crème Brûlée there, too, sometimes, though not for long, since it was against Daddy's lease to have pets. Sometimes I went back to the diner, and sometimes not. There had been days when I'd changed clothes after a ball and got back just in time to make biscuits at four A.M.

I was worn-out.

Daddy kept dancing and humming. I didn't know if he was practicing or just so excited that he had to dance. I didn't care. I collapsed on the bed in the spare room and immediately fell asleep.

- - - - - - -

Crème Brûlée was sitting on my chest snuffling my face. His whiskers tickled my nose. I couldn't figure out what was happening as I came out of my heavy napping fog. I glanced at the clock by the bed. It was seven thirty.

Oh my God! There were only thirty minutes until we had to be at the masquerade!

I'd never tried to be the belle of the ball, but it was nice to have time to take a shower and get ready. I stumbled out of the bedroom. "Daddy, why didn't you wake me?"

"Hmm?" He looked away from his reflection in the mirror. He was wearing black tie and tails. His elaborate mask—a gold and purple dragon—was on the dressing table beside him. "What do you think about my tie, Zoe? Is it crooked?"

"It's seven thirty, Daddy. I'm not dressed. You were supposed to wake me at six."

He frowned. "Sorry, honey. I got a call from a major stockholder at the bank. I guess I lost track of time."

"I'll do what I can to be ready, but we might be late."

I hadn't seen the gown for the ball yet. My father's personal assistant had picked it out for me. She'd done a good job on the other dozen gowns, so I trusted her. Heaven forbid anyone should wear the same gown twice during a season!

I stripped down for a quick, hot shower. My hair was damp, but not wet when I got out. I covered it with a towel while I slapped on some makeup. The eyes were a problem, because Daddy's assistant thought I should use glittery purple eye shadow and large fake eyelashes.

No time for that.

I shook out my hair and put my fingers through it like always. I used plenty of gel to hold it in place. A large gold and purple feather comb looked like a good idea, and it would match my mask. I pulled the curls back, except for some at the sides of my face. The feather added height and interest to the look.

The plastic bag came off the huge, ornate gown with very little difficulty. It was stunning. There were what seemed like hundreds of layers of gold and purple nylon net covered by hundreds of layers of gold and green chiffon. The bodice was a little snug but did good things for my bust. I had a feeling no man would be looking at the feather or my mask that night.

I slid my feet into glittery gold slippers and walked out as Daddy picked up his top hat and cane. "I'm ready."

He nodded as he walked around me. "You look great, Zoe! Don't forget the mask."

I grabbed my mask, and we left for the ball. We arrived with only minutes to spare at the older building where the ball was being held. Tardiness, my father had told me, wasn't tolerated for King Felix.

From outside, the old redbrick building looked as though it needed to be demolished. It had once been a shipping warehouse, according to the cement plaque at the door. NEWLAND AND SONS, 1830. But it had only been for lease recently.

It was hard to imagine there was an elegant ball going on inside, but there were the white-gloved men at the door in their red coats, welcoming people in who possessed the coveted handwritten invitations. I could hear the swell of music streaming out into the night air each time the door opened.

This idea of holding the secret societies' balls and other functions in buildings that no one would ever think of as elegant, or even safe, was part of keeping their activities known to only a few, according to my father. I had no doubt that the Mistics of Time had held an event at this spot since their inception in the 1700s—even before there was a building. Everything about Mobile's carnival secret societies and parade krewes was steeped in tradition and folklore.

Another white-gloved gentleman in a mask opened the big doors inside for us. The outside of the building might not have looked like much, but the inside was palatial. Gold walls and purple carpets stretched as far as I could see. Crystal chandeliers glittered on sterling silver laid out on pristine white linen tablecloths.

There were flowers everywhere, dripping from the walls and lanterns, huge colorful sprays perfuming the air. Music from a string orchestra was subdued, but I knew before the night was out it would get louder.

I was almost too tired to appreciate the enormous buffet that had been spread for the ball, despite my devotion to being a foodie. The tables were thirty feet long and covered in gold cloth that shimmered in the light from hundreds of candles.

On the tables was every kind of carnival food imaginable. There were dozens of flavors of MoonPies—two round graham cracker cookies filled with marshmallow and dipped in chocolate or flavored icings. Lemon. Orange. Strawberry. Banana. They all looked yummy.

The king cakes were enormous. King cakes are a supersweet braided coffee cake that hides a lucky baby statue somewhere inside. They were frosted in the traditional colors of green, purple, and gold.

I couldn't imagine any seafood that wasn't there from shrimp to flounder. It was cooked in every way possible. Fried, boiled, baked, in gumbo, and with rice. The bounty of Mobile Bay and the Gulf of Mexico was well represented. There was spicy jambalaya, platters of roasted corn, and crawfish étouffée.

Whiskey dominated all the colorful (and powerful) drinks, and there were also Sazeracs made with absinthe. I enjoyed it, but it was an acquired taste. Of course there was plenty of sweet tea and a thick, sugary chocolate drink that was served hot and cold.

The idea was to sin as much as you could before Lent. Gluttony, drunkenness, promiscuity—these were the hallmarks of the carnival. Dance. Laugh. Drink until you fell down. Eat too much—for a time was coming when you'd have to give all that up for Lent to prepare for Easter.

You didn't have to be Catholic, as were the first revelers to join in the celebrations. I imagined that most people didn't even know why they were celebrating anymore. But it was fun, so who cared?

Visitors came from across the country to partake of our festivities each year, but no one outside certain select families would ever see the secret balls and masquerades preceding the parades and other amusements.

Everyone in the huge room was dancing. They were masked,

too. The costumes were amazing—women in gowns with hooped skirts and panniers that were five feet across, their hair as high as Marie Antoinette ever wore hers. The men were dashing and daring with their faces hidden and swords at their sides. Tonight was a time to revel.

I was with King Felix, regent of the ball and all festivities for this year. I had no choice but to dance. As we swirled around the room, I could see men and women wrapped in close embraces behind veil-like draperies against the walls. Couples disappeared into side rooms with their arms locked around each other. I wondered how anyone could tell who they were going off with.

Maybe it didn't matter.

I finally decided that I had to sit out a dance or two. My feet in the glittering shoes were hurting. It was hot in the large, layered gown, too. I needed a break if I was going to make it through the rest of the evening. Daddy wasn't short of partners. He didn't really need me again until the massive picture taking that went on at the end of each ball.

I quietly put a small amount of food on a purple glass plate and looked for a chair. I wanted to try everything on the table, but I knew I couldn't hold even a taste of each dish.

I was also storing up recipe ideas for my future restaurant. I had a food truck now, but my goal was a wonderful stationary eatery where hundreds of people waited each night to come in and be amazed. It would be a must-eat spot in all the tourist brochures and on all the travel websites. *No one should go to Mobile, Alabama, without eating here!*

That was a long way off. Right now my recipes were confined to what I could sell out of my food truck. I tried to make them interesting and different, but serving them through a cutout window got restrictive sometimes. Someday it would be different.

I slipped out on the patio that was at the back of the

building. It was surrounded by tall redbrick walls, probably to stop prying eyes from guessing at the identities of the Mistics of Time. I knew those names were a closely guarded secret. In the old days, someone might expect to be killed if they violated the rules and told anyone about the membership of a secret society.

Most of the members had family names that dated back to the founding of Mobile in the 1700s. They were statesmen, bankers, clergymen, and even soldiers. You couldn't buy your way into a parade krewe or a secret society. You were either part of it from birth or you were never part of it.

The lighting along the brick walls came from colorful but subdued lanterns that were hung on trees. Fountains splashed along the cobbled walkway between thick bushes and tall flowering plants. There were plenty of cozy spots for meetings between lovers and secluded benches where they could sit and cuddle.

I took a swallow of champagne and relaxed with a sigh of relief. I didn't dare have Sazerac tonight. Any misstep would be embarrassing for my father. Maybe others felt comfortable getting drunk here, but I didn't. I didn't want to mess this up for him.

My eyes followed the walkway and located several couples who'd sneaked out together to enjoy the night. It was February. The breezes from the bay kept the temperatures pleasant. In only a few months Mobile would be hot and humid.

On a bench immediately across from me was Death.

You had to know Mardi Gras lore to know that Death and Folly were frequent characters during the festivities. I was never really sure why they were used so frequently or what their symbolism meant—a lack of attention on my part. I should have known.

But there he was, slumped over as though he'd been dancing too much. Death was always dressed in black with a skeletal face and form etched on his costume. He wasn't scary like from a horror movie. At least I'd never thought of him that way. Maybe it was because I'd grown up seeing him everywhere during carnival.

He slumped further to the side as I watched, his head hanging at a painful angle that seemed unnatural, even for Death. I got up from the bench, becoming more alarmed, and walked across to him. "Hello? Are you okay?"

Death didn't reply. Instead he slipped silently to the ground at my feet.

TWO

I knelt down beside him. It wasn't an easy task in my stiff gown. I had to jerk my bodice up twice before I could lean over at all. Whoever had created the gown had no breasts, I decided, as I struggled to remove Death's hooded mask.

I glanced around, but the garden patio was empty. Where had the couples I'd seen out here gone? I didn't have my cell phone to call for help.

A waiter passed. He grew very pale at the sight of the Death's real face as I finally got the mask off. There was blood everywhere. That was when I saw the gun in the grass, close to Death's left hand. Had he dropped it when he'd fallen off the bench?

"Can you get some help, please?" I asked as the waiter gaped at me.

I was pretty sure the man playing Death was really dead. He had no pulse that I could find.

He was a good-looking young man, maybe in his twenties. Blondish hair and clean features. He was holding something in his left hand—a piece of paper with some writing on it. I couldn't make out what it said. It looked like a piece of newspaper.

I closed his fingers around the paper again and called for help.

None was forthcoming, though I could hear the sounds of the party inside going loud and strong. The music had switched from quiet waltzes and easy listening to loud jazz. It had been the same way at the rest of the balls we'd attended.

With no help in sight, I reluctantly left the Death character on the cobblestones and ran inside to alert someone to what was happening in the dimly lit garden.

The first man I saw was another waiter. "I need help outside. I think a man playing Death is dead. Where's a phone?"

He stared at me like I was crazy. I felt crazy saying it.

"Security." He pointed to a man dressed all in black. "Maybe he can help you."

I was still wearing my mask—a smiling mermaid face with rosy cheeks and green curls. I threw it aside to make myself heard above the music and laughter.

I reached the security guard and told him my story. He quickly escorted me to my father. Was I speaking in a foreign language? What was wrong with everyone?

"I was wondering where you'd slipped off to." My handsome, slightly inebriated father smiled and downed another Sazerac.

"Someone needs help in the garden, Daddy. I think he may be dead. I think he was shot."

"King Felix," he reminded me, puffing out his chest.

I rolled my eyes. "Okay—King Felix. We have to call an ambulance and the police."

"Relax, Zoe," he whispered so the crowd surrounding him wouldn't hear. "I'm sure it's all part of the act. Get a drink. Find a nice young man to make out with."

First of all, I had a nice young man already. Miguel couldn't come to the ball because it was a secret. I didn't plan to make out with anyone, as my father suggested. I'd see Miguel tomorrow.

"Daddy, I don't think this is an act. If you won't call an ambulance and the police, I will."

Second—how could I relax when I thought there was a dead man on the patio?

I thought I had finally penetrated his alcohol-and-dancing-induced haze. I couldn't tell for sure, because his dragon mask covered half his face. It had slipped while he'd been dancing. I righted it and peered into his brown eyes. "Seriously, Daddy! I need your help!"

"All right, Zoe." He took my hand and leaned against me. "Let's go."

He excused both of us to the group he'd been with. They were all wearing traditional masks—I couldn't tell who any of them were. My mind had started working overtime after seeing the dead man in the garden. *What a great place to kill someone. How would anyone know who did it in this masked crowd?*

We walked slowly outside. My father was leaning so heavily on me that I was afraid we might both fall. It was darker in the walled garden, but I could still make out the shape of Death on the ground.

"See? I told you. Something is wrong."

Daddy knelt on the bricks, despite his expensive costume. He felt the man's pulse as I had and came away with bloodied hands that I could see in the dim light from the lanterns above us. "I think you're right, Zoe. We need to call the police. This man is dead."

"There's a gun over there, too. I think he was shot."

"Who would do such a thing?" My father sat down hard beside the dead man, no longer able to stay on his knees. His voice sounded more sober when he spoke. "Tonight of all nights. What a mess!"

I helped him to his feet, and we went back inside. He spoke to several people in the crowded room, no doubt the right people who could take charge of this embarrassing, and what was sure to be controversial, event. I had no idea who any of them were with their elaborate masks and costumes. I wasn't privy to their secret meetings and activities.

But I might have known them if they were unmasked. Many of the members of secret societies were highly thought of bankers, city officials, and even famous celebrities from Mobile.

They were finally convinced to trudge outside and gaze upon the dead man's face, but they didn't recognize him. I could tell by their outraged tones that they were astounded that an outsider had crashed their secret party.

Surely that wasn't enough reason to kill him, and yet, here he was.

No one had a cell phone in their fancy dress clothes. A young man with white gloves who was obviously working at the party was sent to make the call on a landline somewhere in the building.

I waited with my father, standing against the wall while the word passed around the room. There was a slow but steady exodus toward the front door we'd come in. It seemed the only thing worse than giving away your secret party location was being found there with a dead man.

"The police aren't going to like that everyone is gone," I told my father. "Who are they going to question?"

He fumbled but finally removed his mask. "You don't understand, Zoe. The Mistics of Time have been around since 1702. We're one of the oldest secret societies in the city. People can't know who our members are. It's been that way for three hundred years. No one wants it to change."

I could hear the police sirens headed our way. "I hope the

police are sympathetic. It's been my experience that they don't care much about people being uncomfortable or unhappy when it comes to murder."

I had hoped my friend, Detective Patti Latoure, would catch the case. Instead it was a younger man with an impatient air about him. He stalked toward us in the main ballroom, which was now mostly empty. He was flanked by several uniformed police officers.

"Mr. Chase? I'm Dan Frolick, Mobile Police Department." He shook hands with my father. "What happened here?"

"I'm afraid there's been an accident of some kind." My father explained about me finding the body in the garden.

Detective Frolick turned to me. "And you are?"

"I'm Zoe Chase. It happened pretty much like my father explained. There's a gun on the ground near him. I didn't touch it."

Detective Frolick immediately sent officers to find spotlights that would illuminate the dark garden. He walked briskly toward the walled area, and we followed.

After spending a moment with the dead man, Detective Frolick had one of his officers start going through the bushes, as though he thought someone could be hiding there. "And where are the rest of the partygoers? I assume this is one of the secret societies? Which one is it?"

"I'm not at liberty to answer that question," my father told him. "My lawyer will be here shortly."

"Lawyer? Are you guilty of something that you need a lawyer for, Mr. Chase?" Detective Frolick stared intensely at him.

"I have nothing else to say." Daddy sat down on the lacey ironwork bench and folded his arms over his chest.

"What about you?" Detective Frolick glared at me.

I didn't know what was wrong with my father. This wasn't

the way to handle a problem with the police. I'd been in enough situations to know.

"I'm not bound by any secrecy to the society," I told him. "It probably won't do you any good to know who was here— they'd all deny it. This is the last masquerade ball of the season for the Mistics of Time. There were probably three hundred people here. They all left when they found out you were coming."

"Zoe!" My father's voice was indignant. "You have no right to expose us."

"Thank you, Miss Chase." Detective Frolick snickered. "What else can you tell me?"

There wasn't much to tell beyond what I'd already said. I was sorry I'd blurted out some of the group's secrets. I hoped my father didn't get in trouble because of it. But I was also hoping the rats hadn't left the sinking ship thinking that we were going to take the fall for what had happened, either. It seemed odd to me that there were only the two of us left out of the dazzling company.

I knew everyone in the Mistics would deny knowing anything about the young man in the garden, or even being at the ball, on the grounds of protecting their identities. Would the police take that into consideration before they bothered questioning us? Secret societies were the norm here. I was sure they'd encountered them before.

I got my answer a moment later when the police commissioner himself joined us. He was still wearing his white tie and tails, though he had taken off his mask. He'd been at the ball —one of the first men Daddy had talked to about the situation. Now he was pretending that he just got there.

"Frolick!" Commissioner Chadwick Sloane barked his name. "What's going on?"

I'd noticed the commissioner at the ball with a slender

young woman in a gorgeous sea green gown. She'd been wearing a butterfly mask. He'd been wearing a very distinctive embroidered waistcoat that he hadn't bothered to change when he'd come back for the investigation. I also recognized him by the antique watch he was wearing pinned to his chest like a medal. He'd removed his dragon mask, which had been similar to my father's.

Frolick immediately told him what had happened. He was visibly shocked to see his boss there. It was doubtful that the commissioner came out often for street crime.

The detective explained that other members of the Mistics of Time had disappeared before he could question them—all except me and Daddy. "These are the only two left," he said. "Maybe we could get a court order to get the names of the guests."

Commissioner Sloane's sharp features turned toward my father after dismissing the detective to the other side of the garden. "How did you learn such a thing, Frolick? No member of a secret society in this city would give up their affiliation."

"I told him." I couldn't let Daddy get thrown out of his society. They couldn't do anything to me. "I'm sorry, but someone is dead. I was upset. I didn't mean to give it away."

My father protectively put his arm around me. "Zoe isn't to blame."

Sloane pivoted toward me. "You had no right."

"Leave her alone. She just meant to help."

"Frolick!" Commissioner Sloane quickly walked away from us. "Get their statements. Find out who the dead man is. Report only to me. Do you understand? No press, for God's sake."

"Yes, sir." Frolick gestured to the other officers to let the EMS people examine the dead man.

Sloane pointed at me. "I'll deal with you later, young woman!"

I wasn't sure what he'd meant by it, but I shivered in my daringly low-cut bodice.

My father held me tighter and whispered, "Don't worry about a thing, Zoe. He's all bluster. He can't hurt you or me."

The commissioner left. We gave our statements to Frolick. Crime scene teams moved into the garden and began going over everything. I wondered who the dead man was behind Death's mask. I wasn't sure how the police would find out with all the secrecy that surrounded the event.

Daddy's driver was waiting out front for us when we were finished. My feet were killing me. I had passed the point of exhaustion about two hours earlier. The nap I'd taken was long gone. I just wanted to go home and forget this had ever happened.

"Who do you think that was in the garden?" I asked Daddy as his driver smoothly navigated the empty city streets.

"Two people in the society are chosen every year to play Death and Folly. I'm not privy to that information. The committee that sets things up would know."

"I saw Commissioner Sloane at the ball. He's a member of Mistics of Time, too, huh?"

"Don't mention it to anyone else," he warned. "People have been killed for giving away secrets. I don't want you to be one of them."

"That sounds a little melodramatic. Don't you think that's over the top, even for a secret society? This isn't the 1700s anymore."

Daddy put his arms around me in the back of the car. "I mean it, Zoe. Don't tell anyone what you've seen and heard tonight. I can smooth things over with Chadwick. Just keep all of this to yourself. Promise me."

I promised, surprised by his earnest entreaty. "Maybe you shouldn't belong to this society anymore."

He laughed. "Not belong? My ancestor started the Mistics. I don't think he'd like me to abandon our heritage."

"All right. I won't say anything. But let me know if you find out who that poor man was in the garden."

He kissed my forehead. "Forget about this, sweetheart. Pretend you didn't see any of it. That's what I plan to do."

THREE

Tiffany Bryant, one of the PR people for Mobile Mardi Gras, was reading through a list of dos and don'ts for food truck vendors who'd been invited to take part in the festivities this year.

I kept falling asleep.

It wasn't my fault. With the schedule I'd kept since last fall, and the shock from last night, I was lucky I could get out of bed that morning. Keeping up with the Biscuit Bowl, getting up five days a week at four A.M., was hard enough. Staying up half the night smiling and wearing costumes when there were events and then getting my food truck out on the street by six A.M. had been a nightmare.

But I loved Daddy, and he'd always been there for me. I didn't want to let him down. Now the showy secret parties were over. All I had to do was keep my food truck open most of the day, and night, for the next two weeks.

I was going to need a vacation when it was over.

The hectic schedule was starting to show in dark circles under my eyes, which are on the violet side of blue, and a general lack of attentiveness. I'd fallen asleep three times while working in the last week alone. Only Ollie had saved me from going headfirst into the deep fryer.

"Zoe?"

I heard my name in the midst of what sounded like mumbling and perked up. "Yes?"

"You were sleeping again." Tiffany's voice expressed her disappointment and frustration with me.

I felt like I was in school again.

"Sorry. I was at the King's Masquerade last night until two after working all day." I yawned. "There's not enough caffeine to keep me awake right now."

That statement didn't make Tiffany any happier. Her pretty face screwed up into a petulant frown, and her green eyes narrowed. "You know this is the chance of a lifetime and that dozens of other food truck drivers in our area would love to be in your shoes, right?" I was sure they would, too.

When I'd signed up to be part of the big food truck rally during carnival, it had seemed like a wonderful opportunity. I remembered being excited about it at the time. But that was before dozens of balls, masquerades, and Daddy's coronation as King Felix had taken their toll on my energy.

I wanted to say it out loud, but I'd already caused enough trouble. "I'm sorry. I'll try to get some extra sleep. I've read the instructions, if that helps. I know where I'm supposed to park and what I'm supposed to do."

"I suppose that's better than nothing." Tiffany took a deep, dramatic breath and plunged into the rest of her long recital.

There were twelve food trucks that had been invited to take part in the carnival celebration. It would all come to a head in two weeks with Fat Tuesday and the parades and festivities across the city before Lent.

There were bound to be thousands of people who would eat my food and remember my name later when they were looking for someplace to eat lunch. Despite my general lack of caring at that moment, I was counting on all the attention I could get while I was there. Tiffany was right—it was a fantastic opportunity.

Suzette's Crepes food truck was represented. I saw them regularly on Government Street at police headquarters where I normally parked Monday through Friday. Charlie's Tuna Shack was there, too, along with Yolanda's Yummy Yogurt. Yolanda had a great food truck with fake fruit hanging off. She always played Bob Marley music, which I thought was a big draw, too.

Mama's Marvelous Mojitos was there, as well. I was surprised, because they basically only served mojitos and not much food. But maybe that was their attraction. I never served anything to drink. There wasn't enough room in the food truck to hold cold drinks.

The other food truck vendors that had been invited were newcomers. Each week it seemed there was new competition on the streets. It was getting harder to find a good space on Government Street, South Royal Street, or even close to Mobile Bay where the cruise ships berthed.

Not that I was worried. My deep-fried biscuit bowls had wowed crowds for almost a year. The publicity from last year's Sweet Magnolia Food Truck Race had also helped. I hadn't won the grand prize, but everyone knew me from the TV show.

Tiffany finally pronounced us all fit to take part in food truck sales at the rally. I knew good sales in the next two weeks could mean adding to my savings account, too. That meant being able to remodel my diner into one of the best restaurants in the city more quickly. That had been my goal from the beginning. My plan was starting to unfold.

My friend, and assistant in running the Biscuit Bowl, was waiting impatiently outside the meeting for me. Ollie—no last name—was about forty. He was well over six feet, a large man with a wicked skull tattoo on the back of his head and neck. He'd been a marine until some bad things had happened to him, but that was a long time ago. We didn't talk about it.

"What were they doing in there, tattooing *The Biscuit Bowl* on your back or something? Nothing should take that long that doesn't have food or money involved. Did you eat without me?"

"No. But there were hundreds of rules and regulations to learn, and I had to sign a dozen legal documents. You don't want to know the rest."

"This thing better be worth some money, young'un, or you've exhausted yourself for nothing." He scowled, but Ollie's natural look is a scowl.

It didn't help that he'd broken up with my other cooking assistant, Delia Vann. It made for some unpleasant moments in the very small kitchen where we worked. People needed to get along in a four-by-eight-foot space inside an Airstream motor home.

In the future I planned to ban romantic relationships between employees—and friends.

"It's going to be great for business," I enthused as we walked down Dauphin Street to meet our ride. "Look how many people come out for Mardi Gras each year. They're all going to eat our biscuits and love them. The aftermath will be even bigger."

He stalked along beside me on the sidewalk. He managed to keep his much longer stride in check so my short legs could keep up with him.

I was five-foot-two and three quarters—not exactly short, but compared to Ollie, everyone was short.

February had brought rain and cool temperatures to

Mobile, Alabama. I hoped, as everyone else did, that sunshine would grace the parades and festivities. But weather was fickle and something we couldn't control. It was the same for rainy days on the street with my food truck. Rain meant fewer customers and ruined biscuits that couldn't be used. No one likes an old biscuit.

"Are you all set on the food?" Ollie asked. "You know what you're serving for the next two weeks?"

"I think so. I'm working on homemade MoonPies tonight."

"That sounds like something I could get into. I love MoonPies." He grinned and rubbed his big hands together. "But they're labor-intensive, aren't they? I think it might be hard to make enough for all the people who'll be here for carnival. Have you got a plan for that?"

"I do." I wasn't sure what it was and thought he might be right. MoonPies were complicated to make, but they tasted so good. "MoonPies have been around almost as long as Mardi Gras, you know. I've heard so much carnival lore and legend the past few months that I could take a test on it in my sleep—which is where it would have to be."

"Have you worked out how to make the marshmallow good and sticky? That's an important part of a MoonPie. The icing has to be just right, too. It can't be too thick. I've had it that way. It's no good. Are you doing flavors or just chocolate?"

"Chocolate, at least right now. We'll see if we can keep up with making them for more than just the first day."

Ollie was a good cook. I respected his opinion. He'd given me so many delicious ideas for sweet and savory foods to go in my biscuit bowls. As independent as I liked to think of myself, I wasn't sure I would have made it as far as I had without him.

We'd finally reached our destination. My boyfriend, Miguel Alexander, had been meeting with a client. He had a car—an older Mercedes—and had promised us a ride back to the old diner where I lived and worked.

It was too expensive to drive the food truck all over the city, and I'd given up my Prius to make ends meet. Taxis, buses, and Miguel's car were basically my mode of transportation unless I was selling biscuit bowls.

The dark sky above us looked threatening as the wind whipped up Mobile Bay. The first few drops of rain were starting to fall when Miguel came out of his meeting and saw us.

"Glad you're here." He unlocked the car doors. "It looks like that big storm front is moving in from the Gulf."

We got into the car just in time as a deluge came crashing down on us.

"Whee!" Ollie laughed as heavy rain pelted the car. "We were lucky this time."

"How was your meeting?" Miguel asked me.

"Boring." I yawned. "How was yours?"

"The same." He started the car, windshield wipers slapping against the window. "Mr. Anthony wants my help, but he doesn't want to plead guilty even though it would mean a lighter sentence."

Miguel was a lawyer but also worked for himself. We could empathize with each other's small business problems. He made more money than me, usually, but my work was a lot more fun.

"You'll talk him around." I pushed back a wing of black hair that had fallen into his face. I loved his wonderful brown eyes and his sexy baritone. He was a wonderful listener, and our relationship was going along pretty smoothly.

He kissed my hand. "Thanks for the encouragement."

I yawned again. "I hate to say it, but I'm getting too old to party all night and work all day. When I was a kid, it wasn't so hard."

"You're barely thirty," Miguel reminded me with a laugh. "You'd better start working out."

"That's the ticket," Ollie said from the backseat. "I work out two hours every day." He showed us his formidable biceps. "Both of you are spring chickens compared to me, but I could outlast both of you together."

Miguel pulled his older Mercedes into the heavy street traffic. As soon as it started to rain, drivers seemed to be divided into two categories—those who drove faster because of the rain and those who drove slower because of it. Either one made the journey to the diner take longer.

I didn't mind. Ollie and I talked about making MoonPies and other delicious foods we were going to serve from the Biscuit Bowl during the parades.

Talk about being the luckiest woman in the world—I had Miguel and Ollie on my side and a spot for my food truck during carnival. Life was good for me. Everything was going my way.

And then we got back to the older shopping center where the diner was located. Mr. Carruthers's car was out front. "Oh no!"

"What's wrong?" Miguel drove slowly through the broken pavement and potholes that made up the shopping center parking lot.

"I completely forgot that today is my health inspection on the diner. What am I going to do?"

My diner wasn't much to look at yet, but it was going to be a good stepping stone for me—once the Biscuit Bowl had made enough fans and money. People would come to the diner for a while after that. From there my fans would follow me to my nicer restaurant. I wasn't sure where that would be yet. But the diner was an important part of my plan.

At one end of the shopping center was the homeless shelter

where Ollie lived and was now part-time director. The home-less men who lived there all appreciated a rainy day where my food didn't sell so well. Ollie and I shared the leftovers with them.

I also needed my diner to make food and bake biscuit bowls. That meant it had to pass inspection. So far I'd made no real connection with Mr. Carruthers as I had the previous health inspector. My goose was cooked.

FOUR

"What's the problem?" Ollie demanded. "Just tell him to get lost."

"It doesn't work that way. You need a health inspection to stay open. If I can't make food for the Biscuit Bowl, we can't be part of the food truck rally."

"Maybe you can reschedule," Miguel suggested. "These things aren't written in stone. The inspector is supposed to let you know when he's coming."

The car had stopped beside Mr. Carruthers's vehicle. I grabbed my bag that had been specially made for people involved in the carnival food truck rally. It had lots of food truck slogans and pictures of food, including my biscuit bowls. "I've already put it off a dozen times. There was so much going on. I think this may be my last chance."

I held my bag over my head. I should've brought an umbrella—another casualty of remembering anything. It was better for my souvenir bag to get wet than it was for my black curly hair. The bag could be dried, and everything would be fine. My poor curls were already suffering from the damp weather and had responded with enormous frizz.

"Hello, Mr. Carruthers." I smiled as he rolled down his window. "Maybe we should reschedule this inspection. The weather is awful, isn't it? We could do this on a nice day when you don't have to walk through this downpour."

To demonstrate how wet it was, I splashed around in the puddles that engulfed my feet. My shoes were going to be ruined. I should have worn tennis shoes.

Mr. Carruthers had the kind of face that looked as though he'd been carrying the weight of the world on his thin shoulders for most of his life. His clothes were clean and neat but had seen better days. I knew nothing about him personally, but the man generally seemed long-suffering and unhappy.

"Miss Chase." He enunciated both words with painful clarity as he glanced down at the clipboard he was holding. "This is the *final* opportunity we have to inspect your premises. If we don't accomplish that today, I'm afraid I'll have to shut your so-called diner down."

"Oh no! Let's not do that. I can run in to get an umbrella so you won't get wet." I stared at the top of his balding head. "At least your head won't get wet."

His thin lips stretched into what might have been a smile. "I'll be fine. Lead the way."

I ran to open the door to the diner, praying that I had done everything he'd asked since the last time he was there. There were one or two things he'd passed with the idea that they would be repaired before he returned.

Miguel and Ollie followed me inside, holding the door for Mr. Carruthers.

"Gentlemen." Mr. Carruthers stared at both of them and then at me. "Don't tell me you're serving customers here, Miss Chase. You know you aren't licensed for that."

"No." I had left the kitchen in a mess during my haste to get to the meeting. I straightened up, quickly wiping everything down as I moved. "These are my friends. I don't serve customers here yet. I know that would be wrong. That's why I have the Biscuit Bowl." I pointed to the Airstream in the parking lot with the spinning biscuit on top.

"Of course." Mr. Carruthers consulted his clipboard. "You were approved to use the kitchen in the diner to make food for the truck. Let's start with your food storage area, if you please."

I walked toward the pantry and freezers, but I noticed him running his fingers along the counter as he came around. It was probably still covered in crumbs from working with the MoonPies that morning.

We looked at the freezer, which was in good condition. I'd repaired cracks in the walls and ceiling in the pantry. I watched him mark his paper as I showed him the improvements.

I quickly closed the office door where I slept. I couldn't afford my apartment, the diner, and the Biscuit Bowl on the money I'd taken from my 401k and savings to open my business. It wasn't legal to sleep at the diner, but it was the only way I could get started.

"Your cleanup area next, if you please." His dour face didn't give anything away. What was he thinking?

I had replaced the sink and drain boards on both sides of the counter next to it. I also had to put in a new water heater that had the necessary temperature to kill germs. There was also a new industrial dishwasher and new tiles on the floor near it.

"All right." He scribbled on the paper again. "Let's look at the cooking area."

I'd bought a new oven that would bake enough biscuits at one time so that I didn't have to do double and triple baking. I hadn't replaced the old griddle, but he'd said it would be fine if I cleaned it. There were other replacements and additions. I hoped it was enough.

Mr. Carruthers finally sat at the counter and worked on the paper. Miguel and Ollie were seated at one of the old booths that I hadn't replaced since I couldn't serve customers, anyway.

I waited impatiently for him to give his verdict. It didn't have to be great, just passing so I could keep using everything here. I watched as he took out one of the cards that would mark my grade for the diner. Maybe everything was going to be okay. I crossed my fingers behind my back.

Then suddenly there was my cat, Crème Brûlée. He was a hefty cat with large bones who loved his food. His white Persian face and tabby stripes made him look larger than if he'd been a black cat. Nature had played a cruel fashion trick on him.

I couldn't believe he was on the counter. Crème Brûlée never jumped. He wasn't active enough to do more than hiss and sleep on my bed. I must have forgotten to feed him or he didn't like the food I'd left.

Mr. Carruthers looked at him as though he'd never seen a cat before. "What is this, Miss Chase?"

"That's my cat, Crème Brûlée." I moved quickly and picked him up. "He's very friendly."

Crème Brûlée hissed at me and bit my finger—no doubt to embarrass me. Then he proceeded to hiss at Mr. Carruthers. I handed him to Ollie who wasn't at all happy about it. He took Crème Brûlée, anyway, holding him awkwardly in his arms.

"You can't have a cat here, Miss Chase. It's unhealthy and against regulations for a cat to live at a restaurant." Mr. Caruthers got to his feet. "I can't give you a passing grade with the cat here. He'll have to go."

"What? No! Wait! He doesn't live here." I glanced at Miguel who was shaking his head. "Crème Brûlée is only here because my apartment is being painted. He couldn't stay there with the wet paint and the painters."

Mr. Carruthers held his pen right above the line he had to sign to give me a passing grade. He was only an inch away. "All right. I'll take your word for it, Miss Chase. I'm going to give you a temporary passing grade on your inspection. It will be good for thirty days, but I'm keeping my eye on you. If I stop in, that cat better not be here."

"He'll be gone tomorrow." I grabbed the temporary license. Lucky for me he didn't see all of my personal stuff—including my bed—in the office. A human living at the diner would be even worse than a cat. "Thank you, Mr. Carruthers. This means a lot to me since my food truck is going to be part of the carnival festivities. Would you like one of my throws?"

"No, thank you. I have all the bangles, Frisbees, and other nonsense that I need. I'll see you sometime in the next thirty days. Good luck with your food truck."

Mr. Carruthers nodded at Miguel and Ollie as he walked out the door. He didn't unbend enough to smile.

At least everything was legal for a while.

"I want one of the throws," Ollie said. "I didn't know you had any. Let me see."

I opened the box that had just come in that morning. I'd bought a thousand white plastic cups decorated with Mardi Gras colors of purple, green, and gold. They had the Biscuit Bowl name on them.

"These are awesome." Ollie raved. "Is the Biscuit Bowl going to be in one of the parades? We'll have to be careful not to hit someone in the head with one of these."

"We won't be in a parade, but I thought we could give these out with every order until we run out."

"Great idea. Can I have one now?"

"I hate to be a killjoy," Miguel said. "The cups are cute,

but what about lying to the inspector? What are you going to do with Crème Brûlée for the next month?"

"For the next two weeks leading up to Lundi Gras—Fat Monday—he'll be staying in the Biscuit Bowl with me. There's a parade every night, and I'm supposed to keep the Biscuit Bowl parked in the same place for the whole time. Someone is always supposed to be there with it. It's part of the agreement with the carnival committee. Crème Brûlée will be with me."

"That's two weeks." Miguel got up from the booth and picked up a cup. "What about the rest of the time after Mardi Gras?"

"I don't know about being a killjoy," Ollie said, "but you're sure a pain in the butt, Miguel. This is Zoe's moment in the sun—possibly the greatest moment of her life. She'll be serving biscuit bowls to all the revelers and krewes in the city. That's one of the biggest honors I can think of."

I didn't exactly agree with Ollie. I hoped this wasn't the greatest moment in my life. As good as it was, I knew it could be better.

And I knew what Miguel was trying to say. "Don't worry. I'll figure something out. I could stay with Daddy, but Crème Brûlée couldn't since he can't have a cat."

"I'm not trying to give you a hard time," Miguel said. "I know how important this is to you. I just don't want it to get messed up."

"I know." I put my arms around him and gave him a big kiss for worrying about me.

"It's getting too mushy in here," Ollie said. "I'm going back to the shelter. Zoe, you're not planning to stay alone in the food truck at night, are you?"

"I am. I don't want anything to go wrong. Last year there were some break-ins at the food trucks that were out on the streets. I don't want the Biscuit Bowl to have graffiti all over it, or half my food to be gone in the morning, either. Keeping the trucks in one place keeps the drivers from jockeying for position each day the way we do everywhere else, too. That's why the committee did it that way this year."

"I wish I could help you," Ollie said. "I can be there all day, but the terms of being a part-time director at the shelter means I have to be there at night. I could give it up if you want."

"No. I'll be fine." I smiled at him. I knew he'd do it if I asked him. I didn't plan to let that happen. Having the part-time job at the shelter and working part-time for me was as close as Ollie had come to having a normal life for years.

"I'd be happy to spend the nights out there," Miguel volunteered. "Who sleeps during carnival, anyway?"

"And I'd be glad to have the company. I just don't want you to feel like you have to be there. I'm not worried about getting hurt or anything. I don't think people on the streets having a good time are dangerous, just a little careless."

"I'll take a look at my schedule and see what I can do." Miguel kissed me. "I have to go. I'm due in court shortly. Let me know if you need a ride anywhere."

Ollie and Miguel walked out together, but Ollie waved to him as he turned to go to the shelter. Between the homeless shelter and the diner was a popular consignment shop and two shops that were empty. One was an old tailor's shop with dusty sewing machines still in the window. The other had some old mannequins in it.

Crème Brûlée meowed loudly as though he was protesting them leaving the diner. I knew better. He tolerated them, but that was about it.

A moment after they were gone, Delia sneaked in. "I saw Ollie leave. Is it safe?"

She removed her large dark glasses. Her long black hair was loose on her shoulders, framing her smooth, cocoa-colored face and large brown eyes. She was built like a fashion model, or a dancer, with long legs and a lean body.

If I didn't love her so much, I would be jealous. My body was stocky. I was no great beauty. I couldn't even make it through ballet lessons when I was eight. I kept gaining weight—how many cooks do you know who are superthin?

Miguel seemed to like my curves—and my naturally curly hair. That was good enough for me.

"You and Ollie have to get over this," I told her. "We're going to be too busy during the next two weeks to have you arguing in the kitchen."

"I came to talk to you about that, Zoe. My sister Hazel is having surgery. My mother can't be there, because Hazel lives in Atlanta. I told her I'd come to help out with the kids and all. I'm so sorry. I didn't know what else to say when she asked."

"Of course you have to go." This couldn't be happening. First the diner issue and now Delia wasn't going to be there during carnival. "We'll make it work without you. It'll be fine. Take care of Hazel."

Delia hugged me. "If you don't want me to, I won't go. I told Hazel I'd have to ask you first."

What could I say?

I had kind of rescued Delia from working at a dirty bar downtown. I knew helping me with the food truck wasn't much of a job, probably only a means to an end. I wanted her to do better.

I knew about her big family and all their financial hardships. Delia had kept them going, paying for her sisters' education. I couldn't ask her not to be there when one of them needed her.

I pulled back from her hug and smiled at her. "Of course I want you to go. I hope everything is okay with Hazel. Come back when you can."

"You know I'll be back as soon as I can. What a time to need appendix surgery—just in time for Mardi Gras!"

She hugged me again and then told me she had to pack. Delia had found a small place that she was sharing with a friend. It was better than a cot in the kitchen at the diner. But I missed having her there.

I waved good-bye to her as she left in a taxi and wondered what I was going to do without her for the next two weeks.

FIVE

I awoke on Sunday morning to the news anchor on TV telling me that a man's body had been found in an alley near midtown on Saturday night.

"Jordan Phillips was a staff reporter for the *Mobile Times* newspaper," the anchorman explained with a somber expression on his face as they showed the reporter's photo. "Mr. Phillips had been shot, according to Mobile Police detective Dan Frolick. The investigation into his death is ongoing."

Oh my gosh!

I was stunned as I switched off the tiny TV in my office/bedroom at the diner.

That reporter was the dead man in the garden at the masquerade ball on Friday night.

Crème Brûlée cuddled close to me, his whiskers tickling the side of my face.

"Are the police lying about when and where they found Jordan Phillips? Or is this some kind of trap to catch the killer?" I asked him. "That's the man in the Death costume that I found in the garden. What should I do?"

My cat wasn't exactly helpful in that regard. He licked me a few times and then pushed me away with his big paws. While I lay there, he rolled out of bed and started crunching some dry food.

My father had been very clear about not getting more involved in what had happened at the ball. I guess I could understand the cover-up, considering the secret society and the important people who wouldn't want to answer embarrassing questions. But this was much worse than that.

My mind raced with questions as I got up, showered, and dressed. The shower at the diner was a plus that was a leftover from the time when the diner had been a truck stop. I was fortunate to have found it with everything else I'd needed.

Detective Frolick had been the one who'd questioned me and Daddy. He probably wouldn't have done this by himself. Why were they keeping the real location of the reporter's body a secret? Had Commissioner Sloane asked him to do it to keep everything away from the Mistics of Time?

"Saying they found him in an alley, blocks away from the masquerade ball, on a different night was a good way to do it," I fussed at Crème Brûlée.

I knew I should leave it alone. I told myself that a hundred times as I ate the last piece of king cake I'd brought home with me from a party three days before. It was right on the verge of going stale, but it was still delicious. The colorful frosting was good, too, but no lucky baby trinket inside.

I was drinking orange juice and frying bacon to make the breakfast healthier when Ollie came down from the shelter.

"You've got green frosting on your lips." He laughed. "Was that the last of the king cake?"

I nodded as I used my finger to get the bit of frosting and put it in my mouth.

"I knew it!" He smacked his hand on the counter as he sat down. "I should've polished that off when I saw it yesterday. Did you find the lucky baby?"

"No baby. Coffee? Bacon?" My own recipe for home-brewed coffee that contained some chicory was beginning to perk. It smelled wonderful.

"Sure. I'll take both." He got up and got out the milk. "Is that bacon leftover from the food truck Friday?"

"Yes. I'm working on menus for the next two weeks. I'm afraid I may be short if I want to serve something interesting and different every day. Got any ideas?"

"As a matter of fact," he said, "I have some good fricassee notions."

"I only know chicken fricassee. What else have you got in mind?"

We pored over old cookbooks for ideas. The best menus for the Biscuit Bowl had come from them. Some of the books I'd borrowed from my uncle Saul. Others I'd found at various antique sales around the city and at the library.

Ollie was suggesting a fricassee of pork when Miguel walked in. He kissed me and poured himself a cup of coffee. I offered to split the bacon with him, too, but he turned me down.

"What's the difference between pulled pork and fricassee pork?" Miguel asked after looking over Ollie's shoulder.

"A fricassee is more like a thick stew except without the liquid," Ollie explained. "I have a pork fricassee in mind with potatoes and maybe a few eggs."

"That sounds good," I remarked. "Fricassee is different."

"What about sweets?" Miguel wondered.

"I'm making homemade MoonPies. I don't think I'll respect myself if I don't. We'll probably have to do with biscuit bowl fillings later."

"You're gonna need more than that, Zoe, but that sounds

good as a starter!" Ollie echoed my words. "Are we doing that today?"

I glanced at the biscuit-shaped clock near the door. "I'm supposed to drive the Biscuit Bowl over to its parking space and get set up at noon. That gives us a while. We'll have to make the MoonPies here, anyway."

"I'm always ready for a good MoonPie." Ollie slurped his coffee and crunched his bacon.

"Maybe we can have lunch after you drop off the Biscuit Bowl," Miguel suggested with a smile.

"Sure," Ollie agreed. "I'm not busy."

"I think he meant me and him," I explained.

Ollie scrutinized both of us. "Oh. That kind of lunch. Sorry. Those of us who have been uncoupled sometimes forget that there are couples still together out there."

Miguel and I exchanged glances.

"You might as well come with us," Miguel said. "It's going to take all three of us to set up the Biscuit Bowl. We'll go out after that."

"You sure?" Ollie asked.

"Very sure," I said.

So no romantic lunch, but we could at least be together.

We talked about the coming parade season. It was going to be good and bad for the Biscuit Bowl. I'd never have a better chance to reach new customers, and I didn't have to get started so early in the morning.

On the other hand, the Biscuit Bowl had to stay open until at least midnight for the next two weeks and then open early each day. There would probably be more traffic than we'd ever seen, too, without any way to know when people would be coming.

"In all the excitement I forgot to ask how the ball went on Friday night," Ollie said. "Are you riding on a float in a parade?"

I'd been a little tempted to tell Ollie and Miguel about what had happened on Friday. My oath to my father had kept me from mentioning it randomly yesterday while we'd been doing everything else.

Today was a different story. Now the police were saying they'd found the dead reporter in an alley a few blocks away from the garden where I'd found him.

I was still a little worried about what might happen if I said something to them about it. But as far as I knew, Ollie and Miguel weren't part of any of the secret societies. I trusted them, and I really needed to tell someone.

"Something happened at the masquerade ball Friday night." I took out the huge bag of graham cracker crumbs that I'd smashed for the MoonPies. "I'm not supposed to say anything about it, but now something else weird has happened."

Miguel smiled as he moved his coffee cup off the counter before Ollie started cleaning it. "How weird is it?"

"Really weird. And bad."

"How bad, Zoe?" Ollie asked. "What could happen at a masquerade ball?"

"Someone died."

"Like a heart attack?" Ollie tried to pin it down.

"With those societies and krewes, maybe you shouldn't say anything else, Zoe," Miguel counseled. "I've heard terrible stories about people who give away their secrets. If one of their important members had a heart attack and died, they might not want people to know."

"If your father said to keep quiet, you should keep quiet." Ollie nodded.

I pursed my lips, a little annoyed at their fatalistic attitudes. They didn't even know yet how bad it was. "Come on. This is the twenty-first century. It's not like it was back in the 1800s. I'm not scared of them." *Not much, anyway.*

Miguel washed out his coffee cup and put it on the drain board beside the sink. "I suppose it all depends what it is. Is it something illegal?"

"Yes." I got out the marshmallow and chocolate. "It involves the police."

"Don't share." Ollie shuddered. "I don't want to know what a crazy mystic society is doing behind closed doors."

"Even if it involves murder?"

Ollie looked up from drying the countertop. "Especially if it involves murder."

Miguel sat again. "Just say it, Zoe. Neither one of us is going to take it out of the diner. It will help if you tell someone. I'm sure it's not as bad as it seems."

So while I covered the counter in waxed paper and loaded all the crushed graham crackers on it, I told them about the dead man in the garden and the visit from the police commissioner. I even told them that Commissioner Sloane was a member of the Mistics of Time.

Ollie whistled. "Your father is a member of the Mistics? That's one of the oldest societies in the city!"

"I know."

"Were you a debutante and everything?" Ollie grinned. "I'd like to see *that* picture!"

"No. I was never a deb. Or a queen. Or even a princess. I wasn't interested. Daddy might have talked me into it, but Mom was against it."

"I'm sure the police are handling the situation." Miguel studied the marshmallow. "Just because they didn't do anything right away doesn't mean they aren't going to do anything at all."

"Have you heard or seen the news today? The dead *Times* reporter was the man in the Death costume at the ball. I saw his face when I took off his mask. He wasn't found in the alley. But I'm not supposed to say anything. Daddy was very serious about it."

"That sounds really bad," Ollie said with a frown.

"I don't believe the police would purposely hide where they found the reporter, unless it was information that could lead them to the killer," Miguel said. "I can understand that your father would be nervous about you getting involved in it."

"That wasn't the Mistics or Daddy on TV this morning," I reminded him. "And Commissioner Sloane was there with someone named Detective Frolick. They know where the reporter was found."

"Maybe they're trying to keep your name out of it, too, Zoe," Miguel said.

"Or the police just out and out lied to protect the Mistics of Time," Ollie remarked. "I think they're capable of looking after their own."

I stirred the chocolate in the double boiler so it would melt evenly. "What do you think I should do?"

"Your Daddy knows best," Ollie said. "Don't get involved. What difference does it make where they found him? He's dead, right?"

"Ollie's probably right," Miguel agreed. "The police are investigating. If you get into it they'll have to acknowledge where they found the reporter. That could be a disaster for your family and maybe ruin the investigation."

Ollie looked pleased that Miguel thought he was right. "That's not where you want to go, Zoe. Leave it alone. Let's make some MoonPies."

Miguel didn't say anything else about it as we smoothed the chocolate across the top of the graham crackers.

But I had a terrible feeling I hadn't heard the last of the reporter's death.

After the MoonPies were made and carefully put away— Crème Brûlée loved MoonPies—we took the Biscuit Bowl to the assigned area. It was a large municipal parking lot close to the parades and other festivities.

There was plenty of room for all the trucks. A man in an orange vest told us where to park. Miguel was in the Mercedes. He followed me, Ollie, and Crème Brûlée into the parking area.

There were ten times more regulations about how and where to park for the parades than I faced each day as a business owner. All the food trucks had to have their wheels blocked so they couldn't move. Each truck had to have exactly twelve feet between it and the next truck. When serving, each truck was supposed to be responsible for putting out orange cones to designate where customers should stand.

"Good thing you have some chairs," Ollie observed. "There's nowhere to sit and eat."

"They won't let me use my chairs or tables," I told him. "They're supposed to put out picnic tables."

"That's stupid," Ollie replied.

"It was part of the deal the city made with local restaurants who feel like the food trucks might take away their business."

Miguel had to move his car to the street, but he finally made it back over to us. We had about forty-five minutes to get everything set up so it could be inspected. Even if you had a recent health inspection—as I had—you still had to have another one.

"I've been thinking about the reporter's death," Miguel said as he and I were putting the cups, plates, and plastic forks away.

"Me, too. Almost nonstop."

"It could be dangerous for you to ask questions about it."

I knew he still had more to say on the subject. I noticed that he'd waited to say it until Ollie was outside blocking the wheels on the food truck.

I studied his handsome face. "Are you a member of one of the secret societies?"

"Of course not. Why would you think that?"

"You were almost the city's district attorney at one time. I know a lot of people in powerful positions are members." I turned away again to stock napkins. "Not that I'd expect you to tell me if you were."

Miguel had been framed for evidence tampering when he ran for district attorney. He couldn't prove it, but many people knew it was true. He came from a family with very little money and no connections. But that didn't mean that he wasn't a member of a krewe or society. Not everyone in those organizations was wealthy when they started out.

"I'd tell you." He stopped and put his hands on my arms. "I wouldn't lie to you, Zoe."

"Thanks." I smiled. "I didn't find out that my father's family had helped found one of the city's largest secret societies until I was sixteen and Daddy wanted me to be queen of something. He'd kept it from me all those years, and I was his daughter. We both know people like to keep their secrets."

"I don't have to be a member of anything to know that you could be hurt if you get involved with this. The reporter could have been killed because he planned to expose the Mistics of Time membership. I've lived here all my life. I've heard the stories. I know you have, too."

"I suppose that makes sense," I admitted. "But I can't let this poor man's death be swept under the carpet, Miguel. What can it hurt to ask Detective Frolick what he's turned up so far? I don't have to say anything about the reporter being the same man they found in the alley."

"I don't know if Frolick is a member of the society, but if this is a police cover-up, he's under orders from some wealthy, powerful people to keep the reporter's death quiet. Do you think they're going to let you skip around the city asking questions with no consequences?"

I was beginning to get defensive about his attitude. I'm

sure I wouldn't have said what came out of my mouth next if I hadn't been angry. "My father is King Felix this year. His family was one of the two families that started carnival and the Mistics of Time. I'm pretty sure they aren't going to kill *me* for asking what happened."

The look on his face was enough to make me want to take my arrogant family pride statement back, but it was too late.

He finished stocking his side of the kitchen in the Biscuit Bowl and swept a bow in my general direction. "If that's all, milady, I should run and fetch whatever else you need."

Ollie came in at that point, not understanding the hurt sarcasm Miguel was throwing my way. "Too early for the Renaissance festival," he said with a grin. "But I love those things. Maybe we can all go together this fall."

Miguel left the kitchen without another word. I was about to run after him when the health inspector showed up. I couldn't believe my luck—it was Mr. Carruthers, which I thought was kind of creepy. Was he following me or did they assign him to me because he inspected the diner?

"Get Crème Brûlée out of the front," I whispered to Ollie. "Hurry, please."

Mr. Carruthers smiled when he saw me. "Miss Chase. I hope you found another place to keep your cat. He won't be allowed here, either."

SIX

"I took him to stay with my mother for a while."

It was a desperate lie. My mother wouldn't have kept my cat unless it was a matter of life or death. She definitely wouldn't have helped out to keep my business going. She hated the idea that I had my own business and that I wanted to cook for a living.

Mr. Carruthers didn't have to know that.

"Good." He nodded. "They brought in all the health inspectors from across the city for the food truck rally. It was my good fortune to draw your food truck."

"I'm sure you won't find anything wrong in my kitchen." *I hope*. "What can I do to help?"

"Leave." He surveyed the tiny kitchen area. "It's too small in here for more than one person."

I didn't mention that there were normally three of us working back there. I knew the regulations on that were vague. I didn't want to stir up any more trouble. "Sure. I'll wait outside."

I saw Ollie walking toward Miguel's car on the street and followed him. He was stashing Crème Brûlée in the Mercedes as I reached them. Miguel had locked all the doors but left the windows open about an inch. He could've left them open more—it would take half the window for my cat to climb out.

"Is the inspector done?" Ollie asked.

"No. He asked me to leave. Thanks for rescuing Crème Brûlée. Mr. Carruthers already has a black mark against me, I thought I should play it safe. I think he may just not like cats."

"Mr. Carruthers is here, too?" Miguel asked. "That seems odd, doesn't it?"

"Yes. He said they needed all the city health inspectors. It's probably not odd, though. I figure he saw my name on the list and wanted to keep tormenting me."

I smiled at him and moved closer to where he was leaning against the car. I didn't want us to fight about the dead reporter, or anything else. I knew he was worried about me. Maybe he was right about not asking questions. I wasn't sure. But I couldn't forget finding that dead man in the garden, either, and it didn't feel right.

"And you decided to play it safe?" He raised his eyebrows. "At least with the health inspector, anyway."

"I'm sensing some hostility here," Ollie said. "Are you two fighting?"

"No," Miguel and I both said at the same time.

"That's what I thought. I think I'll skip lunch after all. I'm not hungry enough to sit through you arguing. It's bad for the digestion." Ollie saluted and walked away whistling.

"Let me check into this thing with the reporter," Miguel

persuaded. "I know some people who know some other people. I could ask about the health inspector without anyone knowing who I am. At least let me try that before your name gets mixed up with it."

"But what if something happens to you because you were trying to protect me? I couldn't live with myself."

Miguel had a bad past. As he was running for district attorney, his wife and baby had been killed in a wreck. He'd been driving. The verdict had been mechanical failure. But he and I both knew it could have been something more, since he'd also been framed on the fake evidence charge. He understood how dirty the underbelly of the beast could be.

His name had been cleared, but not until the election was over, and he'd lost. At that point, he lost his job, too. I didn't want to think what it had been like for him. No wonder he was more cautious than me.

He put his arms around me and held me close. "I have a good bunch of informants who will do almost anything for a hundred dollars. Let me see what I can do, Zoe. Please."

I hugged him back. "All right. But please be careful. I'm sorry I said those things about my family. I didn't mean to hurt you."

"I understand." He kissed me. "Don't worry. I have tough skin."

"It's just that I can imagine how terrible it is for the reporter's family, you know? They deserve the truth."

"And they might be getting the truth, but that doesn't mean the news media is entitled to it. The police could have a good reason for keeping everything quiet from the general public. It could be part of their investigation."

"I know. I hope you're right. Thanks for understanding."

"Always."

"I think the health inspector is looking for you." One of

the other food truck drivers tapped me on the shoulder and then pointed toward the Biscuit Bowl.

"This should only take a minute. I'll be right back." I thanked the other driver and smiled at Miguel.

I walked back to the Biscuit Bowl. Mr. Carruthers was waiting impatiently for me, tapping his pencil on his clipboard.

"I see a recent inspection was done on this food truck, but apparently either your refrigerator has gone bad since then or the inspector wasn't thorough enough."

"What do you mean? The refrigerator is fine. I replaced it with a brand-new one recently."

"It was one tenth of a degree too warm. You can try turning the temperature down to see if that works, but another inspector will have to come take a look at it before you open for business."

Seriously? One tenth of a degree? "What if I turn the thermometer down and you check on it again in a few minutes?" This was ridiculous. What did he have against me?

"Look around you, Miss Chase. There are a lot of food trucks here. I don't have time to hold your hand through an inspection." He handed me his written decision not to pass my kitchen.

I wanted to throw it at him.

I went inside and turned down the temperature on the mini-fridge. If I couldn't get Mr. Carruthers to come back and take a look in a few minutes, I'd ask another inspector. I just replaced my old refrigerator. I wasn't buying another one because the inspector didn't like me.

Miguel was willing to wait for lunch while I waited for my mini-fridge to cool down. We sat in the car so Crème Brûlée wouldn't be alone. He was on the floor in the backseat making pitiful meowing noises. He wasn't a fan of cars.

"While I was waiting, I called a friend who works for the *Mobile Times*. He said he hadn't heard anything different than the story we heard on the news—nothing about Jordan Philips being found in a garden Friday night. He said the newspaper will go after the story on what happened with a vengeance. Jordan was the son of the owner. He said he'd get back to me if he hears anything different."

"That was smart," I complimented. "It might have been better than approaching Detective Frolick about it."

"Thanks. I can be sneaky if I need to be."

"Not really a good thing to tell your girlfriend." I grinned and kissed him. "I might not trust you anymore if you're sneaky."

"I do what I have to, Zoe." He shrugged. "But I'm never sneaky with you."

"What about what you said about the media? Would Jordan's family know the truth even if they are the media?"

He kissed the frown that had formed between my eyes. "Give it some time. Let's see what the police turn up."

"Okay—for now."

We kissed for a few minutes. My eye was on the clock in the car. I didn't want to wait longer than necessary to check on the mini-fridge. Despite what Mr. Carruthers had said, I'd been through a few health inspections. I knew they didn't take that long, but once the inspectors had gone, it could be hard to get someone else to look at it.

"It's been fifteen minutes," I finally told Miguel. "I have to see if the temperature has gone down. If not, that refrigerator is still under warrantee. I'll take it back and get another one."

He smiled. "You're such a romantic, Zoe."

"Sorry." I blushed when I realized that I had been watching the clock as we'd been kissing.

"I'll go with you."

"I'd appreciate it if you'd stay here with Crème Brûlée.

He'll be more upset—and louder—if he's alone. Thank you, Miguel."

He kissed my hand. "My pleasure. But next time I'm disconnecting the clock before I kiss you."

I laughed at that. I knew he understood my commitment to my business. I felt sure if our positions were reversed that he would've been looking at the clock, too.

I went back to the Biscuit Bowl and found that the minifridge was two degrees colder than it had been. *Really!* All Mr. Carruthers would've had to do is wait a minute or two. The temperature had probably been warmer because I was taking things in and out of the fridge.

And one tenth of a degree—please!

I looked around for Mr. Carruthers but couldn't find him anywhere. All the food trucks were in place, making it hard to see anything around them. He might have been inside one of the trucks and I just couldn't see him.

I decided to grab the first person I saw with a clipboard and an ID badge and haul him or her back to my food truck. It would only take a moment to compare Mr. Carruthers's inspection notes to the temperature in the mini-fridge.

I waved to a few other food truck owners who were also my competition, but it was usually friendly competition. We were all trying to make it in this new foodie world. Sometimes it got a little dirty when it came to parking spots and ways to snag customers. But mostly I'd found that everyone was good-natured and wished one another well.

Where are all the inspectors?

I finally saw my regular inspector coming out of the Suzette's Crepes food truck. He was shaking hands with the owner and heading down the stairs.

"Mr. Sullivan!" I waved to him. "Can you come with me for just a minute?" I told him what had happened. He usually did the inspections at the diner and for the Biscuit Bowl.

"Sure, Zoe." He smiled and glanced at his clipboard. "Let me get through this next inspection and I'll be right over."

"Why did they replace you at the diner?"

He shrugged. "The city is always worried that inspectors take bribes or get too chummy with the restaurant owners, so they change who we work with from time to time. Don't worry. I don't personally know Roger Carruthers—he's new—but I'm sure he'll be a good inspector. You must've just got off on the wrong foot."

"Okay. Thanks."

"I see your Biscuit Bowl truck from here. I'll be down as soon as I'm finished at Harry's Hot Dogs. We'll take care of this."

His smile reassured me. I ran to tell Miguel what was happening and then went back to my food truck to wait.

I opened the large door that had been cut out of the back of the Airstream. I couldn't believe my eyes when I saw another man dressed as Death lying in the middle of the kitchen floor.

I closed the door as quickly as I could and ran away.

SEVEN

I grabbed the first police officer I saw and told him what had happened. I didn't mention that it was the second time it had happened to me. It was hard, but I needed to stay clear on this.

"A dead man?" The officer said it in such a way that I knew he was skeptical. "In your food truck?"

"That's right. Not just a dead man, but Death."

His brows went up. "Death?"

"You know—Death and Folly? Someone dressed like Death. Just come with me and you'll see."

By that time Miguel had left the car and joined us. "What's wrong, Zoe?"

"I found a dead man in the Biscuit Bowl." I tried to make enough facial motions that he'd know what I meant without him asking, *Another one?*

"Let's take a look." The officer studied Miguel. "And you are?"

"Miguel Alexander." He gave him a business card. "I'm Miss Chase's lawyer."

"And you just happened to be here with her today?" There was that skepticism in his tone again. "How's that?"

"He's also my boyfriend," I quickly added. "Can we go now?"

"What makes you think the man in your food truck is dead? He's probably just drunk and passed out. This is carnival," the officer suggested as we walked to the Biscuit Bowl.

"I don't know for sure," I said. "I hope that's all it is. I don't want to think what will happen if a dead man is really in my food truck."

But I knew what it would mean—my food truck would be impounded for testing and there would be no Mardi Gras sales for me.

Mama's Marvelous Mojitos was parked close to me. Mama, a large woman in a brightly flowered dress, smiled and waved when she saw me.

I was about to open the back door of the Biscuit Bowl when the officer asked me to move aside. "I'll handle it, Miss Chase. You stand back."

I held Miguel's hand as the door opened. The three of us peered inside.

The body—or drunken person—was gone.

I was relieved and confused. I knew someone in a Death costume had been on the floor. Where had he gone?

"I don't see anyone," the officer said. "Maybe it's the heat."

But it wasn't that hot.

"Someone was here only a few minutes ago," I defended. "Maybe you should go inside and take a look."

He nodded. "I can do that, but I don't think a full-grown man could hide in your cabinets, ma'am. I'll take a look. You wait here."

Miguel held me back and whispered softly, "Maybe you

should drop this, Zoe. No one is in there. Do you want to explain what happened at the ball that made you think there could be a dead man dressed as Death?"

I stared at him. He seemed really worried—like Daddy had been. But Miguel was generally more worried about things and more serious than I was. It was partially his nature, I suspected, and his experience with life. He'd been through a lot more emotionally than I had been.

"No. I don't want to go into it. But Miguel, there was someone in there, and he was dressed like Death, just like Jordan was. And I don't think he was breathing, although I didn't check. It's too much of a coincidence, don't you think? What's going on?"

"I don't know. Here he comes."

The officer stepped out of the Biscuit Bowl. "I can't find anything in there, Miss Chase. Not a clue. I don't know what to tell you."

I smiled. "I must have imagined what I saw."

He nodded. "Yes, ma'am. I'll be at the street if you need anything else."

I watched him leave before Miguel and I went into the kitchen and closed the back door.

The officer was right about one thing—there was no sign of a person in a Death costume. "I don't understand. He was right here. Where did he go?"

"Maybe he wasn't dead. Maybe he'd been out partying and passed out. He woke up and left before you got back."

It was a plausible suggestion for what had happened. I didn't believe it entirely, but I went with it. I didn't have much choice.

Part of me was slightly worried that it could be a warning. It was too close to what had happened at the masquerade for me not to feel rattled by it.

Mr. Sullivan ducked his head into the kitchen. "Zoe? Are you ready for me?"

Miguel kissed my cheek and went back to his car to sit with Crème Brûlée.

It only took my old inspector a moment to check the mini-fridge. It was fine.

"I'm sorry you're having problems with Mr. Carruthers. Would you like me to speak to him on your behalf?" Mr. Sullivan asked as he gave me a new certification.

"No. I'll figure it out. Having you talk to him might make it worse. Thank you for offering."

He shook my hand, his gaze roaming the kitchen. "You've come a long way, Zoe. Imagine your food truck being part of the celebration. Got to be exciting!"

"You know it," I agreed with a grin.

I put the inspection sign up near the window where my previous inspection sign had been. I looked around the kitchen again, ill at ease in a way that I never was when I was working.

There was no chalk outline where the body had been a short while before, but I could trace it with my gaze. Everything was as I had left it for the inspection. Whoever it was had come and gone cleanly.

The whole thing had probably happened because I'd left my back door unlocked. It was a prank or a drunk, like the police officer had said. It was easy to get more upset about it than normal because I'd found the dead reporter.

"Well, no one is in here now," I said with my hands on my hips. "I have too much to do to stand around thinking about this."

I worked as quickly as I could to make sure everything was ready and then locked the kitchen up tight. The generator outside was running to keep the fridge going. It looked like I was set for the start of carnival.

I hurried back to Miguel's car. I knew being trapped in a car with Crème Brûlée could be a difficult experience. I wasn't sure what we could do with him while Miguel and I had lunch. The weather was cool, but I didn't feel safe leaving him at the diner or in the Biscuit Bowl.

Miguel had already thought about the problem—no doubt inspired by time spent with my cat. "What about eating lunch at Lavender's café? They have those outside tables on the sidewalk. You can hold Crème Brûlée on his leash while we eat."

"What a great idea!" I kissed him. "That's perfect."

We drove across town, taking side streets since most of the main streets were already filled with revelers.

My friend Lavender Blue was too busy to talk. The café was busy, but not many people were sitting outside. Miguel and I sat at one of the cute iron lace tables while Crème Brûlée explored the limits of his leash and harness. We ordered lunch and then sat back to watch the impromptu parade that had started down the street.

It was mostly made up of kids with musical instruments. Some of the instruments were handmade or created from whatever they could scrounge together. They played on glass bottles with sticks and banged pots and pans. There were a few washboard players and even one older man who played the handsaw.

Those sounds were mingled with trumpets and a trombone. There were several banjo players who smiled and nodded as they passed us. One little boy pulled a puppy in a red wagon. Several young women were dancing along with them and handing out candy as throws.

"You never know where the party is going to be." Miguel grinned at me. "That's what I love about this time of year."

"Me, too!" I toasted him with our newly arrived glasses of wine.

We ate fresh hush puppies and poke pie, wilted dandelion salad with maple mustard dressing. There was warm honey gingerbread with heavy cream in tiny purple, green, and gold cups for dessert. It was delightful sitting in the sun with the cool breeze from the bay.

The parade was over before we'd finished eating. Crème Brûlée spent most of the time lying on his back, swatting at a piece of candy wrapped in cellophane that had been thrown our way. He was amused and not getting into trouble. I was glad for the time with Miguel.

At the end of the meal Miguel took my hand and smiled at me. "What are you doing the rest of the day?"

"Taking care of a thousand last-minute details before opening tomorrow. You?"

"I have an appointment with a new client."

I stared into his beautiful brown eyes. "Is something wrong?"

"Just worried about you," he admitted. "I'm sorry you were the one who found the reporter at the masquerade."

"Me, too!"

"I hope finding another person dressed like Death in the Biscuit Bowl wasn't some kind of warning to keep your mouth shut."

From my mind to his lips. "I was thinking the same thing. It's awfully coincidental."

"We're probably both just being paranoid."

"Probably," I agreed with a smile. "It's silly, right?"

"I hope so." He glanced at his watch. "Where do you want me to drop you off?"

"I have to pick up a few things I left at Daddy's apartment. Then I have to get my food ready at the diner for tomorrow."

I picked up Crème Brûlée. He walked on the leash for a few steps and then rolled over on his back to swat at it.

We got in the car, but the lighthearted mood we'd had

during lunch had sobered. I knew the tension was there because of what I'd seen, not between us. Miguel kissed me before I got out of the car. I could see he really wanted to warn me about being careful again, but he refrained. That was good. I was nervous enough all by myself.

I pondered my thoughts about the whole mess as I passed through the luxurious apartment lobby, which was decorated with green, gold, and purple banners welcoming carnival. There were dozens of old photographs of floats and bands from past Mardi Gras parades on the walls. It was very festive.

I was surprised to turn the key in the lock on my father's door and find him home. He was tossing clothes everywhere. Suitcases were piled up in every room.

"Daddy? Are you okay?"

He was pale and still dressed in his workout clothes. "Zoe! I'm glad you got my texts. I was so worried about you." He hugged me tightly, and tears ran down his perfectly tanned face.

I pretended I knew what texts he was talking about and let Crème Brûlée off his leash. He scampered for his bed— poor darling—exhausted by his difficult day.

"What's wrong?"

"We have to get out of town right away. I'm afraid we're both in terrible danger."

EIGHT

I sat on the sofa. *So much for not panicking.*

"What are you talking about?" I checked my phone. Sure enough, there were five texts from him. There was no real information in them about what was going on—just more ranting.

"I had a vision early this morning on my way home from the gym." He scraped his hand across his short black hair and began pacing the room. "I saw the ghost of Chief Slacabamorinico. He was standing right in front of me. He warned me about you."

"Old Slac?" Chief Slacabamorinico was a mythological figure from the late 1800s. He'd led the Joe Cain parade during carnival wearing a turkey feather headdress with a deer tail belt, shell necklace, kilt, long johns, and brown moccasins. Each year someone new took up the costume to lead the procession.

Legends said that Joe Cain (a real person) had wanted to

revive Mardi Gras after the Civil War in 1866. He had dressed up, saying he was a Chickasaw chief named Slaca-bamorinico, riding in a wagon through the streets on Fat Tuesday that year. It seemed to have done the trick.

The ghost of Old Slac was a thing to frighten children. Or at least I'd always thought so.

"Were you drinking?"

"No. I was sober—until I got home. I've been drinking since." He paced the room a few more times. "I tried telling myself that everything would be okay after that reporter's body was found in the garden. I thought it would be taken care of."

"What do you mean? You knew that they were going to lie about where Jordan Phillips's body was found?"

"No. Of course not. But anyone capable of putting two and two together could figure it out. They didn't want the information about what really happened to get out."

"What really happened?" I asked with a silent apology to Miguel for not staying out of it.

"I don't know," he admitted. "Maybe the reporter threatened to do an exposé of some sort. That wouldn't do. Maybe he just wasn't supposed to be there. He probably wasn't invited."

"Daddy—this is wrong. Someone killed that poor man. Maybe somebody who is part of the Mistics. We have to say something."

"That's exactly what Old Slac told me we shouldn't do. Neither one of us should say anything. And knowing you have a difficult time with that, Zoe, I decided we should leave Mobile for the next two weeks."

I was offended by that. "What do you mean? I can keep a secret."

The doorbell saved him from replying. He opened the door after peering through the keyhole. "Saul! Thank God you're here!"

Uncle Saul looked a lot like my father. They were both about the same height—though my uncle was a bit thinner than my father. They'd both inherited the family business, the Bank of Mobile, from their father. My uncle with his wild, curly black and gray hair had gone his own way, running a restaurant in Mobile and ignoring his family name.

One day, he left that, too, and moved out to the swamp where he'd built a log cabin that he shared with an albino alligator named Alabaster.

My father hugged his brother and wept on his shoulder like a child. Uncle Saul patted his back and stared at me with a quizzical lift of his eyebrows.

"Hey, what's this all about?" Uncle Saul stepped away from his brother. "Looks like someone died."

"Someone died all right." My father sniffled. "And then Zoe found his body and led me to him."

Uncle Saul laughed. "Zoe, honey, you must be half bloodhound, girl. You're gonna get a reputation."

"That's not the half of it." My father proceeded to fill Uncle Saul in on the masquerade ball, Jordan Phillips's death, and Old Slac.

Uncle Saul poured himself some of what my father was drinking—it smelled like old whiskey. "That's a pickle. And you say the ghost of Old Slac warned you to get out of town, Ted?"

"That's right. I saw him as clearly as I see you. I'm going to pack a bag and get Zoe out of here."

"The ghost of Old Slac hasn't been seen around here for a hundred years." Uncle Saul downed the whiskey. "Why would he come back now?"

"To warn me! He knows what happened."

It was nonsensical that Daddy was approached by a ghost—no doubt it was his own guilty conscience. I wouldn't be able to convince him of that notion, but there was a lot at stake for me.

"I'm not going anywhere. The Biscuit Bowl is set up to be at all the parades for the next two weeks. I plan to make enough money to get work done at the diner and pull in a thousand new customers."

"We're talking about your life," my father reminded me. "There's always next year. Or maybe you could hire that big fella with the tattooed head to run your food truck."

"I'm already down a worker, Daddy. I can't run from this. And who's to say it will be any better when I get back. It's not like that reporter is going to come back to life. I'll still know he was murdered at the ball. I don't want that on my conscience, do you?"

"Zoe's right, Ted," Uncle Saul said. "If the Mistics are after her, they're not gonna stop because Mardi Gras is over. We have to do something."

"Like what?" my father demanded. "This is real, just like the ghost of Old Slac. I thought you'd understand, Saul."

"I understand. But you can't run forever. You shouldn't have got yourself all involved with those Mistics fanatics."

My father gulped down more whiskey. "*Now* you decide someone can't run away from their problems? You've done it your whole life. First it was about Daddy and working at the bank. Then it was college. You ran away from the restaurant. You know all about running."

Uncle Saul shot to his feet and shook my father. "That's right. I know all about running. I'm telling you that this isn't the answer for you and Zoe. Running is only good if you don't plan on coming back."

Daddy calmed down and sat on the sofa. "I don't know what else to do to protect her. She's all I have."

I felt like crying when he said it. I went to his side and hugged him. "I'll be fine. Don't worry about me."

"As much as it pains me to say it, I think you all should go to the police with this." Uncle Saul sat in one of the uncomfortable chairs and shook his head.

I knew that was a hard thing for him to admit. Uncle Saul hated anything to do with the establishment or any large institutions. For him to tell us we should go to the police would be like me deciding I didn't want to make food again.

"That's exactly what Old Slac warned me against," Daddy said. "He said the Mistics of Time would surely have it out for us then."

Uncle Saul stared at my father. "Don't you think it's more likely that someone dressed up like the ghost of Old Slac just to make you afraid, Ted?"

As my father was considering the idea, the next worst possible thing happened. The doorbell rang. I answered it without thinking.

It was my mother.

She was wearing one of her pale pink power suits with a matching bag and heels. Her short blond hair was perfect—as always. I'd been dyeing the gray out of my black hair since I was eighteen. Sometimes I "accidentally" allow a silver streak to show.

Not my mother. Her blond hair was always exactly the same shade as it had been when I was a child. Her blue eyes were keen, taking in the two men. She entered the room like a force of nature. That's why she always won when she went to court. I could only imagine the fear in someone's eyes when they faced her across the bench when she became a judge.

There was no doubt in my mind that she'd win the election.

"What's going on, Ted?" She didn't even acknowledge Uncle Saul.

I knew they had been a couple before she and my father were married. But that was a long time ago.

My father, being the man he was, spilled everything to her in a matter of seconds. They didn't get divorced because he wasn't willing to do whatever she told him. It was more a matter of the things she *didn't* tell him to do—including other women he enjoyed being with outside their marriage.

Uncle Saul rolled his eyes and got another drink.

"I knew all that secret society and krewe nonsense was nothing but trouble." My mother summed up her beliefs on the subject.

"Anabelle, that isn't true," Daddy defended. "They do a lot of good in this city. This was just a mistake."

"A mistake that could cost our daughter her life!" My mother snarled like a tigress defending her cub. "We have to get Zoe out of town."

"See?" Daddy laughed at Uncle Saul. "That's exactly what I said after I saw the ghost of Old Slac this morning."

"What are you talking about, Ted?" my mother demanded. "How much have you had to drink?"

"Not enough," he drawled.

"Running away won't help this situation, Bella." Uncle Saul tried to reason with her.

I'd never heard him call her by that name before. I'd never heard anyone call her by that name.

She ignored his lapse in judgment. "Go home to your gator, Saul. I think Ted and I know what's best for our daughter."

I was tired of listening to everyone talk about me like I wasn't there. "I'm not going anywhere, Mom. I'm working the next two weeks. Do you know what an opportunity it is to be part of carnival?"

"Quiet, Zoe. Go pack a bag." My mother took out her cell phone—pink like her suit. "I'll arrange for a private plane to take her to New York. She'll be fine there for a few weeks."

"I need to go," Daddy said. "Old Slac said I'm in danger, too."

"Anabelle, Ted, just listen for a minute." Uncle Saul tried to reason with them.

As their arguments grew louder, I kissed Crème Brûlée's nose and told him to be a good boy. "Let's go before this gets any uglier."

He bit my nose a little and licked it before I picked him up in my arms. It was as though he completely understood what I was saying. He's such a smart kitty.

I grabbed my bag, too, and said good-bye to my relatives. As I walked out the door, I heard my mother yell, "She's leaving! Someone do something!"

Her words only brought on more arguing. I closed the door to the apartment and pressed the button for the elevator. It was blessedly quiet on the trip downstairs. Not so much when I walked outside, as a large high school band was marching down the middle of the street.

Two makeshift floats followed them. The street was already littered with beads and tiny toys. Everyone stood on the sidewalk, watching and waving. There was no way to leave the immediate area, but I didn't see anyone who seemed to mind.

"Well, Zoe Chase!" Chef Art Arrington stood before me like the life-sized model of himself that I saw almost every day on billboards around the city and on the sides of his motor home.

He was short and round with a wreath of white hair, bright blue eyes, and a closely clipped gray beard. He was as well-known to the people of Mobile as Colonel Sanders was everywhere else. He always wore a white linen suit with a black string tie like the Colonel, too.

"Chef Arrington!" I hugged him, barely able to reach around him. "What a surprise to see you here."

Crème Brûlée made a grunting noise, since he was caught between us.

Chef Arrington and I didn't have a long relationship, and it was based on odd happenings that had brought us together. But he'd become like my patron saint, encouraging me and helping me find opportunities to get ahead with my food truck.

The best part was being invited to his many famous parties at his old mansion, Woodlands. I'd rubbed elbows with famous chefs from all over the world. Each party was a remarkable experience with amazing food.

"Not so much, Zoe," he admitted. "I have a nefarious purpose for being here. I confess the doorman called to let me know you were here."

I didn't like the sound of that. I knew Chef Art could be sneaky when he wanted to get his way, but he'd been so good to me. I was willing to help him if I could.

"Nefarious, huh? What purpose would that be?" I had to yell the words over the sound of the band that was now dancing in the street as they played. "I have to get back to the diner to get ready for tomorrow."

He laughed. "I don't think either of us is going far during this pop-up parade, do you? Let me buy you a cup of coffee in the hotel café and explain the situation."

He was right. Neither of us was going anywhere. Traffic was already backed up both ways. No doubt a few police cars would soon add to the madness.

"I have to bring my cat."

"Not a problem." He held out his arm, and I slipped my hand into it, accepting his invitation.

When we entered the quiet café, I asked, "You didn't set up the whole parade so I couldn't leave until you talked to me, did you?"

He patted my hand on his arm. "Even I don't have that kind of power, my dear. You know what this city is like at this time of year."

He scanned the café, and I became suspicious. As soon as he saw a man seated at the back of the eatery, away from the windows, he immediately set us in motion to join him.

I'd never seen the man before. He was older, like Chef Art, probably in his seventies. His hair was a full white mop on his head. He had a large ruddy face below it.

He was a big man with a broad chest and shoulders. The shoulders were slightly stooped with age, but he got to his feet easily as we got near the table.

"You must be Zoe Chase." The man held out his hand to me. "Anabelle and Ted's daughter, yes?"

"Yes. And you are?"

"This is Tucker Phillips." Chef Art introduced him as he pulled out a chair for me.

The last name couldn't be a coincidence. The dead reporter's name was Jordan Phillips. What was that old saying—out of the frying pan and into the fire?

I hesitated to sit opposite Tucker Phillips. Chef Art picked up on my reluctance. "That's right, my dear. This is Jordan Phillips's grandfather. Sit down, please. You make me feel short."

I took Tucker Phillips's hand and squeezed lightly before I sat, carefully concealing Crème Brûlée under the large white linen tablecloth. I couldn't believe Chef Art had his fingers in this pie, too. "I'm so sorry for your loss, Mr. Phillips."

Tucker and Chef Art sat, too. A waitress brought us menus, but Chef Art ordered coffee and beignets for all of us. "You're gonna love these, Zoe," he promised with a grin. "Best in the city."

I smiled at him and uneasily glanced across the table into Tucker's blue eyes. "Why am I here?"

"That's something I love about Zoe," Chef Art said to Tucker. "She always gets right to the heart of the matter. The girl is *sharp*."

"My son could do with a few more reporters like that. Any interest in working for the newspaper, Miss Chase?" Tucker smiled as he said it, but I could sense the terrible sadness and heartbreak behind his words.

"No, thanks. I'm a food person. I own the Biscuit Bowl food truck—deep-fried Southern biscuits with a dip in the middle that I fill with sweet and savory foods. I'm hoping to make my mark one day with a sexy new restaurant. The same way Chef Art and my uncle did."

"Saul Chase?" Tucker nodded. "I remember his old place. Excellent food and good prices. Whatever happened to him? Did he finally join Ted in the banking business?"

"No. He lives in the swamp out near Farmington. He's happy there. He doesn't miss the city life. He's in town for Mardi Gras—or did you know that already?"

Our coffee and beignets arrived. There was an awkward moment as everyone added condiments to their coffee. I watched the cream swirl in my cup and wondered where this conversation was leading.

Crème Brûlée was getting bored, but he got quiet when I fed him a piece of my beignet.

Chef Art laughed. "Zoe is a little suspicious sometimes, Tucker. Eat up, you two. These beignets shouldn't be wasted."

I sipped my coffee, not prepared to eat the delicious sugary donuts until I knew what was going on. "I think I have good reason to be suspicious. Let's get to it, shall we? You want to talk about Jordan's death."

Tucker shuddered and put a big hand across his eyes.

I felt terrible that I'd caused him more pain with my careless words. "I'm so sorry, but I've had a rough day. Part of that has been dealing with my parents and their fears about what will happen if I talk about Jordan."

Chef Art patted Tucker's shoulder and then started eating a beignet.

"I apologize." Tucker got himself together as he impatiently wiped the tears from his eyes. "I'm an old man, Miss Chase, with very few things that I still enjoy in life. My grandson was everything to me. His death has been like dying myself."

I reached my hand across the table to him. "I didn't know him, but your loss is terrible."

"Thank you. I thought I had this under control or I wouldn't have faced you this way."

Chef Art slurped his coffee. "Don't worry about it, Tucker. Zoe is a very understanding person. She's also clever, quick on her feet, and notices everything. She can help you."

I stared at him. "What are you talking about?"

"Tucker has a few questions about his grandson's death—understandable, I think. We know you were there." Chef Art held up a beignet. "You have to try one of these."

NINE

Tucker took that lead-in from Chef Art to tell me about the *Mobile Times* newspaper—which his father had founded in the early 1900s. He was editor in chief until his son, Bennett, took over about twenty years ago.

"Bennett brought Jordan into the business the same way I brought him in—and the same way my father brought me into it—working from the bottom up. Bennett was a good reporter, but Jordan had a real zest for it."

I ate the beignet Chef Art had offered me as I listened. A beignet is a fried doughnut sprinkled with powdered sugar and usually served with coffee. This one was exceptional. I hadn't eaten beignets this good since I'd been in New Orleans. The waitress brought fresh coffee, and I ate a second beignet.

I knew I shouldn't have eaten the second beignet, but I was stressed. I needed something to get through it, and they tasted so good. Yes, massage and exercise are better for your body, but I could hardly break out in jumping jacks. And beignets were good for your soul.

"I appreciate you telling me about your son and your family," I said when Tucker paused for a sip of coffee. "But I'm not sure how I can help you."

Tucker leaned closer and whispered, "I know you found my grandson's body at the Mistics of Time masquerade ball."

"What?" I gulped. If those two knew about it, who else knew?

"Don't worry." Chef Art rubbed my shoulder. "It's all hush-hush."

"You mean there's a mole in the Mistics of Time?"

Tucker and Art made shushing noises louder than what I'd said. Everyone in the café turned to look at us.

"Not a mole, exactly. There's someone in the society who was decent enough to tell me what was really going on," Tucker said. "I didn't think things like this happened anymore. My father told me stories about crazy things during carnival in his day. The societies were much stronger then. I just want to know what you saw. I'm trying to figure out why Jordan was there."

"Who told you about it?" I asked.

Tucker sat back, arms folded across his chest. "I can't reveal my source. He came directly to me rather than going to Bennett or the police. I owe him."

"My only part in this was finding Jordan's body in the garden. I'm sorry, but I don't see how I can be much help. I didn't see anything. You should really go to the police. I have a friend who's a homicide detective and—"

"That won't work," Tucker said. "Chadwick Sloane covered the thing up himself. He won't let his officers investigate and drag up dirt on the Mistics."

Did he know Commissioner Sloane was a member of the Mistics? I wouldn't want to be the one who told him. Of course, maybe Sloane was the one who'd told Tucker about his grandson.

"I don't know what you're looking for. It was dark, poorly lit. There may have been some things that I missed. I don't know."

"I appreciate that, Zoe. My son says Jordan was following a lead on a big story. It's frustrating, not finding any answers. You're my last hope."

No pressure.

"I honestly don't know what else I can say." I thought back. "He had a piece of newspaper in his hand. There was blood. It was awful."

Chef Art cleared his throat. "Perhaps you could infiltrate the Mistics of Time using your father's position. Someone in that group knows what happened."

I didn't even ask how he knew about Daddy being a member. Maybe it was just an assumption. They knew about what had really happened at the masquerade. It was probably easy to put it together.

I looked at him, hoping my total disbelief at his suggestion was written on my face. "Are you serious? My father is a complete basket case about this. He wants the two of us to leave Mobile until after Mardi Gras. He says he saw the ghost of Old Slac on the way home from the gym this morning. I've already seen a disappearing version of Jordan dressed as Death in the Biscuit Bowl as I was setting up today. I don't think spying on the Mistics is a good idea."

Tucker's face paled as I finished speaking. He exchanged glances with an equally pale Chef Art.

"You're right." Tucker got up from the table. "I'm sorry I bothered you, Zoe. Best of luck."

I watched him leave as Chef Art called for the check. "What's up with you two?" The abrupt departure was making me nervous.

"Zoe, your father is right. Old Slac—or the ghost of Old Slac—is a sure sign that death is coming. As for you seeing another man dressed like Death in the Biscuit Bowl, I've never heard of it as an omen, but you should leave with your father right away."

"Since when is the ghost of Old Slac a real thing?" I asked. "Is that supposed to be the ghost of Death I've seen, too? Come on, Chef Art. I can't believe you think any of that stuff is real."

He hurriedly gave the waitress a hundred-dollar bill for our coffee and beignets. "You'd better start thinking it's real, my dear. I don't want to see you get hurt. Go away for a few months. Have a nice vacation. Maybe by that time this whole thing will have blown over."

I felt like the proverbial rats were deserting the sinking ship—and I was the ship. Chef Art headed out of the café almost as quickly as Tucker Phillips. One minute they were begging for my help, and the next they were writing my obituary.

Their attitudes were even worse than those of my mother and father.

The parade was over when I stepped outside. Traffic was back to normal. I hailed a taxi for a ride back to the diner, hoping I'd find some sanity in the task of getting my food ready for tomorrow.

I opened the back door of the taxi after seeing the familiar flamingo sticker on the window. It was my uncle's friend, Cole.

- - - - - - -

I wasn't surprised to find Uncle Saul lounging in the backseat. "Get in, Zoe girl." He grinned. "The ghost of Old Slac might want to take a potshot at you from a roof."

I got into the taxi and slammed the door behind me. "I'm glad you think it's funny. No one else does."

"That's Saul for you," Cole said from the driver's seat. "How you doin', Zoe?"

"I've been better," I replied honestly. "I hope you're good, Cole."

"Can't complain. It's time for carnival. Greatest time of the year!"

"I used to think that, too." I stared at Uncle Saul. "So what happens now?"

"I don't know. I left before your mother killed your father. I was hoping we'd bump into each other. Where are you off to?"

"I have food to make," I told him briskly. "This is a big chance for me with the Biscuit Bowl. I know I don't have to tell you that. I'm not wasting it because the ghost of Old Slac, or a disappearing dead man, tells me I'm in danger."

"I think I can help you with that. Disappearing dead man, huh? I didn't hear Ted or Anabelle talking about that."

"It happened this morning while we were setting up the food truck. I didn't have a chance to tell anyone because they were so busy figuring out how to get me out of town."

We talked on the way to the diner with Crème Brûlée snoozing on my lap.

I told him everything that had happened since I'd found the body at the ball. Cole made remarks as we went along. Traffic was heavy as people rushed to get from place to place without finding themselves in the middle of a parade. There were also a few thousand extra people in the city for the festivities.

When Cole stopped to let us out at the diner, he frowned at me. "Bad luck to see the ghost of Old Slac. I'll pray for your daddy, Zoe. You let me know if you need any help."

I reached in the taxi window and hugged him. He always refused my money. "Thanks. I'm going to make you a big platter of food with some homemade MoonPies."

He blushed and muttered a few words I couldn't understand before saying good-bye.

Ollie was waiting in front of the diner. He and Uncle Saul shook hands. "Good to see you, Saul. How's that gator?"

"She's doing better. Bonnie gave her some antibiotics and it picked her right up. Those albino gators get sick easy. That's why they don't last long in the wild."

Bonnie Tuttle was the wildlife officer in Farmington where my uncle lived. I'd had some hopes of them getting together, but it hadn't happened yet. They were still just friends.

I opened the door to the diner while they were talking and switched on the lights.

It was nice to be home, such as it was. I hoped to make enough money to afford a small apartment not too far away. I hadn't figured that into my budget yet because I desperately wanted to spend all my extra money remodeling this place. But I knew the time was coming when Crème Brûlée and I would need a new home. The incident with Mr. Carruthers was just one of several recent problems living in the old diner.

Uncle Saul sniffed the air as he walked in. "I can smell those MoonPies. Chocolate, right?"

I smiled as I put away my bag and set Crème Brûlée at his food bowl. "I wouldn't make any other kind. Did you just come to town for Mardi Gras?"

"No. I wasn't coming this year. It's too loud and too crowded. I came down because Ted called. I was worried about you."

"I've been worried about her, too." Ollie stared down at me. "She's too stubborn for her own good."

"I'm not leaving Mobile and hiding somewhere until whatever happened to Jordan Phillips goes away. We'll just have to figure out who did it. That way, Daddy and I are safe, and I can do what I want."

I knew it wasn't as simple as I'd made it sound. I didn't care.

Uncle Saul and Ollie washed up and put on clean aprons and plastic gloves. They both loved to cook and gossip. I was offering them an opportunity to do both.

Ollie started his potato and pork fricassee by frying the sliced pork as I cut potatoes and tomatoes for it.

Uncle Saul started making his lemon meringue filling for the sweet biscuit bowls we'd probably need after the Moon-Pies were gone. "I'm glad you're not helping Tucker Phillips or his son. That newspaper has always been a rag. You've got enough on your plate without solving their problems for them."

"It strikes me that their problem is the same as mine," I told him as I switched to chopping onions. "We both need to know who killed Jordan and why."

"No wonder they backed off after you told them about the ghost of Old Slac," Ollie said with a shiver.

"It might not have been his ghost," I argued. "Maybe it was just a man in a costume, like the one leading the Joe Cain procession every year. Everyone knows about the legend—why not make use of it?"

"Good point!" Uncle Saul punctuated his words by pointing a lemon at me. "But it still says they're thinking, and worrying, about you and Ted, Zoe. What about you seeing the person dressed as Death again?"

"I don't know. Maybe a warning? That's kind of what Miguel and I both thought."

"Or another ghost," Ollie said. "Speaking of ghosts, where's the salt?"

I pointed to the cabinet above the stove. "I put everything away for the inspector. And what does salt have to do with ghosts?"

"My mama always told me that salt kept ghosts and

demons away. They're afraid of the stuff." He liberally salted the pork fricassee.

No ghosts would want to eat that.

"Taking ghosts out of the equation, let's say whoever killed Jordan is just staging these things for our benefit," I suggested. "They want us to be scared so we don't report it to the police or look into it ourselves."

Uncle Saul nodded as he got out the cornstarch. "That makes more sense to me than ghosts wandering around the city."

"You don't believe in ghosts?" Ollie's voice was surprised.

"Not particularly." Uncle Saul laughed. "I've never seen one. Have you?"

"Yeah. I've seen my share. I saw my grandfather's ghost when I turned thirteen. He was looking at the pocket watch he'd left me. And I saw my aunt Lavinia's ghost. She was eating sugar at the kitchen table."

"How old were you when that happened?" I asked with a smile.

"I was just a kid, but I remember it like it was yesterday. You know that disgusting green ghost in *Ghostbusters* who ate everything? That's the way Aunt Lavinia's ghost was."

Uncle Saul let out a hoot of laughter. "How could you tell it was her?"

"She was wearing the same ugly flowered dress they buried her in. And I wasn't the only one who saw her. Uncle Mattie saw her, too. He took the sugar away from her before there was none left for the rest of us."

"What about you, Zoe?" Uncle Saul stirred the thickening lemon filling in the big double boiler.

"I've never seen a ghost, but I think it's possible. Maybe when some people die they don't have things finished. I could see where they could come back."

"I think it's best if we don't consider these two occurrences as supernatural—not if we want you and your daddy to live through this," Uncle Saul said. "We understand why someone could be trying to scare you off. We just need to know who's doing it. That's the way to put an end to all this."

"There were at least two hundred guests at the ball." I handed Ollie some chopped onions. "Any one of them could have killed Jordan. If Jordan was there to do a story about someone that was going to make the whole society look bad, I could see them ganging up to kill him."

"Did Tucker Phillips say what his grandson was working on?" Uncle Saul asked.

"He said he didn't know. I don't know if I believe him. There was something kind of cagey about him. It seems like his son, Bennett, would know for sure."

"If the man came to you for help, Zoe girl, it's a good bet he doesn't want to get his hands dirty."

"I could go online and look up some past stories Jordan worked on. Maybe I could get a clue from that." I gave Ollie more chopped onions and potatoes.

He took out another large cast-iron skillet. "You said he was trying to impress his father and grandfather. I suppose something big and dangerous would do it. I wonder if he was with a member of the society or if he sneaked in. I'm thinking Tucker wouldn't have needed a snitch if his family was part of the Mistics."

"Good thought." I smiled at him.

"I've heard stories from the past where secret society members killed people who tried to infiltrate them—usually by beheading." Uncle Saul grinned and made a slicing motion across his throat. "You know, I could get into the Mistics of Time and check around. Ted isn't the *only* Chase with a lifetime membership."

"I think that would be a little suspicious, don't you?" I asked as the doorbell chimed, and Miguel joined us.

"What would be suspicious?" He kissed me around my food chopping.

"Uncle Saul joining the Mistics of Time after not taking part in it all his life." I smiled but didn't try to return his kiss. Onions didn't make great perfume.

Miguel was still wearing his blue suit and tie. He took off the jacket and sat on a stool at the bar beside me. "You aren't seriously thinking about looking into what happened to Jordan Phillips, are you?"

TEN

Since that was the topic of conversation as we cooked, I could hardly pretend we weren't considering it. I explained to Miguel about my meeting with Tucker and Chef Art.

"Zoe, you have to leave this alone. You said yourself that Commissioner Sloane is involved. You aren't a private investigator. I understand that you don't want to leave town. But stay out of this."

Ollie and Uncle Saul both stared at Miguel's harsh words and then went back to cooking. I was still cutting onions, potatoes, and tomatoes for the fricassee or I would've invited him into the parking lot for a private discussion.

"I don't see where I have much choice. No one else is doing anything," I reminded him. "Whoever killed Jordan thinks he can scare me and Daddy off with ghosts. That's not happening."

Miguel glanced at Uncle Saul and Ollie. "Will the two of you help me talk some sense into her? These secret societies can be dangerous—Jordan's murder is an example of that."

"We kind of agree with Zoe," Ollie told him. "We were just trying to figure out what we could do."

"Have you had some run-ins with a group?" Uncle Saul asked with a sober face.

"No. Not me personally. But I know some people who have." Miguel turned to me again. "What can I say to get you to leave this alone?"

"Unless you know someone who can make Death and the ghost of Old Slac go away, I don't know what else you can do."

Miguel looked a little frantic. He ran his hand through his thick dark hair and took off his blue tie that I'd bought him for our two-week anniversary.

"Okay. I can see you're not giving up. Let's get the police involved."

"How can we when Commissioner Sloane covered it up?" I asked him.

"You only have Tucker Phillips's word for that," he said. "I think we should talk to Patti Latoure. She could keep it quiet. If there's corruption in the department, she could involve Internal Affairs."

"What if you tell her and she's part of the cover-up?" Ollie asked.

"It isn't even her case," Miguel said. "And I don't believe she'd be involved. I've known her for years. She is a good, decent person."

Uncle Saul took a little lemon filling out of the double boiler. He set it on a plate to cool so he could taste it. "I think the man has a good point, Zoe. Tell Detective Latoure. If she's mixed up in it, you'll know right away."

"I think it's a bad idea," Ollie grumbled. "You want to get Zoe killed?"

I smiled at Miguel. "Okay. Let's see if we can talk to Patti."

- - - - - - -

Detective Patti Latoure's husband wasn't happy about her agreeing to meet with us on her day off.

"Keep it short." She eyed her stocky husband, who was drinking lemonade at a stand in the park where we'd agreed to meet.

She was a good cop who'd helped me out of a few jams I'd managed to get into since opening the diner. I liked her as a person, too. Her blond hair was loose on her shoulders for a change instead of tied back from her face in a ponytail. Her sharp blue eyes scanned the area, watching everyone around her.

"I'll be as brief as I can." I blurted out everything that I knew about Jordan's death.

"That's a pretty serious charge against Dan Frolick and Commissioner Sloane, Zoe." She looked alarmed. "You don't have any pictures of them with the body at the ball, do you?"

"I didn't have my cell phone with me."

She sighed heavily. "I don't like the way this sounds. Maybe you should get out of town for a while so it can blow over."

I shrugged. "That's what everyone says. But I have my food truck open for the parades. I can't just leave, Patti. You know how it is."

"I know how it is when you're dead!"

"Can you look into it?" Miguel asked her. "I don't want Zoe to investigate on her own—and I don't want to help her."

"I don't blame you." She glanced at her husband. "Let me see what I can find out. Don't do anything. In particular, don't repeat this to anyone."

"We won't," Miguel promised. "Get back with us as soon as you can, huh?"

"I can't promise anything. This is some serious stuff you're throwing at me on my day off—and during carnival. I'm not even sure how to check on the commissioner, but I can ask around about Frolick. I don't know him that well. Still, I find it hard to believe he'd move Phillips's body away from the crime scene."

"I'm glad someone isn't afraid of the Mistics of Time." I looked at Miguel and smiled.

"I'm not saying I'm not afraid of all the crazy secret societies. And I'm not doubting what you think happened, Zoe. I'll take a look at it—but not at the ghost of Old Slac. I'm not a ghost hunter."

Patti went to join her husband, putting her arm around him. I knew he hated her being with the police department. I was sure it was for reasons like this. He was a lawyer and had expected her to be one, too. She'd confided that a friend's death in college had changed her career path.

"What do you think?" I asked Miguel.

"I think she has a healthy fear of people wanting to kill her. I think you should copy her."

We started back to his car. I'd left Ollie and Uncle Saul cooking at the diner.

I stopped walking and put my hand on his chest. He'd left his suit coat at the diner and was wearing a thin white shirt.

"What's wrong with you? You've acted weird ever since I told you about the ball. I can't believe you're that scared."

He took my arm, and we started walking again. "When I got out of college, a friend of mine was asked to join one of the secret societies. We both thought it would be fun. He told me he was going to an initiation of some kind. We were supposed to meet the next day and talk about it. He didn't show. I learned later that his body was found in the bay."

"That's terrible. Was it the Mistics? I hope not."

"I don't know. My point is that they don't fool around. You definitely saw something you weren't supposed to. I don't want them to find you in the bay, too."

I put my arms around him and hugged him tight. After his wife's death, I should have realized he might be more than usually nervous that I could be killed, too.

Not that I *wasn't* worried about it. I was just more worried about what had really happened.

"I understand. We've given it to Patti now. She can handle it. I need to concentrate on my food truck, anyway."

He kissed me. "I'm sorry if I wasn't being supportive, Zoe. I just don't want anything to happen to you."

"Thanks. Let's go back to the diner and see what's going on with Uncle Saul and Ollie, shall we?"

- - - - - - -

I had no idea how much food the two men could make in the short time that we were gone. Uncle Saul had finished the lemon filling and started on some icing for the sweet biscuit bowls. Ollie was letting the pork fricassee cool before putting it in the refrigerator. He was sampling a MoonPie when we got back.

"These are exactly the right consistency," he called out when he saw me. "You didn't make enough, but the ones you have are really good."

"It would probably be hard to make enough MoonPies for a whole day," I reminded him as I stashed my bag in the office. "How did the fricassee turn out?"

"I took some out for you." He handed me a small plastic container. "Tell me what you think."

I tried it. It set my mouth on fire. "You added chili peppers to it?"

"Sure. We all need some spice." He patted his flat stomach. "It's good for you."

"How did the meeting go with Detective Latoure?" Uncle Saul asked.

"She said I should keep my mouth shut and stay out of trouble." I summed up her response.

"She's looking into it," Miguel added.

"That's good news!" Uncle Saul did a little happy dance behind the counter. "I hear they have a parade going on over by the cruise ship that just came in. Maybe we should head over there for a celebration."

"Sounds good to me!" I agreed.

"Not me," Ollie said. "Talk about being too touristy. That would be the worst."

"Okay." Uncle Saul modified his plan. "How about some Sazerac at Jumbo's Joint. It's not too far from here."

"I have a new client," Miguel said. "I'll buy the first round."

Everyone was ready for that. Uncle Saul and Ollie finished up what they were doing. I put the pork fricassee into covered containers and shoved it in the fridge along with the lemon filling.

I couldn't make biscuits until morning—no one likes a soggy biscuit. I planned to leave someone else at the food truck while I baked each morning. I hoped I had enough people to make that happen.

I went in the bathroom to check my hair and makeup before we left for the bar. The men stood around talking in the kitchen. They weren't worried about what they looked like. I grabbed some business cards for the Biscuit Bowl. It couldn't hurt to give some away while I was out.

My heart felt light and happy as we watched a crown-shaped float go by on the way to a parade. I squeezed into Miguel's car with Uncle Saul and Ollie. I didn't even have to call shotgun—Miguel chased Ollie out of the front seat.

We stopped at the parade by the docks. It wasn't very big, but there were several good bands playing and sequin-costumed dancers. There were people dressed as dragons spouting fire. I could hear the oohs and aahs from the hundreds of visitors that were there with the cruise ship.

I thought it was fun. Ollie thought it was too commercial. We had a good time arguing about it over cold shrimp cocktail and Sazerac at the bar. Miguel and Uncle Saul were in a deep discussion about whether or not parade floats should throw food as they went by. Miguel only had one drink when we first got there since he was driving.

I admit that I'd had one or two extra Sazeracs by the time my phone rang around one A.M. I'd already decided I wasn't sleeping that night and would make a ton of biscuits back at the diner before heading over to the Biscuit Bowl.

We'd had a good time, and I was sure my voice sounded like it when I answered. "Hi, there. You've reached Zoe Chase—food truck driver and extraordinary cook."

"Zoe?" It was my mother, of course. "Where are you? Are you all right? You sound strange."

"I'm fine, Mom. Out with some friends." I tried to sound more sober than I was.

"Something has happened. Come to the hospital right away. Your father is in surgery."

ELEVEN

"He was found by someone from one of those secret societies—the Knights of Revelry," Mom told me. "I think that's the group with Folly dancing on the rim of the big champagne glass."

We were sitting next to each other at the hospital. Uncle Saul and I had taken a taxi while Miguel took Ollie home. Daddy was in surgery after a sketchy attack of some sort. There weren't many details. She'd told me it wasn't that serious, but it seemed to me that anytime someone had surgery, it was serious.

Uncle Saul came back from the snack area with Patti Latoure at his side.

"How is Mr. Chase doing?" she asked. "What happened, ma'am?"

My mother eyed Detective Latoure. "I think he fell or something. He was at a bar, so he was probably drunk." She looked at me next. "Like some other people—celebrating this stupid holiday."

Patti took out her notebook. "I'm sorry something happened to your husband, Mrs. Chase. If you have any details from him, I'd appreciate if you'd share them with me."

"He's not my husband anymore. Thank goodness. As far as details, he was unconscious when they brought him in. You can talk to that officer on the phone over there. He gave me a brief account of what he knew."

Patti excused herself and went to speak with the uniformed officer who was talking on the hospital phone at the nurse's station.

"You don't have any idea what happened?" Uncle Saul kept his voice low.

"I know what happened—so does Zoe, but she's probably too stubborn to admit it." My mother's voice was equally low. "It's this crazy thing with the dead man that Zoe found at the Mistics' ball. I told them both to leave town. I'm sure this is a message after Ted saw what he thought was the ghost of Old Slac."

Uncle Saul shook his head. "That's what I was afraid of."

"The question is—is someone going to get some sense and leave before it's too late?" Mom glared at me.

"Don't start that again, please. We don't even know for sure what happened to Daddy. And I'm not going anywhere." I thought I might as well get that in before everyone started arguing about it again.

The doctor came out of the surgery unit, still wearing green scrubs with blood on them. "Mrs. Chase? Your husband is going to be fine. The knife missed any vital organs. The wound wasn't very deep. We'll keep him a day or two, but I'm sure he'll make a full recovery."

There was a fine mist forming in my mother's blue eyes. I was sure she'd never admit to crying over Daddy, but I could see she was very emotional about the doctor's news.

"He's not my husband." She took a tissue out of her bag

and delicately blew her nose. "Thank you, Doctor. I'll check on him again tomorrow."

"It's okay, Mom." I awkwardly patted her shoulder. She wasn't the kind of person who enjoyed random hugging. "He said he'll be fine."

She viciously turned on me. "And what about you? Do I have to get this call for you, too, because you won't do the smart thing and leave Mobile for a while?"

"Please don't start that again."

"Fine! But don't say I didn't warn you." Mom turned on her heel and headed toward the elevators.

"Maybe she's right, Zoe," Uncle Saul said. "This is definitely another warning. Your father could have been killed."

"He wasn't. Let's not talk about it anymore."

"I think we need to talk about it, Zoe." Detective Latoure had joined us again while I wasn't looking. "There's a family room. Let's go in there for a minute."

We went in the tiny white room. There was a table and a few chairs as well as two recliners where people could relax as they waited to see their loved ones.

It wasn't that I was all that brave or that I didn't think I could be hurt. I just knew I couldn't back out of this opportunity. It would never come again if I suddenly left town. There had to be another way to make this better.

We all sat around the table. Patti took a deep breath and plunged right in. "I'm sorry this is happening to your family, Zoe. I've tried to look into it, but it's difficult. Detectives don't like to share information about their cases. Talking to Frolick was like talking to a stone statue. I can't just walk in and ask Commissioner Sloane what happened at the ball. I probably shouldn't even know he was there."

"I understand. You're doing the best you can with a difficult situation."

"But I'm hoping to get some information under the table

from the medical examiner's office. I have a friend who works there. I know she can keep her mouth shut. I'll let you know about that. In the meantime, I caught this assault on your father. It gives me a legitimate reason to question things he's been involved with."

Uncle Saul thanked her. "We appreciate all you can do, Detective."

"Just doing my job." She sighed as she got to her feet. "I'm going to the bar where your father was found to see if I can find any witnesses. I'll keep in touch."

Uncle Saul and I kind of stared at each other, not saying anything. I held his hand and he smiled at me.

"We'll figure this out. There's bound to be something we can do."

I wasn't sure what that could be. Whatever it was hadn't occurred to me yet.

Before I left the hospital, I gave the nurse my cell phone number so they could let me know when my father was awake. I had to head over to the diner to get Crème Brûlée. I didn't want to think what kind of emotional wreck my cat would be if he had to stay by himself.

Ollie hadn't gone back to the shelter. He and Miguel were waiting downstairs for us. Everyone was much more sober than they should have been. It was as though the Sazerac had fallen away from us along with the good time we'd had at the parade and the bar.

"Would you mind taking me to get Crème Brûlée and then over to the Biscuit Bowl?" I asked Miguel. I'd explained what happened to Daddy and his condition.

"I'd mind," Ollie said. "You go stay at your daddy's place the rest of the night. I'll stay at the food truck. It's all decided, Zoe."

"What about your job at the shelter? I thought you were supposed to be there at night."

"I explained everything to the director. He's good with it."

"I'll help you with the biscuits in the morning," Miguel added. "You've been through a lot."

"Thanks." I had tears in my eyes as I hugged both of them. "You two are the best."

"I'm staying at the apartment with you, Zoe," Uncle Saul said. "I'd say at this point that we can't be too careful."

I hugged him, too, completely crying by this time, and then hugged Ollie again. I would've hugged Miguel again, but he kissed me instead. I guess he was past the random hug stage.

"You good to drive?" Uncle Saul eyed Miguel.

"You know it. Hop in."

Miguel and Ollie dropped me and Uncle Saul in front of Daddy's apartment building. Marvin, the doorman, held the door for us. "I heard about your father, Miss Chase. I hope he's all right?"

"The doctor says he's going to be fine." I summoned a smile. "Thanks."

He nodded. Uncle Saul and I passed through the lobby and up the elevator. We didn't speak until we got in the apartment.

I put my bag on the table and stared out the window that overlooked the city.

"Uncle Saul, I know we're all afraid, but I don't see any way around trying to figure this out."

He sat in the uncomfortable chair and nodded. "I know, Zoe. I see it, too. How are we gonna work that out with you running the food truck almost nonstop for the next two weeks?"

"I don't know yet, but there has to be a way."

- - - - - - -

It felt like I had barely closed my eyes when the alarm went off. I dressed hastily in jeans and a Biscuit Bowl T-shirt and headed out the door.

Miguel was waiting at the curb at four A.M. He was a man of his word—something I loved about him. I hopped in the front seat, and we headed over to the diner.

"Is there something I can do to help make biscuits?" Miguel asked as we let ourselves inside.

"Definitely!" I yawned. "You could make some coffee."

I switched on the lights. Crème Brûlée took a quick peek at who was there and then sashayed into the office/bedroom and went back to sleep. "It's going to be a long day."

The words were barely out of my mouth when I heard a tap on the window. I'd locked the door behind us, not exactly feeling safe these days.

It was Mr. Carruthers. I couldn't believe it.

I went to the door and opened it. "It's four A.M."

"Actually, closer to four thirty." He glanced at his watch. "I'm back for your next inspection."

TWELVE

Miguel was furious. "I don't think it's legal for you to stalk her this way. I don't know all the rules and regulations you follow, but this seems over-the-top."

I kind of agreed with him, but I also wanted Mr. Carruthers out of my life. If I could get through this inspection with him, I hoped the city would do a quick change-up before next year. I might not get Mr. Sullivan again, but anyone would be better than Mr. Carruthers.

I had already closed the door to my office/bedroom. Crème Brûlée was snoring on my pillow. He didn't look at me when I checked on him.

I hoped that was one problem out of the way.

Mr. Carruthers was going through his checklist on his clipboard again, but rapidly, without really looking at anything. We stood in the kitchen where I glanced at the clock. The biscuits weren't made, but the coffee was on. Usually, I was out on the street at six A.M. for a good spot at police headquarters. At least I didn't have to get things ready before eight A.M. for the food truck rally.

"I guess this looks pretty good now, Miss Chase." He kept slowly reading through his notes.

Impatiently, I poured myself and Miguel a cup of coffee.

"Could I have one of those, too?" Mr. Carruthers took a seat at the counter. "It's a long day starting this early, but so many restaurants are open for breakfast. You have to inspect them while you can. Nobody likes an inspector hanging around while the customers are eating, you know?"

"I can only imagine." Since he wasn't in any hurry to leave, I started my biscuit dough. Miguel helped me out by getting some of the ingredients from the pantry.

Crème Brûlée scratched at the door to get out.

My heart started pounding. Miguel had heard, too, and turned on the radio. I gave him a grateful smile and began cutting the vegetable shortening into the flour.

"I've heard people talk about your biscuits," Mr. Carruthers said with a crooked smile. "Only good things, mind you."

I returned his smile and thanked him. Was he never going to leave?

He started talking about his years as an inspector and about the Navy—he was a sailor for six years in his youth. I listened with half an ear. The other half was listening to Crème Brûlée, hoping he wouldn't start meowing loudly from the office.

"I have to go now, Zoe." Miguel's words were carefully chosen. It wasn't his normal speech pattern, so I knew something was up. "I'm going to take that container of shortening out of the office over to the Biscuit Bowl so it can heat up."

I had no idea what he was talking about, but I knew he had something in mind. "Okay. I'll see you later."

He did a quickstep into the office, closing the door

immediately behind him. I kept working the biscuit dough. He came out a few minutes later with a large covered container.

I realized he was trying to smuggle Crème Brûlée out of the diner.

"I'll get the door." I started to clean my hands.

"No need," Mr. Carruthers said. "I can get that for you."

Miguel and I stared at each other as Mr. Carruthers opened the front door. I looked down at the biscuit dough, hoping I hadn't kneaded it for too long. Too much kneading made for tough biscuits. If I could just get through the next few minutes, maybe this would be over.

The door closed behind Miguel. It was getting light. I could barely make him out as he walked to his car and stowed the container in the backseat.

"I guess I should be going, too." Mr. Carruthers stood up and handed me my inspection card. "You've passed, Miss Chase. Good luck with your food truck."

"Thank you, Mr. Carruthers."

"And sorry to hear about what happened to your father. I hope he gets well soon."

I watched him leave the diner, thinking that bad news traveled fast—or he was a member of the Mistics. I was probably just being paranoid. He'd probably just seen it in the paper or on TV and put me and Daddy together.

That had to be it, right?

"My hero!" I kissed Miguel. "Brilliant plan."

"He started howling right after I got him to the car."

"Poor kitty. He doesn't know what to make of his new life. Our old life was very sedate and routine. I didn't drag him around this way. He loved watching cooking shows with me. I'm sure he never dreamed he'd actually be involved."

Miguel waited a few minutes after Mr. Carruthers's car

was gone to get Crème Brûlée. He came back in with the container and let the cat out in the office. "That was close."

"Thanks for thinking of that. What a morning."

I made and baked another five trays of biscuits. I could never be sure how many biscuits I'd need in a day. Since biscuits were my specialty food, they went fast.

I knew I would probably have to come back and bake again since the parade days would be longer than my usual seven-to-six working days. I thought five trays was good for a start and would take me through until lunch.

We packed the car with MoonPies, lemon pie filling, biscuits, and bottled water before heading over to the Biscuit Bowl. It was already almost seven. The food trucks had to be open at eight A.M.

The streets and parking lot were empty as we approached the area where the food truck rally was being held. It would be a good spot to sell food, away from the main parade routes, but close enough for easy access when the parades were over.

Food truck operators were outside talking, laughing, and smoking in the municipal parking lot as they waited for the day to begin. As promised, the city had set up picnic tables so our customers could sit and enjoy their food.

"Thank God you're here," Ollie joked when we reached the Biscuit Bowl with the first load of food. "There was a man who staggered through the parking lot on his way home from a party. I was worried sick that he might be hungry. But I didn't need to panic. All the other food truck operators jumped on him trying to sell him breakfast. Poor man said he wasn't hungry and threw up all over that big joker who owns the crepe food truck."

"Nice story. Sorry you were bored. Mr. Carruthers came by again. This time the diner passed inspection."

"So early in the morning?" Ollie glanced at Miguel. "Was he crazy or drunk?"

"Neither one, as far as I could tell," Miguel replied. "I'm not sure it was right for him to be there, but it's done, anyway."

"Let's get this food in the Biscuit Bowl," I suggested.

Miguel said he'd go back to the car for Crème Brûlée. I smiled and thanked him.

I could see that it was going to be harder for me to be here each day than it was for some of the other drivers. Many food truck owners made their food right in their food trucks. I could only finish my food here.

I was used to going back to the diner at five or six P.M. and then getting ready for the next day with the Biscuit Bowl in the diner parking lot. For the next two weeks I was going to have to transport all the food here every day. Dragging the food over here was going to be an extra challenge, but one well worth the effort.

We got all the food stowed away by eight. The deep fryer was on, already hot and bubbling. I'd heated up the water in the warming trays and added the fricassee so it would stay hot. I could throw a small amount into the microwave and heat it up for individual servings if I needed to.

Ollie, Miguel, and I sat down for a cup of coffee and egg biscuits at a picnic table. It was very quiet, but we were surrounded by marvelous smells as other foodies got their day's menus ready. The breeze was cool. The first day of the rally promised to be fair.

I hoped those moments were the quiet before the customer storm. Crème Brûlée was fed, and I'd walked him on his leash in a small patch of grass so he could go potty. He was asleep again in the front of the food truck.

Two hours later we were still waiting for customers. Miguel went home to get ready for an appointment with a client. The other food truck drivers started walking around and sampling one another's food. I wasn't hungry, but Ollie made the rounds. He passed out some of our biscuits—food truck drivers eat, too, right?—and he brought back samples from the trucks around us.

"These tuna nuggets from Charlie's Tuna Shack are really good." His mouth was full as he spoke. "And these spicy onion rings from Betty's Blossoming Onions are awesome. Betty wasn't half bad herself."

"Great." I was a little depressed at our lack of customers. "I can't believe they want us out here so early every morning and no one is eating."

"You go out at this time every morning during the week," he reminded me. "What's the difference?"

"I only go out so early to get a good spot. We already have our spots here. I'm just here doing nothing."

He brought out a kabob with chunks of pineapple, tomatoes, and pork on it. "Try this. It's from that new place, Flo's Flaming Kabobs. I love it! Everything is served on fire. We should try that."

"Flaming biscuits don't sound very good."

"You're just in a bad mood, Zoe." He ate the kabob. "Why don't you call the hospital and see how your daddy is doing? That should make you feel better."

"Maybe."

He shrugged his broad shoulders. "Unless he took a turn for the worse during the night."

"Ollie!"

"Sorry." His grin was wicked. "I'm sure he's doing fine. I'm going to try one of Ducky's Dancing Shrimp. Sounds good, right? Want me to bring one back for you?"

"What's a dancing shrimp?"

"They kind of cut them up to look like little ballerinas. Cool, huh?"

"Yeah. Bring me back a dancing shrimp. I'd like to see it."

"Want one with coconut or lime?"

"Whatever."

I took out my phone when he left and called the hospital. I knew they had my number and could've called me, but what if they forgot?

"Your father is doing fine, Miss Chase," a nurse told me. "He's going to sit up in a few minutes and try to eat something. Your mother is with him. Maybe you should give her a call."

"Thank you." I looked at the phone, wondering if it was really my mother with him or one of his girlfriends. It was hard to believe my mother had gone back to have breakfast with him. I knew they were still involved with each other— mostly because of me. I thought they cared about each other somewhat, but this seemed out of proportion for their relationship.

The back door to the kitchen area opened. I expected it to be Ollie with a dancing shrimp.

Instead, it was Police Commissioner Chadwick Sloane.

"Hello, Miss Chase."

THIRTEEN

He reminded me of a gator with his sharp features and tiny dark eyes. I didn't think he would hesitate to chew up and spit out anyone who crossed him. He was a big man—probably used to using his height and weight to intimidate others.

Maybe it was just the impression I had from him.

He took his hands out of his overcoat pockets. "I wonder if I might have a few words with you."

I didn't respond—still amazed to see him there.

He must have assumed that meant it was all right. He sat down on the edge of the counter where Ollie had been with his kabob only moments before.

"What can I do for you, Commissioner Sloane?" I felt trapped in the small kitchen even though I could easily have run out through the partially open back door.

I think it was the whole situation that made me feel like I couldn't get away. For all the tough words I'd spouted about staying in Mobile, I was terrified. But I was more afraid to lose my livelihood and have to admit to everyone that I'd been wrong as I had to look for another job.

"Miss Chase, you and I seem to have a small problem."

"Really? We barely know each other. How could that be?"

"You've been trying to stir the pot, haven't you? Asking questions about that reporter's death, trying to set my own people against me."

I swallowed hard, hoping he wasn't talking about Patti. I didn't want her to get hurt in this. "Maybe you could just tell Jordan Phillips's family what really happened to him and that would take care of the whole problem."

"There are two reasons I can't do that. First, the investigation into Mr. Phillips's death is ongoing. We don't know who killed him or why he was killed. Second, his family is in the newspaper business. They'd be likely to report what I told them."

"I understand what you're saying, Commissioner. But you lied about him being found in an alley." My voice trembled. I squared my shoulders and pretended I was my mother. Her voice wouldn't have wavered. Neither would her resolve. "Was that to protect the killer, the investigation, or the Mistics of Time?"

"I'm not protecting anyone. I'm just trying to make sure this young man's death gets the investigation it deserves."

"By saying he was found in the alley instead of in the garden at the masquerade ball? Was he a member of the Mistics? Was he trying to do an article about the secret societies in Mobile?"

"You know I can't talk about members of the order of the Mistics of Time. It's against our rules."

This was getting me nowhere. "What is it you want me to do, Commissioner Sloane?"

"Run your little food truck." He smiled as he glanced around the kitchen. "Enjoy carnival. The police have this well in hand. I have an officer keeping an eye on the situation—on *you*, Miss Chase!"

"Did someone tell my father that before they hurt him?"

He got to his feet. "I wouldn't know, Miss Chase. I'm sorry that happened to Ted. He's a good man. Take care now. This can be a dangerous city."

I sat there with my hands shaking when he was gone. He'd made it pretty clear that I should leave Jordan's death alone. It made me angry that he'd treated me that way, and that he might even have had a hand in what had happened to a young man who was only trying to impress his father and grandfather.

I couldn't leave the Biscuit Bowl, but I took out my laptop and started looking at stories Jordan had written just before he'd died.

He was a wonderful writer and crusader. He'd written stories exposing hospital fraud, problems with child care in the city, and senior citizens being scammed out of their retirement money.

When Ollie came back about twenty minutes later, I was reading an article about a bank taking advantage of their workers. Thankfully, it wasn't Bank of Mobile, my father's bank.

"Here you go." Ollie handed me a shrimp with a piece of lime.

It really looked like a tiny ballerina. "It must take them forever to cut each shrimp this way." I stuck it in my mouth. "But it tastes good."

"I thought that, too, and there's only one person working the kitchen. I don't know if he'll make it with any crowds. This is his first time out. Makes you wonder, doesn't it?"

"You mean how they chose the food trucks?"

"Exactly. Here I was thinking they chose us because we have experience and street cred. This guy doesn't have either."

"But he does have interesting food. Maybe Tiffany Bryant is a fan of fancy shrimp." I glanced at the clock again. "What took you so long? Are there long lines of customers at Ducky's Dancing Shrimp?"

"Nah. Just talking to Ducky. There aren't any customers at any of the food trucks."

I yawned. "We do better than this in front of police head-quarters on a Monday morning. Where is everyone?"

"Maybe it's too early for people to be out at parades. We'll catch some later."

"But somebody is probably making money in our usual spot."

He shrugged and sat on the counter. "What are you reading?"

"Articles written by Jordan Phillips."

"I thought you weren't going to mess with that, Zoe. I'd say it could be bad for your health."

"Commissioner Sloane paid me a visit while you were gone." I smiled. "He was pretty convincing that I shouldn't ask so many questions. But I don't think we should look the other way. He was so smug about the whole thing."

My phone rang. It was Patti Latoure. "Zoe, I may have overstepped."

"Anything to do with the police commissioner?" I told her about him stopping by the Biscuit Bowl. "He wasn't interested in food, either. I hope you aren't in trouble."

"No. I'm fine. I spoke with Dan Frolick. I thought we could do this detective to detective. I was wrong. I don't know why he has such a problem with this. The man is annoying. I'm glad he's not my partner."

"Thanks for checking into it, anyway, Patti. Maybe we should both back off, huh?"

"No way. Not after what you told me. We need to know what's going on. I'd like to say that Mobile has more secret societies than it knows what to do with, but that may not be the case. Maybe Phillips was targeted for something else and dumped at the ball for this very reason."

"I won't back off if you don't."

"That's where the problem is. I'm a police detective. You're a food truck operator. I'm better equipped to handle this kind of thing. Don't be stubborn. I'll take care of it."

"Thanks, Patti. I know you'll do your best." I said good-bye and ended the call.

"What was that all about?" Ollie snacked on some other food he'd brought back with him.

"Patti doesn't think I should help her look into Jordan's death."

He laughed. "The Biscuit Bowl better get busy then. That's the only way I see you staying out of it."

We both looked out the customer window at the gray morning light. Rain began falling as we watched. Within a few seconds it was a downpour. With it came cool air from the bay sweeping the streets where people were ready to party.

"Oh brother." Ollie slapped a hand to his head. "Go on. I'll keep an eye out here. But you'd better watch the weather. If the sun comes out, hightail it back here."

"Thanks." I shut my laptop and left it there for him in case he got bored. I knew Ollie wasn't crazy about the Internet or any other electrical devices. But I thought if he got desperate, it would be something to do, anyway.

"Where are you headed in case Miguel drops by?"

"Tell him I'm headed to the *Mobile Times* office. I want to talk with Jordan's father." I put on my rain poncho.

"You'd better not say anything about the ghost of Old Slac so you don't scare him off, too," he suggested. "That seems to get people right away, even if it is an old myth. I believe it. I guess other people do, too."

I thanked him, left the kitchen, and headed out of the

parking lot, my head down as the rain poured on me. Ollie was right—the only people in the parking lot were bored food truck drivers. I hoped the whole day wouldn't go like that. I had a lot of money invested in food for the next two weeks. I expected to break even, anyway.

There were no taxis on the street. I didn't know if it was the weather or because there were extra tourists in the city. I was standing fifty feet from a bus stop as the bus rumbled up. I ran to catch it and managed to find enough change in my bag to pay.

The bus was empty, too—unusual for this time on a weekday. I knew carnival interrupted almost everything from school to government. Maybe no one was out yet because of the rain. Later there were bound to be crowds on the street.

I got off in front of the big white *Mobile Times* building. It had been here for as long as I could remember. It was one of the older buildings, probably historical. Daddy had read this newspaper when I was growing up. It wasn't as "highbrow" as some of the other newspapers in the city—his words, not mine. He also enjoyed reading about Hollywood gossip.

My mother, on the other hand, only read legal briefs and law reviews. It was no wonder they hadn't stayed together.

I stepped inside and spoke to a young woman behind a desk in the front lobby. She called to see if Bennett Phillips had time to see me. I looked at all the old front-page stories about carnival that were on the walls. It was a nice way to celebrate. Some of them were from the 1800s. The floats had lanterns and candles on them. It was interesting to see all the changes that had taken place through the years.

"Mr. Phillips says he'll see you, Miss Chase." The girl smiled. "I know you. My fiancé and I have eaten at the Biscuit Bowl. We love your gumbo!"

"Thanks. We're part of the food truck rally for carnival this year. You should come by and check out our homemade

MoonPies." It was nice to be known for something I did instead of someone I knew.

"Sounds great. Your biscuit bowls are delicious."

I took a nice warm glow up on the elevator with me. It was great to meet people who loved my food. I could only imagine what it would be like to open my restaurant to hundreds of people every day. I couldn't wait.

It was easy to find Bennett Phillips's office. It was on the third floor—the only thing there. He had his name in bronze letters by the door with *Editor in Chief* right below it.

There was another woman—this one in her fifties or early sixties—seated at a desk outside the closed door. The name plate on her desk said, Belle Wood. "You're Miss Chase?" she asked.

"Yes."

"Mr. Phillips will see you in a moment." She didn't look up at me. "You'll only have about sixty seconds to talk to him. He's squeezing you in between important matters. Have a seat over there, please."

I sat in one of the chairs where she pointed. Obviously he knew who I was, since he'd agreed to talk to me. I tried to think of ways to say what I needed to say in sixty seconds. I tend to be a blurter, so that could work for me in this case. I hoped he hadn't already talked to his father about me and decided that I was too frightening to be around. I only had a few questions. Maybe we could get to them before he kicked me out.

I should've brought a biscuit bowl filled with lemon pie. That might have gotten his attention. Food was a good distraction. I could've talked while he was eating.

The phone rang on the assistant's desk. She immediately told me to go in. I thought I recognized her from somewhere but couldn't place her.

I didn't waste any time taking her up on the invitation.

The office inside was huge. Bennett Phillips sat with his back against three large windows. I could see the bay from here. It was gray with the rain. Very few boats out.

His desk was big, too. There were pictures of him with the mayor, with a state senator I recognized but whose name I couldn't remember, and with his father and Jordan.

"Well?" he barked. "I assume my secretary told you I don't have long. Get to the point."

"I've been researching your son's stories. They have a common theme of Jordan trying to bring problems with large institutions to light. Was that what he was trying to do at the Mistics of Time ball?"

FOURTEEN

The expression on his face was one of astonishment. He looked a lot like his father, except that his hair was cut short instead of a mop on his head. He was thinner than Tucker, too. At one time Tucker had probably looked a lot more like Bennett.

Jordan didn't look like either of them. He must have taken after his mother.

"You know nothing about my son." His words were terse, but I felt the pain behind them.

"You're right. I never even met him. But I have to tell you that he's had a huge impact on my life. In fact, I'm worried about that life right now. My father was attacked yesterday, and Commissioner Sloane paid me a visit this morning. I need help trying to figure this out. I don't think that help is going to come from the police, do you?"

He reached out to his phone on the desk and pushed a button. "Alice, hold my calls." She said something back that

I couldn't understand. "Hold him, too. I'll see him when I'm finished with Miss Chase."

And I didn't have to give him a biscuit bowl at all. I was pleased and impressed.

Bennett came around to my side of his big, old desk and leaned against it. "I apologize for my hostile attitude when you came in. I read about your father—I gave the okay for the article about his attack. Darn shame. He's a longtime subscriber and a good friend."

"Are you a member of the Mistics of Time, too?" I thought I might as well get to the point.

He frowned. "No. Is your father a member? I saw that he was crowned as King Felix this year for carnival. I didn't know which society he was with."

So much for secret societies. Give me a month and a membership list, and everyone in Mobile would know which krewe or society everyone else was with. I wasn't good with secrets.

"Are you a member of *any* secret society?"

"I don't understand what that has to do with Jordan's death."

I blurted the entire story to him in probably less than sixty seconds. He knew everything I knew since the night of the masquerade ball. I would be a terrible spy. They wouldn't even have to torture me to find out everything.

"Do you know what you're saying?" His bushy brows came together in a large line across his forehead, like a gray caterpillar. "This is police misconduct, if what you're saying is true. Can you verify any of it?"

"I don't have pictures or documents, if that's what you're asking, Mr. Phillips. But I've been threatened and so has my father, who was the second person to see your son dead in the garden that night."

"Are you willing to swear an affidavit to that effect? Would Ted be willing?"

"I want to help. But I don't think that would be in my—or my father's—best interests right now."

"Then what? What are you offering me that I don't already know?" he grumbled as he went back to his chair. "What can you possibly do to help find my son's killer?"

"I'm not really sure. I thought if I could figure out what he was working on when he died that it might give me something."

"The police already cleared out his desk. I don't have any of his notes. I'm not sure how I can help."

"You were his editor. Didn't he have to talk to you about stories he was writing?"

"In a cursory kind of way, yes." He shook his head. "Jordan had the right temperament for this game. I let him have his head. Sometimes we talked—sometimes we didn't. He always delivered something fresh and insightful. That was what mattered."

If there was no way to get a look at what Jordan had been writing before he died, I wasn't sure if we could do anything. He liked to stir the pot, as Commissioner Sloane had accused me. But we needed to know which pot he was stirring.

"Did you know your father talked to me about helping him find Jordan's killer?"

"No! Why on earth would he do that?"

"My friend, Chef Art Arrington, encouraged him. They both knew Jordan was found in the garden instead of the alley, like the police say. They know something about the Mistics, too. They were talkative until I told him that my father had seen the ghost of Old Slac."

"That old thing." He shook his head. "Chef Art, huh? He likes to cause trouble. He and my father go back a long way. I'll give Dad a call and ask him what that was about."

"I wish there was more we could do." I thought about what had happened to Miguel with his career in the DA's office and losing his family. I didn't want that to happen to me. I wanted to make everyone tell the truth about Jordan, but how much was I willing to risk?

"Me, too," he said gruffly. "But with the police covering this up, we don't have a chance, do we?"

"I don't know." I got to my feet. "I'm sorry I wasted your time."

He stood, too, and offered me his hand. "You're a brave soul, anyway, Zoe Chase. It was a pleasure to meet you." He scribbled a phone number on the back of a business card. "My personal line. Don't talk to anyone else about this."

I gave him my cell number in return. "It was nice meeting you. Maybe we can still figure this out."

"I hope so."

I passed Belle Wood, the slightly rude assistant outside Bennett's door. There were also three police officers waiting, along with Detective Frolick.

Frolick stood and came over to me. "Miss Chase. What brings you here today?"

"My father was attacked, Detective. I hoped there was more news than the paper had printed. Mr. Phillips told me that was it. I guess I'll look somewhere else."

"Around here, we call what happened to your father a warning," he told me. "I'd take it to heart if I were you."

I didn't want to antagonize the man or give anything away. I smiled, nodded, and walked quickly to the elevator. He didn't follow me.

The elevator door opened as Frolick and the officers stepped into Bennett's office and closed the door.

"Excuse me, Miss Chase." Belle got up from her seat and came toward me with a worried glance over her shoulder.

She reminded me of an older, plus-size version of Delia with reddish hair. That's when I knew who she was. "You were the Mistic's Queen of Carnival when I was about ten, weren't you?"

"Yes." She seemed surprised that I recognized her. "That was a long time ago."

"You haven't changed that much. I remember how beautiful you were that night and what a gorgeous gown you were wearing."

"Thank you." She cleared her throat. "The police asked me for Jordan's cell phone yesterday. He didn't have it with him when they found him. I only found it this morning. He'd left it here as he was walking out. Sometimes he wrote on it while he was waiting for people. I haven't looked at it yet. Maybe there's something worthwhile on it."

She held out a cell phone. It was one of the bigger ones with a wide screen.

"Why are you giving it to me?" I asked.

"I don't think Jordan is getting a fair shake from anyone," she whispered, her voice choked with tears. "Maybe you can help him. I don't know what happened or why, but something isn't right. He shouldn't have died that way."

I took the phone from her and put it in my bag. "Thank you. I'll let you know if I find anything."

"I know you'll do your best. I knew your father once. He's a good man."

Cole's number was on my cell phone. He was waiting at the street by the time I got out of the building. It was still raining, but poncho-clad revelers were out now. If there had been a parade scheduled, it wasn't happening in the rain. Many of the floats were made of tissue paper and cardboard. Only the big parades at night would continue despite the dismal weather.

But that didn't stop street musicians from playing jazz at the corner or a few clowns who were handing out throws along the street. Everyone was eager to party—and hopefully to eat.

"I hope I have some customers now," I told Cole as I closed the back door to his taxi. "The Biscuit Bowl is parked with the food truck rally. Can you take me there?"

"I sure can. How's your daddy doing? That was a terrible thing that happened to him. You think it really was the ghost of Old Slac?"

We talked about all of the old myths and legends surrounding the carnival in Mobile. Most people thought our city had copied the celebration from New Orleans, but it was the other way around. Mardi Gras happened in Mobile fifteen years before New Orleans was founded. Their celebration might be better known, but it was certainly not as old. I liked to think that our carnival was more exciting, too.

"I'm glad you gave me a call," Cole said. "I've wanted to taste your homemade MoonPies ever since you mentioned them. My mouth has been watering. I'm going to put up my no-call sign and eat an early lunch with you, Zoe, if that's okay?"

"That sounds great." We'd just reached the food truck rally in the municipal parking lot. Maybe I'd left it empty, but there were people everywhere now. "Looks like we're busy."

I walked quickly past Ducky's Dancing Shrimp and Betty's Blossoming Onions, which both had lines going around their trucks. My heart started pumping as I reached the Biscuit Bowl—a huge crowd was waiting outside.

I took Cole into the kitchen with me. Ollie was zooming around like a madman.

"Where the fudge have you been, young'un?" he demanded, not stopping between dropping biscuits into the hot oil and drizzling white icing on some that were already fried. "These people are crazy. They want every kind of biscuit bowl we have. Some of them just bought plain biscuits so they wouldn't have to wait."

"You know what I was doing." I took off my poncho and put on my apron.

"How'd that go?"

"I don't know yet." I took over the biscuits in the deep fryer, and Ollie went to the window.

"Let me give you a hand with these napkins and such," Cole said as Ollie floundered, trying to find the plates, plastic forks, and napkins.

"Thanks." Ollie smiled at Cole. "You're exactly what we need right now—another pair of hands."

Cole had a smoker's wheezing laugh. "I've never seen so much activity since my wife had twins."

We all laughed at that and then had to pay attention to what we were doing. Ollie took the orders and set up the food. I cooked the biscuit bowls and filled them. We were already running low on MoonPies. I put three aside for us to make sure we got some before the crowd devoured them.

The customers kept appearing. It wasn't long before we were running out of pork fricassee. I could see the bottom of the last metal container we'd brought with us. There were still plenty of biscuits and lemon pie filling. But what were we going to do about our savory biscuit bowls? It wasn't even lunchtime.

"I have to go back and get something together," I explained to Ollie. "I was prepared for our usual crowd at police headquarters. These people are eating us out of food."

He nodded. "You go on. I can hold 'em off."

"Can you take me back to the diner, Cole?" I asked him.

"I can, but I sure hate to miss this." He grinned. "This is a lot more fun than driving a taxi. And it smells a lot better."

"I'd really appreciate it. I'm making you a plate right now."

"Okay, Zoe. Let's go."

I got his plate of food, including a MoonPie, and covered it with plastic wrap. I started to push open the back door and almost pushed it into Miguel. "What are you doing here?"

"I came by to see if you needed any help." He glanced at the long line of customers. "It looks like you do."

I hugged him. "I have to go back to the diner and find something savory for the biscuit bowls. I completely underestimated what we needed. We're almost out of food."

"Miguel! My man!" Ollie handed three sweet biscuit bowls out the window to a customer. "I don't think I've ever been so happy to see you—except for that time the police hauled me in for breaking and entering. Step up here and deep-fry some biscuits."

Miguel removed his suit coat and rolled up his sleeves. "It's a good thing I've got some experience with this. Hurry, Zoe."

Cole and I waded through the crowd to reach his taxi. There were so many cars parked outside the parking lot that the police had shut down the street. It was going to be difficult to get back to the diner.

But Cole maneuvered his taxi through the cars with one hand, the other wrapped around a MoonPie. "This is the best MoonPie I ever ate. You are a good cook, Zoe. No wonder people love your food."

"Thank you. That means a lot."

Uncle Saul called as we were trying to get across town to the diner. Other roads had been closed due to impromptu parades that were choking traffic across the city.

Cole and I were behind a group of musicians marching down the middle of the street, their instruments covered in plastic to protect them from the rain. There was also a group of scantily clad young women wearing crowns and sashes. They rode in convertibles with the tops down despite the rain. They waved and smiled even though their hair was wet and their faces were shiny with water.

"They're releasing your father," Uncle Saul said. "I'm at the hospital now. The doctor said he shouldn't stay by himself for a few days. Your mother is taking him home with her."

"Is that a good idea?" I had disturbing memories of some

of the last fights between my parents. I couldn't believe that would be good for someone who was just discharged from the hospital.

"I offered to say at his apartment with him. She won't hear of it. I'll be over there at your mother's if you need me. How's business?"

"I didn't even come close to making enough food. I'm on my way back to the diner to get more. Ollie and Miguel are holding down the fort."

"I'll see if I can come over and give you a hand after we get your father settled in. I'm sure your mother will go back to work. I could leave him with her housekeeper. The doctor said he'll sleep a lot for the next few days."

"You just take care of Daddy, Uncle Saul. I'm glad he's going home. We'll work out the food at the Biscuit Bowl. Bye. Love to you and Daddy. Keep an eye on Mom."

He chuckled. "Maybe I should've brought Alabaster to guard your father. See you later, Zoe."

Cole had made it to about a block from the diner by weaving in and out of traffic. People had abandoned their cars to stand on the sidewalk, watching parades and the occasional homemade float go by. Sometimes I forgot how exciting carnival was. With so much going on, there was no time to be bored.

"I'll walk the rest of the way," I told him as he was beating his hands on the steering wheel to keep time with the music outside.

He glanced at me in the rearview mirror. "You sure? I don't mind waiting if you don't."

"It's gonna take me a while to get all the food together, anyway. Maybe you could come get me after the parade is over."

"Sure thing. I'll be there."

I got out of the taxi. I could see the diner from there. I was surprised to see a strange car parked at the door. It couldn't be a customer. I wondered who the shiny brown BMW belonged to.

Thank goodness it wasn't the car Mr. Carruthers drove!

I danced a little to the music flowing up the street. Even here, beads, tiny stuffed animals, and other throws had been left behind by the festivities. When I was a child, I picked up the leftovers whenever I could. My mother said they were dirty. I thought they were the most beautiful things in the world.

But I was an adult and couldn't go around picking up beads—or even the tiny pink plastic elephant on the ground.

Or maybe I could.

I snatched up the elephant and stuck him in my bag. I looked around like I was expecting someone to be watching me. I hugged the secret that I'd done something I wasn't supposed to like I would have a recipe from Uncle Saul.

I didn't have to wonder for long at the occupants of the BMW. Chef Art and Tucker Phillips emerged as I got there.

Could this day get any more complicated?

"Good morning, Zoe," Chef Art said. "I guess almost afternoon, eh?"

"Miss Chase." Tucker nodded as the breeze from the bay played with his long hair.

"Gentlemen—I don't know why you're here. But if you have something to say, it will have to be while I'm cooking. The Biscuit Bowl is about to run out of food. I'm facing a cooking crisis."

"Well, let me help you with that," Chef Art volunteered as I opened the diner door. "You and I have made some sweet sustenance together in the past."

"That's true enough. I'd welcome the extra hands."

"I'm not so good in the kitchen," Tucker admitted as he held the door open for me. "I'm here because I got a call from my son. You've been a busy lady."

FIFTEEN

I went inside, dropped my bag behind the counter, and peered into my refrigerator and freezer. What could I throw together for the rest of the day? I was prepared for such emergencies, though I'd never experienced them before. When there was a sale on any food I thought I could use, I bought it in mass quantities. I would never use a frozen biscuit, but I would certainly cook with frozen chicken, steak, or vegetables.

I was going to have to go shopping or entice someone to do it for me, probably tomorrow. I had enough chicken to make some spicy chicken stew that might go the distance. I also had some frozen berries that I could make into compote. I didn't see the lemon pie filling lasting all day, either.

"I hope you're not beating yourself up about running out of food." Chef Art had already removed his white linen jacket and carefully rolled up his white shirtsleeves. "There isn't a professional cook in the world that hasn't faced that problem at one time or another. It's what we all secretly yearn for and yet despise."

I passed him an apron. "You're quite a cooking philosopher, sir. I hope you're as handy cutting vegetables."

"I think you'll probably be faster at that. Let me take the stove. I'm superior when it comes to actual cooking."

"Okay. I'm superior at chopping. We're a good match." I took out the frozen chicken. "We're making stew for my savory biscuit bowl. And a berry compote for my sweet. I'm not sure how many biscuit bowls we'll need. I guess I'll do five trays. We'll see from there."

Chef Art chuckled as he put the chicken into a pot. "I hope you don't use frozen bird all the time. I understand an emergency. And may I suggest that you get an oven in that little food truck kitchen of yours?"

"It just can't handle the electricity. I took out the microwave during the food truck race, but I need it on a regular basis."

"Maybe you need a new food truck."

I put a plastic container full of fresh carrots, celery, peppers, and onion on the counter to chop. "For that money I can remodel the diner. Eyes on the prize, right?"

"That's right."

"I hope I'm not interrupting," Tucker said. "But my son said you have some ideas about Jordan's death. Perhaps you could share those with me?"

"Only if you're interested that my father was attacked—probably to keep him quiet about Jordan. Having a visit from Commissioner Sloane was inspiring, too."

He frowned. "Chadwick Sloane tried to warn you off? What did you say?"

"I didn't say much of anything." I chopped carrots a little faster thinking about it. "But then I started wondering what Jordan was doing at the ball and why that got him killed. I went to your son hoping he might have some ideas. Someone gave me Jordan's cell phone. The police had already confiscated his laptop. I haven't had a chance to look at the phone yet."

"Where is it? Let me see it."

"It's in my bag." I pointed under the counter. "Take a look."

Chef Art and I worked in comfortable silence for a while with only the sound of vegetables being chopped and chicken sizzling with garlic and onion. When the veggies were in pieces, I started defrosting the berries I'd saved from last summer. I'd got a good price on a large quantity from the produce market.

"I can't see anything on this," Tucker said. "I think it's broken."

I took a quick peek at it. "Nope. It's password protected. We'll have to figure out what password Jordan would've used."

I showed him how to try different passwords and left him to it. I could hear him muttering for the next twenty minutes as he tried words and phrases that didn't work.

"I can't think of anything else he might have used." Tucker shook his head in frustration as he stared at the phone. "Maybe I could hire someone to do it."

"Someone who might be a member of a secret society who will tell everyone what we have?" I reminded him as my first batch of biscuits was baking.

"I suppose that's true."

"Have you tried things from his childhood?" Chef Art asked him. "That's what I use as a password on my phone."

Tucker went on trying everything he could think of as he muttered, and occasionally cursed, under his breath. "This is stupid. Why does anyone do such a thing? I open my phone and there it is."

"I guess you don't have anything to hide." I added sugar and some lemon to my mixed berry compote.

"What did Jordan have to hide?" he asked.

"Maybe something he was killed for." A tray of biscuit bowls came out golden brown and smelling like heaven.

"That stuff smells mighty good," Tucker said. "It's getting close to lunch. Maybe I should call Bennett and see if he has any idea what the secret password could be. Did he give you the phone?"

"No. I can't say who it was. I'm sorry."

"Kind of crazy giving a reporter's phone to a foodie." Chef Art laughed. "You were bound to try foods as passwords."

"What about a girlfriend?" I suggested. "Was Jordan dating anyone?"

"Yes. He was going out with a lovely young lady the last few weeks. I can't think of her name right now." He got to his feet. "I'm going to call Bennett."

The door to the diner closed behind Tucker. "This has driven him crazy," Chef Art said. "Not that I blame him. We've been driving all over the city trying to find out what really happened to Jordan. I'm glad I don't have children. They're a nuisance when they're small and a worry when they're grown."

I grinned at him. "You really are full of philosophy today."

"Things like this make a man reevaluate his life." He tossed some spices and herbs into the pot with the chicken and vegetables.

"Mind how much liquid is in there," I mentioned. "You might have to drain some so it doesn't soak into the biscuit."

He stared at me. "I don't know another chef I'd take that from much less a food truck cook."

"That's because you're Chef Art. No one knows more than you about cooking." I smiled to ease the sarcasm. Only a year ago I would've felt the same way about him. Knowing him personally made him more human, easy to tease.

"That's right," he agreed with a grin. "I wouldn't have minded having a daughter like you, Zoe. A girl after my own heart. I'm afraid if I'd really had a daughter, though, she would've been made out of marshmallow cream and would've hated to cook."

"Is that what you've been reevaluating?"

"That, and my mission here on earth." He stirred the chicken. "I've been thinking about starting a cooking school. I'd start here in Mobile. Maybe go nationwide after we test it. You could come and work for me."

"I appreciate the offer, but I don't think teaching is my calling."

"You could do it part-time when you aren't working the food truck," he continued. "You could make extra money toward your remodeling project."

It was tempting, but my time was limited. I couldn't splinter my energies. I had to stay focused. "Thanks. I don't think so."

He shrugged as I moved another tray of biscuits out of the oven.

Tucker came back inside with a wide smile on his face. "I think I figured it out. You were right, Miss Chase. It was his girlfriend's name—Lisa."

I looked at the phone again. "You did it! Now you have to search through the files to see what he was working on that might have gotten him killed."

I had the last two trays of biscuits in the oven. The chicken stew was done, and the berry compote was in a metal container ready to go.

My phone rang. It was Ollie. He was hyperventilating because all the food was gone. "Are you coming back soon?" he asked. "If not, I'm closing down. People are really angry when you don't have food in a food truck."

"No! You can't close down. It's against the rules. I'll be there in a few minutes. Give out flyers and tell people they get a discount when they come back."

"Okay. But don't blame me if they eat the flyers."

I ended the call. "I have to go. You keep working on that phone, Mr. Phillips. Let me know if you find anything."

"Let us give you a lift to the food truck rally," Chef Art offered. "It's the least we can do."

The front door chimed again. "Delia!" I was surprised and happy to see her. "How's your sister doing?"

She looked wonderful in a lemon yellow top and skinny jeans. Both men appraised her as they might have a valuable painting.

"She's gonna be fine, Zoe. I was glad I was there during her surgery, but I knew you needed me. Mama and the other kids are still there with her. They understood when I told them I had to go. I got back as soon as I could."

She walked over and hugged me despite my being covered in flour and vegetables.

"I'm so glad to see you." I tried not to get her dirty. "I could really use an extra hand."

"What can I do? Where's the Biscuit Bowl?"

Out of the corner of my eye, I saw Cole's taxi bump into the parking lot outside. "We're about to move a lot of food over there now. Let's get it out to the cars."

I was lucky to have the taxi, and I took advantage of the BMW. There was just enough room for everything and everyone that needed to go to the food truck rally.

I would have felt bad not riding with Cole, even though I would've liked to have a look at Jordan's cell phone. Now that he had it, Tucker didn't seem to want to let it go. Not that I blamed him. Knowing everything that was in *my* phone, I could see where it would be bittersweet for Jordan's grandfather to look at it.

Delia rode in the BMW—in the front seat with Chef Art. They'd had a brief relationship that had ended soon after we'd met. It wasn't a serious relationship, but I wondered what they talked about going back across town.

I knew Delia had some wishful thoughts about Chef Art at one time. He was rich. I understood her quest for a better life. She'd been raised very poor with a large family. She was always looking for a way to move up.

I wasn't much help with that. All I could offer was friendship and what wages I could afford. That's why I always encouraged her to look for something better. She was my friend. I hoped she'd find what she was looking for.

It took five of us to transport the food to the Biscuit Bowl from the street. It was a stupid rule not to allow any vendors' cars into the parking lot. I was sure I wasn't the only one having a food problem.

We got there just in time for lunch. There was a big parade going on a few blocks over in midtown. The crowds from this morning had evaporated—probably to watch the parade. I was sorry we'd had to turn some people away but was hoping to be ready for the next rush.

Ollie was standing outside with a forbidding expression on his face and dozens of flyers in his big hands. I wasn't sure if anyone would have dared to ask for a flyer. I couldn't fault him for being in a bad mood.

"It's about time," he said. "Miguel and I have had it rough. There were a few people whose heads I would've liked to knock together. I didn't. But only because I didn't want you to get a bad reputation."

I hugged him. It was like hugging a rock. "I'm so sorry. I appreciate that you stayed here and handled it. Where is Miguel?"

"Walking Crème Brûlée in the grass." Despite the hug and the apology, he was still stiff and angry. "That cat has a personality problem. He tried to scratch me again."

"Where do you want this food, Zoe?" Cole struggled with a large container of berries.

"Thanks. Let's get it all in the kitchen."

I waited while Cole, Chef Art, and Tucker took what they were holding into the kitchen. There wasn't enough room for all of us in there at one time.

I went to find Miguel and Crème Brûlée. My cat was doing his usual tricks—standing and staring, alternating with meowing and rolling in the grass.

"I can't tell if he likes being out here or not," Miguel said with a smile.

At least he was still smiling.

"He really likes being out here. He's just being difficult." I took the leash from him. "Thanks for thinking of him."

Miguel put his arm around me. "I think he only likes you, Zoe."

I lifted my cat and cuddled him. He swiped at me with his paw and nibbled on my chin. It wasn't painful.

"I hope you've got a lot of food." Miguel followed me to the front of the Biscuit Bowl. "Those people this morning were really hungry. I felt like we were in a bad zombie movie."

I laughed as I made sure everything was set up for my cat. Crème Brûlée was exhausted from his trip outside. He settled down right away and was snoring before I closed the door.

"Thank you for being here. Ollie is still mad at me. I hope he'll take the rest of the day off and come back tomorrow. Delia is back. I think the two of us can handle it."

"I still have some time," he said. "I can help."

"That's very nice of you, but I don't want to take advantage. I might need you tomorrow. I don't want you to see my call on your phone and ignore me."

He put his arms around me and kissed me. "I don't think so. I'll stick around so you can let Ollie go home."

"You're the best. I'm surprised someone didn't snatch you up before I could find you."

"I don't think that was possible." He kissed my nose and smiled.

"If we're finished with the lovefest out here," Ollie interrupted, "we need to get this food put away. I'm not even sure there's room for it."

He was right. He was also still angry. Chef Art and Tucker had dropped off the food and left. Delia was already in the kitchen working. Cole was relaxing in the shade at a picnic table with the food I'd made him earlier.

I left Miguel and took Ollie's arm until we were behind the Biscuit Bowl so we could talk. "I'm really sorry this happened. I didn't do a good job planning for it. I don't know what I would've done if it wasn't for you being here. I hope you'll forgive me."

He glared at me. "Zoe."

"Yes?"

"Nothing." He grabbed me and gave me a big bear hug that took me off my feet. "You did the best you could. I'm not mad—not at you, anyway. We should've been able to close if we didn't have any food. That's a stupid rule for the food truck rally. That's what I'm mad about. Okay?"

"Okay. Thanks." He put me back on my feet. "Why don't you take off the rest of the day? I might need you later and you won't be so tired."

"I'm not tired. I'm good." He motioned to the Biscuit Bowl. "Is *she* okay with me being here?"

I knew he meant Delia. "Let's not go through this again. I need you to work together even though you broke up. You said you could do that."

"And I can. I'm just saying *she* might not be able to do it." His face was set in tense lines. He wouldn't admit how much the breakup bothered him.

"All right. We need to get all this food put away and get ready for lunch. Miguel is staying, too. Let's hope the crowd is as big as it was this morning."

SIXTEEN

It didn't take long to find out.

We'd barely put the food where it belonged when crowds began surging through the parking lot.

"Looks like the parade is over." Ollie took his spot by the open window.

"How do you want to do this, Zoe?" Delia asked.

"I'll handle frying the biscuit bowls," I told her. "Ollie has the window. You fill the dessert bowls, and Miguel fills the savory bowls."

"I see them coming!" Ollie called out.

It was the last sane thing anyone said for three hours. It was an onslaught of hungry revelers wearing beads and carrying stuffed animals and Frisbees. They wanted everything—ten savory biscuits and ten sweet biscuits. They ordered in dozens instead of singles. It was like nothing I had ever done.

Our downfall was not having something to drink. People ordered biscuit bowls and asked for soda or sweet tea. We had neither. Some of them went to look for food and drinks together, leaving without my biscuit bowls.

It had always been a problem for me, but at the usual spots there were other food trucks that only served beverages, or people brought their own drinks from home. Once in a while someone might not be happy that they had to go to more than one food truck, but not often. It was very noticeable here.

"There goes another one," Ollie said. "We gotta do something about this, Zoe. It's too hard to get through this crowd loaded with biscuit bowls and find someone with a Pepsi."

"I know, Ollie, I know." I was busy getting another dozen biscuit bowls out of the fryer. "There's nothing I can do about it right now."

"We don't have room in here for drinks, too." Delia passed several more sweet biscuits to Ollie.

"Maybe you need a big ice chest with bottled or canned drinks," Miguel suggested. "When this calms down, we could get something and set it up."

"Good idea." I smiled at him. "I like originality from my highly paid employees."

He grinned as he passed five savory biscuit bowls to Ollie for an order. "We aim to please."

We worked well together. It went so quickly that I hardly had time to look up before it was three P.M. and the crowd was finally disappearing.

"I hear there's another parade getting started on Dauphin Street. It's one of those put on by a big krewe, Cosmic Cowboys of Wragg Swamp. Should be a good one." Ollie turned away from the window. "I'm glad they're gone. I hope there's food left. I'm starving."

We took what we could find to eat and went outside to drop down at an empty picnic table, exhausted, eating lunch quietly under the cloudy skies. The rain had stopped, but it still looked threatening for later in the evening. We could hear the sound of marching bands and cannon fire sprinkled with fireworks.

"I have to go back to the diner and make more food." I was almost too tired to eat a chicken stew biscuit bowl. It was delicious but almost too much work. "First I have to buy food. I'm out of everything but flour, shortening, and baking powder."

"Make me a list," Miguel said. "I'll shop for you. You can get started on the biscuits."

"Great idea." I was grateful for his support. "How am I going to keep up with this for two weeks? I'm already exhausted."

Delia rubbed my back. "We probably need to do this in shifts. That way everyone has a chance to rest. Miguel and I could take a shift, and you and Ollie could take the next shift."

"Miguel already has a job," I said.

"Which is going to be slack for the next two weeks, anyway, during carnival," Miguel reminded me. "Most people put things off until after the holiday. I can work with you."

"Thank you." I smiled at him and yawned. "Maybe we can do this thing."

"Of course we can!" Ollie devoured three biscuit bowls with pork fricassee that he'd saved for himself from the morning rush. "I gotta tell you, Zoe: that chicken is good, but not as good as my pork."

I laughed. "I guess I'll get more ingredients for another fricassee."

"I'll be glad to make it for you during my off shift. I like to cook at night."

"Sounds great. Thanks, Ollie. I want to go visit Daddy for a few minutes before I go back to the diner."

After dividing up all our ideas, I was so grateful to have such wonderful people working with me. I hoped someday to be able to repay them for what they'd done.

My phone rang as I was making a shopping list for Miguel. It was Tucker.

"I think I've found something, Zoe. Jordan had a lot of writing in the phone. He also had interviews and appointments with people he was researching. I think I know what he was doing at the Mistics of Time ball. Can you meet me somewhere?"

"You can meet me back at the diner. I'll be cooking there for a while in about an hour. Let's see what we can find."

Delia agreed to stay at the Biscuit Bowl. She was still kind of fresh compared to the rest of us. There didn't seem to be a big rush on the way until supper. We could restock and be back by then.

Miguel dropped me off at my mother's house. I felt bad that I hadn't seen my father since he was conscious. Miguel left me with a quick kiss after scanning my shopping list to make sure he understood everything. He might not be a cook, but he was the best assistant ever—with benefits.

"I'll see you back at the diner," he said. "Be careful."

"It's just my mother," I joked. "How bad can it be?"

"You know what I mean. You're still involved with whatever happened to Jordan Phillips. Don't take any chances."

"I won't. I'll see you later."

My mother's housekeeper, Martha, greeted me at the door, but I paused at the downstairs bathroom to freshen up a bit before going to see Daddy—I knew I smelled like fried biscuit bowls. My face was sunburned and my hair was going crazy. There wasn't much I could do about either of those things. I washed my face, smoothed back my hair, and spritzed on some perfume. That was the best I could do.

"He's in the blue bedroom." Martha was waiting when I came out of the bathroom. "Can I get something for you— tea, lemonade? Wesley made some wonderful cookies this morning."

Wesley was my mother's chef. Normally I would've jumped at the chance to eat anything he'd made, but I was still too full. "Nothing to drink, thanks. But I'll take a few cookies to go."

She went to get them and I went upstairs.

This house on Julia Way would always be home to me. It was a two-story 1920s Victorian that didn't show a bit of its age. It had been wonderfully cared for up until my mother took possession of it when I was a child.

Since then she'd obsessed over every aspect of the house and grounds. Her legacy to whoever got the house from her would be dozens of improvements and additions. I loved the old place, but I wouldn't have wanted to live there.

Someday I pictured myself living in an apartment above an exclusive restaurant—my own, of course. It would be in one of the older parts of the city with a wonderful view of the bay. I added to my dream on a regular basis as I watched home improvement shows between cooking shows on TV.

I wondered if Miguel would be part of that. We weren't to that commitment stage in our relationship. I wasn't sure if we ever would be, and I didn't really care at that time. I was doing what I'd always wanted to do with great friends around me. I couldn't complain.

Tiptoeing across the floor upstairs to reach the guest room, I thought Daddy might be sleeping. I didn't want to disturb him if that was the case.

I peeked in the doorway and immediately flattened myself against the wall, barely breathing.

My mother and father were kissing. It was enough to addle my brain.

What should I do? I dared another glance.

She was almost lying across him. They were as entwined as the moss in the big oaks outside. I hadn't seen them do anything like this—well—ever. I felt sure they had at some time, but maybe not since I'd been born.

I decided to clear my throat in a polite manner. They'd break apart and try to be presentable.

I cleared my throat. Neither one of them looked my way or moved.

I did it again. *Louder.*

That worked. My mother got quickly off the bed, smoothed her hair and top. Daddy smiled at her and squeezed her hand.

What are they doing?

They'd been divorced for twelve years. Was this some knee-jerk reaction to my father being attacked? Obviously they hadn't thought this through before going at it that way.

I put a big smile on my face and walked into the room as though everything was fine. "How are you feeling, Daddy? I'm glad you're out of the hospital. I'll bet you'll be glad to go home—to *your* apartment—soon."

"I'm doing just fine, baby girl." He held out his hand to me.

I have to say that he didn't look as pale and pathetic as one might expect a person to be after going through what he had. His eyes were sparkling and there was a lot of color in his face.

"I thought I'd stop by to see if there was anything I could do before I start making food again for the Biscuit Bowl. You wouldn't have believed the crowds that were out this afternoon. I expected that I had enough food for the whole day, but it didn't work out that way."

"Zoe, your father needs his rest," my mother said. "We should talk about things downstairs."

Was she kidding? She was all over him. Was that a hickey on her neck? I still couldn't believe what I'd seen.

"In a minute." I smiled at her. "I have a few questions for Daddy."

"I'll just wait downstairs, then," she said. "Don't be too long."

Once she was gone, I desperately wanted to ask him about

the two of them. Had this been going on for a while? Were they getting back together?

Instead I chose the easier subject—Jordan's murder and Daddy's attack.

"Did you see anything or anyone?"

"I didn't, Zoe. I admit to having had a few too many. I walked out of the bar and some crazy person attacked me with a knife. I was lucky other people were coming out of the bar, too. They scared him away."

"It wasn't the ghost of Old Slac, was it?"

"No, of course not. But I think seeing him was a warning that this was going to happen."

"Daddy, I know this is a difficult topic, but is there any way to find out if Jordan Phillips was a member of the Mistics?"

He closed his eyes. "I wish you wouldn't pursue this, honey. I don't want to visit you in the hospital. You don't understand how important secrecy is for the Mistics of Time."

"So you think your people did this to you as some kind of warning to keep your mouth shut?"

"No. Of course not. I'm just saying that we take a sacred blood oath not to talk about our membership. I have to respect that."

"Daddy, a man is dead. I don't know if he was killed because he infiltrated your society or if it was something personal."

"I know, honey. But—"

"Was he a member of the Mistics of Time or not?"

"He wasn't," he blurted. "But I don't think he was killed because of that." He took a breath and frowned. "I think you were channeling your mother there for a minute, Zoe. You looked and sounded just like her on a bad day."

That made me stop and think. The one person I didn't want to grow up to be was Anabelle Chase.

"I'm sorry, Daddy." I hugged him.

"Mind the stitches, honey."

Seriously? After what I saw?

"I didn't mean to interrogate you, but I'm having some problems with Chadwick Sloane. I think he was threatening me. And I saw what looked like the Death figure, in the food truck. It was the same as finding Jordan Phillips."

"Hush!" He put his hand over my mouth and looked around the bedroom as though he was afraid someone might hear me. "Where did you see Death?"

"In the back of my food truck. I told the police."

"Bad idea." He shook his head.

"I was afraid it was another dead man."

"And you aren't supposed to know that was Jordan Phillips in the garden," he scolded. "All right. You already know. You have to *pretend* you don't know."

"Daddy, his father and grandfather are devastated. They want to know what happened to him. Imagine if this was me. Wouldn't you do whatever you could to find out how I died?"

"Zoe, I'm sure Chadwick put this in blunter terms than I'm going to. These are warnings. Stay out of it. Yes, I feel terrible for the young man's family. I wish I could help, but I can't—and neither can you."

His eyes were intent on my face as he spoke. I could tell he was still scared for me and him. I hugged him again and promised not to do anything else that could cause trouble.

I didn't mean it, but I said it to keep him from worrying. I had another piece of the puzzle—Jordan wasn't a member of the Mistics. I hoped I could take that information, scanty as it was, and find the other pieces that would lead us to his killer.

SEVENTEEN

My mother met me on the stairs going out. I was ready for whatever she wanted to say about me leaving town, forgetting about Jordan, anything. I wasn't going to argue with her. I had to get back to the diner.

"Zoe, we need to talk."

"Not now, Mom. I really should be baking. Daddy is sleeping. I love you both. See you later." I thanked the housekeeper for the plastic container of cookies.

"You can't ignore this." She followed me to the front door. "I want to know what you're doing to find that young man's killer."

I wasn't ready for that. I gawked in surprise but managed to pull my act together. "Nothing. Daddy asked me to stay out of it. I'm too busy running the food truck to do anything."

"Don't lie to me, Zoe Elizabeth Chase! I know you're

probably running all over town asking questions and other crazy things. I want to help."

"Are you a replicant or a pod person?" I touched her blond hair. "You can't be *my* mother."

"I don't know what in the world you're talking about. Is that some kind of street talk?" Her blue eyes bored into mine. "I knew you'd pick up some bad language out there!"

"Never mind. Why do you want to help? You wanted me to leave town and not get involved."

"That was before someone tried to kill your father. I heard what you said to him about the police commissioner and finding one of those ridiculous people dressed in a Death costume in your food truck. I think I could be useful. I can bring a strong understanding of the law and moral fortitude to the table. You need me."

Okay. So I was wrong about someone not listening to our conversation upstairs. "I really have to go, Mom. I'll talk to you later."

Her eyes narrowed. "You need a ride, don't you? You didn't bring that big food truck with you, did you? I hope not, for heaven's sake. What will the neighbors think?"

"I'll call a taxi."

"Martha," she yelled to the housekeeper. "Have the car brought around."

And that was that.

I knew I was beaten. I got in my mother's silver Lexus and we drove to the diner. I barely had a chance to breathe between her intense questioning. I was glad I'd never had to face her on the witness stand.

"So this dead man's grandfather is meeting you at the diner with the purloined cell phone." She nodded as she swerved crazily in and out of traffic.

I hadn't ridden with her in a long time. Maybe this was

why she usually had someone drive her places. I wished I was driving as I held on to the door handle. "Yes. But you can't question him like he's a suspect—like you just did me. This is a delicate situation. He just lost his grandson."

"I know how to handle people, Zoe. Don't you worry. I have a reputation for this kind of thing."

That worried me a lot.

True to his word, Tucker was at the diner with Chef Art again. I was surprised to see Uncle Saul there, too. I'd wondered if he'd gone home after getting Daddy back to the house. I was happy to see him. Maybe he could help me curb my mother.

"Chef Art Arrington!" My mother parked the car and hit the pavement running. "I haven't seen you in ages. What have you been up to?"

"Anabelle Chase!" Chef Art gave her a quick air hug and then slipped her hand into the crook of his arm. "What a terrible business this is. I am so sorry to hear about what happened to Ted. May I introduce Tucker Phillips? You probably know him from his years running the *Mobile Times*."

I opened the door to the diner knowing what she was thinking: *Not that rag.*

"Yes, of course." My mother lied as smooth as buttermilk pie. "We always had a subscription to your paper. I'm so sorry about the loss of your grandson."

I'd forgotten how sweet she could be.

"What's going on, Zoe?" Uncle Saul asked as we got inside the diner. "Why is Anabelle here—and talking that way?"

I thought about telling him what I'd seen in the blue bedroom but decided against it. My mother and father kissing had nothing to do with cooking for the food truck or with Jordan Phillips's death. I decided to stay away from that subject. It was too distressing.

"She wants to help figure out who hurt Daddy and killed

Jordan." I shrugged as I switched on the lights. "I'm trying not to think about it. What are you doing here?"

"I called Miguel, and he said you were coming here to make biscuits. I thought you could use a hand."

I hugged him. "I could use at least a dozen hands right now. I don't know how to plan to make food for the next two weeks. It's nothing like going out for a day at police head- quarters with the Biscuit Bowl. We've already sold out twice. If I have to come back here four or five times a day to make food, it's going to eat into my profits and drive me crazy."

He laughed and kissed my forehead. "Why didn't you say so? I had this problem plenty of times at the Carriage House. I know what you need to do."

I dropped on a stool at the bar and nodded. "Please. What- ever you can tell me."

We both looked outside where my mother was still talk- ing to Chef Art and Tucker.

"Go ahead," I urged. "They might be a while."

What Uncle Saul had to say was really simple. I just hadn't thought of it that way.

"What's the most important food you sell?" he asked.

"No doubt my biscuit bowls."

"They are also the most time-consuming. And you have a problem serving them fresh, right?"

"You know I do."

"Then you have to pay more attention to the biscuit bowls than to what's in them. You're not gonna like this advice, but you can make, freeze, and store what's going in the middle. All you have to do is plan for it."

"I don't know. What if it tastes like it's been frozen? I did that today and worried about it. What if the customers hate it?"

"Focus on what sells your food and what's most important,"

he said again. "If the biscuit bowl is fresh, everything else will be tasty inside it."

I started to raise another objection. He held up one hand.

"It's not like you have to do this all the time, Zoe. We're talking about the next two weeks. It may be the only way you're gonna make it through."

I decided to think about it while I made several batches of biscuit dough. It made sense. I needed to give my time to the biscuits. I'd have to think about what I could make to go inside that would be less labor-intensive than I was used to.

It wouldn't be easy—I was used to letting my creative cooking imagination run wild. I got up every day with a new menu in mind. But I had never run out of food before. That had been humiliating. I couldn't closely estimate what I needed each day like I did normally.

Uncle Saul made coffee. "Don't look now, but they're coming in."

The door chime rang, and my mother walked in before Tucker and Chef Art. They were talking about what had happened to Jordan. I hadn't seen the phone in Tucker's hand yet. I wanted to take a look at it.

The three of them sat in one of the old booths. The seats were lumpy, and the tabletop moved if you touched it. It didn't matter, because I didn't need them for my food truck. Once in a while some of the men from the shelter came down and ate what I had left over from the day. That was about it. Still, it was a little embarrassing. I knew all three of them were used to much better surroundings.

"Would you like some coffee?" Uncle Saul asked them. "It's Zoe's own concoction, but it's pretty good."

Chef Art and Tucker each had a cup. My mother only wanted water. I tried not to let it hurt my feelings. She normally only drank water.

With the oven full of biscuit bowls for the next few

minutes, I walked around the counter to ask Tucker about Jordan's phone.

As I did, Mr. Carruthers burst through the front door like an avenging inspector angel. "Aha! I knew there was something more going on here. You're not supposed to have customers at the diner, Miss Chase. You're only allowed to use the cooking facilities for your food truck."

All conversation stopped at his entrance. Everyone stared at him.

"These aren't customers." I wanted to ask what was wrong with him. Was he stalking me, looking for problems with what I was doing?

"They have something to drink in their hands," he said. "They're seated in your diner."

Chef Art had to nudge Tucker out of the way to get to his feet. "Do you know who I am, sir?"

Mr. Carruthers stared at him. "You're Chef Art Arrington. I'd know you anywhere."

"That's right. Are you bothering my young protégé? I've looked after her every step of the way since she started her food truck."

It wasn't exactly true, but I wouldn't argue with my famous champion.

"I had no idea, Chef Art." Mr. Carruthers looked stricken. "I'm only doing my job."

Tucker joined them. "My son is the editor in chief of the *Mobile Times* newspaper. I was in his place for almost forty years. I think it's been a while since we did a story about health inspections in the city. I don't recall people hiding out and watching to see if someone was doing what they were supposed to do."

Even my mother got to her feet. "You know, I believe this card on the window says this diner passed inspection. It's recent, too. Is that your signature, sir?"

Mr. Carruthers had gone from stricken to terrified. "You're Anabelle Chase. You're running to be a judge. What are you doing here?"

"Answer the question, sir, and don't elaborate. Is this your signature on this card or not?"

"Yes, ma'am."

"And did you certify that this diner has passed the inspections needed to be open?"

"Yes, ma'am, but—"

"Then I don't understand why you're here harassing my daughter."

Mr. Carruthers stared at me. "You're her daughter?"

"Yes."

"You should have said something. I didn't know."

"Are you insinuating that a good review is easier to get for someone you know?" my mother demanded.

I was actually starting to feel sorry for Mr. Carruthers.

"Of course not. We have a set of standards that we use to inspect every food facility."

"Then I suggest you go and inspect some other facility that you haven't already inspected. This one seems to be in order."

"Yes, ma'am."

Mr. Carruthers hastily went back to his car, which was parked on the side of the building, and crept out of the parking lot. Everyone watched him go. I would've burned a tray of biscuits if Uncle Saul hadn't rescued them.

I finally took a deep breath. My mother, Chef Art, and Tucker sat down. I put in two more trays of biscuits and asked about the phone again.

Tucker handed it to me. "I don't see anything in Jordan's notes or projects that has to do with secret societies or the Mistics of Time. Take a look, Zoe. See what you can do."

I sat at the counter between trays of biscuits baking and

glanced through Jordan's phone. It felt weird looking at everything he had in there. I was embarrassed to search his private notes and thoughts. I had to keep reminding myself that it could help us learn who'd killed him. I'd want someone to take the time to look through my phone if something had happened to me.

I also made a mental note to take any embarrassing personal items off my phone that I didn't want people to look at when I was dead.

"Is this Jordan's girlfriend?" I asked Tucker.

"Yes. Lisa. She's good-looking, isn't she? She was one of the queens at last year's carnival. Her family is quite prominent in the area."

A prominent family could mean they belonged to a krewe or secret society—maybe the Mistics. Usually, the queens were chosen from families with connections to them. "What's her name?"

"Lisa Rakin. Her father owns one of the local TV stations," Tucker said. "Lovely girl. We were hopeful Jordan might settle down. He was starting to get a reputation as a Lothario, though it wasn't deserved. He was infatuated with his work. That was why he went through so many young ladies."

I kept looking through Jordan's pictures and was surprised to find someone I recognized. "Tiffany Bryant? She's one of the PR reps for the food truck rally."

Tucker frowned. "I think her last name is Sloane. The commissioner's daughter. She was a very nice girl, too. I think they dated at the end of last year."

"The commissioner's daughter dated Jordan? How long did they date? Why is her name different?" I asked.

"They dated a month or two. Not long. I think her mother and father are divorced. I believe she and her mother use her mother's maiden name so as not to be tied to the commissioner. He's a man with many enemies. Why do you ask?"

"Because the commissioner might not be covering for the Mistics. He might be covering for his daughter. He was with someone at the masquerade. It might have been Tiffany, like I was there with my father."

"Why didn't you think this was relevant, Tucker?" Chef Art asked. "I can't believe you didn't put the two together!"

"How did they split up?" my mother asked. "Could she have killed him because he was too busy to pay her attention and then started dating someone else?"

"That wouldn't explain why Jordan was at the ball," Tucker said. "He wasn't a member of the Mistics and hadn't seen Tiffany since last December as far as I know."

"But it's a start," I told him. "This has to be more than a coincidence."

It could certainly explain why Commissioner Sloane had been so aggressive about people not looking into Jordan's death too closely. Protecting the Mistics was one thing. Protecting his daughter was another story.

"If she was at the masquerade she could definitely be our suspect." I was still gazing at her picture on Jordan's phone.

"How will we find out?" Chef Art asked.

"I see a lot of her. Maybe I can get her to tell me if she was there—kind of woman to woman." I realized that I was volunteering, but that was all right. This was the best breakthrough we'd had about Jordan's murder. Tiffany might even reveal more if we talked. Maybe she'd tell me that she killed Jordan.

That was probably wishful thinking.

I took another pan of biscuits out of the oven. Miguel drove up and waved as he got out of the car.

"So we don't think Jordan was doing some kind of exposé on the Mistics of Time, then." Tucker nodded. "Maybe this girl killed him out of spite?"

"Perhaps." Chef Art squeezed his friend's hand. "I'm so

sorry about this, Tucker. I hope we can find some justice for the boy."

Tucker and Chef Art left the diner looking for Sazerac. I'd promised to let them know if I found out anything else about Tiffany attending the masquerade.

My mother had heard enough about what was going on. She had an appointment with her publicist. "You know I never cared for these krewes and such," she said. "Maybe this will be a wake-up call for people to abandon them."

"I don't think anyone's death is enough to do that," I told her. "I'll see you later."

Uncle Saul and I helped Miguel bring in the groceries. The car was stuffed full of them. He also had a large plastic barrel with Coke written all over it. It barely fit in the trunk. He explained how he'd got it free when he'd purchased a ton of soda and ice.

"This should solve your drink problem, Zoe. I hope so, anyway."

I examined the insulated barrel. It wouldn't fit inside the Biscuit Bowl, but we could have it right in front of the window so Ollie could keep an eye on it. "Thanks for thinking of it."

He handed me the shopping bill. I almost collapsed on the tile floor. I was putting out a lot of money with no guarantee I could make it back.

But hadn't that been what it was like from the beginning? These next two weeks could make or break my business. I started cooking with Uncle Saul's suggestions in mind. There's nothing like cooking in mass quantities to relieve anxiety.

I wondered what I could say to Tiffany to get her to tell me that she'd killed Jordan out of jealousy. We didn't exactly get along.

And there was that pesky problem of why Jordan had

been at the masquerade. Obviously he'd sneaked in, but why? If he'd broken up with Tiffany in December, I doubted that he was stalking her or even wanted to see her.

Had Tiffany done the famous *I just want to see you one last time* routine? Would Jordan have fallen for that and gone to the masquerade?

It was possible, I supposed. People in love did silly things.

EIGHTEEN

We got the groceries put away—mostly on the counter, since I was going to use them right away. Uncle Saul started a large pot of pork fricassee—with apologies to Ollie. I hoped he wouldn't be upset because we'd made it without him.

I took the last two sheets of biscuits out of the oven and glanced at the biscuit clock. We had to get moving.

"I guess we'll make everything we bought today and hope we have enough to get through dinner." I shrugged at Uncle Saul. "It looks like it would feed hundreds of people. I hope we have that many customers."

"You may have to consider portion control," Uncle Saul said. "Have you ever measured how much fits into a biscuit bowl and how much fills it? Every extra ounce cuts into your profits if it's not needed."

"I wouldn't even know how to do that. We fill them to the top of the biscuit bowl. I can't see any other way to do it."

He had the pork sizzling when he came over to me and

took out a one quarter cup measuring spoon. "Let's try this and then we'll know. You could use a measuring cup so you'll know what's going into the biscuit bowl."

"I don't know. Using frozen food and cutting portions? I feel like a fast food joint."

"They're the best at knowing what makes their customers come back without using more than they need." He hypothetically filled a biscuit bowl with one quarter cup of rice. It came to just below the top.

"I can't do that right now. I appreciate your advice, Uncle Saul, but I can't look at it like this."

"You might have to—at least for the next two weeks. Survival is what's important here, Zoe. Don't forget that."

I didn't want to forget it, but I didn't want to shortchange my customers, either. I wanted them to go away full and happy so they would tell other people how good my food was. If I lost that, I lost everything.

I chopped oranges for my orange-raisin sweet biscuit bowl. Oranges were cheap and plentiful this time of year. I also made more icing to drizzle over them. This was good and fresh. It would yield enough to feed a few hundred people. I hoped it was all that I'd need.

After I'd finished with the oranges, I started on vegetables for the fricassee. I told Miguel what we'd learned regarding Jordan's death. He'd met Tiffany when I received my invitation to the food truck rally.

"If this was revenge, she took her time," he remarked. "Most rejected lovers strike right away. She would've been sitting on this for a while."

"I know, but it makes sense, too. Commissioner Sloane is personally overseeing this investigation. If Tiffany is involved, he'd be extra careful."

"True."

"Again, though," Uncle Saul said, "you have the issue with

how she got him there. Did she lure him there with something? What could she have used to entice a man who was done with her?"

"An insider's view of the Mistics?" I suggested. "If she knew him at all, she knew his career meant everything to him."

"Maybe." Miguel nodded. "It would make a good article for the paper, I suppose."

"And he liked exposés," I said.

"Did you look at his texts while you had the phone here?" Miguel asked. "That could be the answer."

"No. I didn't think about it. I should have, but there were interruptions." I chopped a bunch of onions holding a wood matchstick in my mouth. It was hard to talk around it.

"What's with the matchstick?" Miguel asked. "I've seen you do that before. Is that some cooking mojo?"

Uncle Saul laughed. "I taught her that. The sulfur in the matchstick keeps the onion fumes from making you cry. I guess that's my contribution to the world."

I removed the matchstick from my mouth. "How can you say that? You've done wonderful things for the world."

He stirred the onions I'd already chopped into the fricassee. The aroma was starting to fill the diner. "I'm going to be sixty later this year, Zoe. A man starts to think about what he's done with his life at my age."

As someone who had recently turned thirty, I could relate to that. It was one of the big reasons I'd quit my job at the bank and started the food truck. "You've done so much already. You've had your own restaurant. You built a log cabin. You saved Alabaster. You've done a lot."

"But I'm not leaving anything behind—no kids, no lasting accomplishments. When I die, everything I've done will go with me."

I didn't know what to say. His words, and Jordan's death,

had lent a somber air to what should have been a fun-filled carnival atmosphere. I sighed and finished chopping a mountain of vegetables.

My phone rang. It was Delia. Things were starting to pick up at the Biscuit Bowl again. She was almost out of food.

"We shouldn't be long now. Hold on," I told her.

"Considering this fricassee is gonna sit around in a warming tray for a while, I'd say it's in good shape," Uncle Saul said. "Why don't you and Miguel go back to the food truck rally with the biscuits and the sweet orange filling? I'll bring the fricassee along in a bit."

"Thank you." I hugged him. "I'll never forget you. You've always made a difference in my life."

"You're sweet, Zoe girl. I love you, too. Now scoot. We don't want to go back to an empty food truck again."

"That's for sure." Miguel shuddered. "I never knew hungry people could get so ugly."

"I hear you." Uncle Saul laughed. "I used to dread lunch on Sundays at the Carriage House. Those people coming in after hours of preaching could get downright scary."

Uncle Saul helped me get the orange-raisin filling packed up. I also brought the white icing and biscuit bowls with me. We took everything out to Miguel's car and planned to stop for ice for the Cokes on the way.

There was no way to plan for the children's parade along our route to the food truck rally. Hundreds of children of all ages marched down the middle of the streets. Some played homemade instruments. Some sang at the top of their lungs. There were children in wheelchairs and those with hairless heads from chemotherapy.

It made me cry watching them. Miguel handed me his handkerchief. "I don't know what it is. When I see a children's parade during carnival, I cry."

"It's okay. Everyone has their soft spots."

I handed him back his handkerchief. "Thanks. What's your soft spot?"

"People who get in trouble and can't get out by themselves. That's why I do what I do. I realized when the DA framed me for falsifying evidence that sometimes people need others to stop and listen to them. I like helping those people."

I hugged and kissed him—maybe a little longer than I'd planned. The parade had gone around a corner, and the driver behind us started honking his horn. "You don't have to worry about the legacy you leave behind, either, Miguel."

He started forward again, squeezing my hand. "Let's talk about that again when I'm sixty."

That was a tender moment.

But as we sat a few blocks down watching the pet parade go by, we were a little more impatient. Delia had called again, agitated by only having one biscuit bowl left. All I could tell her was that we were on the way.

"How do you plan to find what you need to know from Tiffany when you see her again?" Miguel asked as we waited.

I laughed at a huge Great Dane that was wearing a costume that included boots. "I don't know. We don't exactly get along, but I thought if she went to the masquerade with her father like I did with mine, it would give us a common point of reference. We could talk about our dresses and where we go to get our hair done. That kind of thing."

"And you'll suddenly question if she killed Jordan?"

"Not suddenly. I can be subtle. I'll hint around about it."

He pointed at a star-studded Pomeranian. "Look at that!"

The driver behind us, the same one that had been following us since the children's parade, impatiently honked his horn again. He obviously wasn't from Mobile. There was nothing we could do about the parade. It would be this way for the next two weeks. He might as well get used to it.

The pet parade ended abruptly with a cat being pulled in a red wagon by an adorable child in a matching costume.

We finally reached the food truck rally in the municipal parking lot. I was amazed to see two of the food trucks missing. When Miguel and I started taking supplies to the Biscuit Bowl, I asked Delia if she'd seen them leave.

"I talked to two of them—the woman with the blossoming onions and the man with the dancing shrimp." She shrugged. "They both ran out of food. They couldn't get anything back fast enough and had to shut down. That little witch who runs the rally told them to leave."

"You mean Tiffany Bryant?"

"That's her. She stopped and asked me if we had enough food for the dinner crowd. I lied and said we did. She kind of acted like she was disappointed."

I couldn't believe it. I needed to be on her good side. She was probably just stressed. I had to figure out a way that I could help her with her job so she'd feel compelled to be nice to me.

It was the start of my plan to get her to confess.

I was glad for my team of friends and relatives who were helping me survive this. I wouldn't have made it without them. We got the supplies unloaded, including the plastic barrel that would hold the Cokes, but we'd forgotten the ice. Miguel went back out for that.

I took Crème Brûlée for a walk in the grass. He looked up at me so cute that I had to pick him up and cuddle him. He bit my nose and finger, just love bites, and then licked me. I gave him some extra snacks for being such a sweetie.

With the orange-raisin filling in the mini fridge and the biscuits ready to sell, Delia carefully asked about Ollie. "Is he going to work at different times than me, Zoe? I know he must hate me now."

"I don't think he hates you. He's angry and upset, but

he'll get over it. Breakups are hard. Some more than others. I'm sure the two of you will be okay again. This is a very small kitchen. Any hostility is too much."

"Don't I know it?" She frowned. "I never meant to hurt Ollie. He just doesn't want what I want. He's happy living at the shelter. I can't let myself think that way. I've had to fight too hard to get where I am. I want better than a cot at a shelter, you know?"

I hugged her, understanding what she was saying. Not everyone could share Ollie's philosophy about life.

Two people walked up to ask for biscuit bowls. I was glad they wanted the sweet bowl. They also wanted one chicken stew bowl. That made us officially out of stew. I took their money and called Uncle Saul. We really needed that fricassee.

Miguel set up the barrel of Cokes right outside the window. I knew we could have some loss from that—someone couldn't constantly watch to make sure no one took one without paying. But we'd be okay.

Miguel came in to ask if there was anything else he could do before he had to leave again. "I have an appointment this evening. I'll check on you later." He kissed me good-bye.

Delia sighed as he left. "You better hang on to that one, Zoe. He's a prize. If I'd known he was free when he represented me, I would've snatched him up."

Two more customers came up and wanted savory bowls. We had to turn them away. One of them took a sweet orange biscuit bowl instead.

I remembered what Uncle Saul had said about putting in too much filling. Was he right about that? I didn't want to lose money from being naive about what I should do, but putting the customer first was important, too.

There was a knock on the back door. Tiffany peeked around the corner. "Zoe? I'm so glad to see you here. Is everything okay?"

Facing her made me gulp. This was my chance to talk to her woman to woman, and I couldn't think of a single clever thing to say. "Everything is fine. I had to get supplies, but we're ready for supper."

"Great! I may not have gone over this when we went through the rules for the rally." She took out a long sheet of paper. "The owner or manager of the food truck must be on hand during all hours of operation."

"Okay. Thanks for telling me." I was sure I hadn't heard that rule before. *Come on! Think of something to bond with her. Quit stalling.*

"Do you have a designated manager who can be here when you're not?"

"Yes." I glanced at Delia. "This is Delia Vann. She's one of my designated managers. I also have Saul Chase, Miguel Alexander, and Ollie."

She stopped writing the names and looked up at me. "Ollie? Is there a last name?"

"Ollie Oliver," I lied. I had no idea what Ollie's last name was. He never used it. But I felt okay telling a white lie about what was basically just a formality.

"Okay." Tiffany surveyed my list of workers. "Thank you. I'm glad you're not trying to go this alone. Already, we've lost two trucks. Some people weren't prepared for the situation. I guess next year I'll ask about preparedness before I sign anyone for the rally."

"Thanks." This was it. Delia was talking to several other customers who'd come up to the side window. It was the perfect opportunity. "Having a good time during carnival?"

Lame! But it was the best I could come up with.

"Yes, thanks. You?"

"Great now that we're this close to Mardi Gras. Those balls and masquerades got to be a bit much, huh?" *Better. Much better.*

Tiffany didn't seem surprised to hear me mostly admit that my family was a member of a secret society. She smiled. "I know what you mean! I hate those big parties, don't you? I avoided them this year since I knew I was working during carnival."

"Oh." She might be lying, but I couldn't think what to say next.

"Well, excuse me. I have to get back to work, and I can see that you have customers!"

Tiffany waved and left the kitchen. Uncle Saul got there with fricassee just in time. Ollie had come with him. He stared at Delia for a moment. She moved away from the customer window, and he took his usual spot.

That was it. I'd expected more friction between them.

"I can stay if you think I can help," Uncle Saul said. "Otherwise, I'm going to head over to the house to sit with your father."

"No! Don't go over there!" I thought how upsetting it might be for him to see my mother and father in the bedroom as I had. What would he think? "I really need you here for a while."

"Okay." He hugged me. "Don't get so stressed out that you fall apart, Zoe. You won't stay in business long that way."

"I tried talking to Tiffany," I confessed, changing the subject. "I wasn't very good at it. I think it's going to take some practice."

"Don't worry about it too much. These things have a way of coming to light no matter how hard people try to hide them."

I agreed with him, even though this secret seemed pretty well buried. With all the cover-ups, the Phillips family might never know what had really happened to Jordan. I had to do better next time with Tiffany, even if I might be the least sneaky person I knew.

A steady flow of customers began coming to the window as we got the fricassee put away. With Ollie there, I wasn't as worried about the Cokes disappearing. All he had to do was stare hard at people to make them nervous.

Delia set up plates, napkins, and forks. Uncle Saul handled filling the savory biscuit bowls, and I did the sweet bowls and deep-fried the biscuits.

We were in sync as a team before the crowd arrived and steamrolled across the food truck rally. I barely had time to look up before a new group was there, hungry for biscuit bowls. The food passed quickly from person to person in the kitchen.

A Dixieland band was playing somewhere as night settled on Mobile. We heard the occasional sounds of firecrackers and laughter but couldn't experience it firsthand. I wasn't sure this was something I'd want to do every year during carnival. I was missing all the fun I could have been sharing with Miguel. Maybe by next year I'd be more certain of the Biscuit Bowl's future. Being out here felt like an act of desperation with all the fun I was missing.

The steady stream slowly became a trickle of customers. At midnight when it was time to close, we still had some food left and the parking lot was empty. It was going to be a long night sleeping in the front of the food truck with Crème Brûlée. I hoped I was exhausted enough that it passed quickly.

NINETEEN

Crème Brûlée wasn't ready to settle down. I took him for a walk. We played with his favorite squeaky toy. Every time I was almost asleep he crept across the seat and batted at my face with his paws. I guess he'd slept so much during the day that he didn't want to sleep when I did.

I could hear other voices in the parking lot and the sounds of people getting their food trucks ready for the next day. The generator was a steady humming beside the Biscuit Bowl. All the sounds and smells were different than I was used to—even in the diner.

It was two A.M. and I needed to use the portable toilet. I got out of the front seat of the food truck hoping Crème Brûlée would settle down while I was gone.

It was very lonely in the parking lot. The overhead lights left deep shadows among the trees that surrounded the area. The wind whispered through the leaves.

Most of the food trucks were dark or only showed light from a television or a laptop inside. Music was still playing, and distant laughter echoed down the street in front of the parking lot.

It was eerie walking to the portable toilet, but I didn't have much choice. There was certainly no room in the kitchen for a makeshift toilet. I knew I was lucky to have one so close to the food truck.

All I could think about as I crossed the pavement was finding Jordan the night of the masquerade, how he'd looked in the dark garden dressed as Death. Not great thoughts when I was nervous already. I believed he'd been posed on that bench waiting for someone to find him.

I thought about the newspaper he'd had clutched in his hand. Now that I knew he was a reporter, it made sense. He was probably working on a story—but what story? And was it worth his life to write it?

There were many gruesome ghost stories in Mobile. I hadn't thought of them in years, but I thought of them then. Every rustle of the leaves made me wonder if Jordan was resting in peace. Was his ghost haunting the walled garden where he'd died?

I remembered being fascinated by those stories when I was a child. There was the old French woman who walked through the graveyard behind the main branch of the library. People said she begged for alms to save her dying child. There were ghostly sailors who'd drowned in Mobile Bay and who came into the city on some nights during the full moon. People said Dauphin Island was haunted by a restless Native American tribe that had been killed by the Spaniards.

When I was a child, I'd believed every ghost story I'd ever heard. It infuriated my mother, who said she'd never believed in ghosts. Not Daddy, though. He knew some great old stories.

In time, I'd grown out of them. I'd never seen a ghost, so I just came to the conclusion that they weren't real after all.

On a night like this, with the sound of partying still going on in the distance and a church bell tolling the hour, I remembered all of them, and they seemed real again. A sleepy owl called out from under the eaves of the old municipal building that was being converted to a museum.

It was a night full of ghosts that flitted through the streets during carnival.

I ducked into the portable toilet and locked the door behind me. Even though it wasn't someplace I'd normally want to be, I was grateful for the shelter. I lingered longer than I normally would have but finally stepped back outside. I could only hold my breath for so long!

There was a lazy Alabama moon drifting through some clouds above me. I told myself not to look around. Just go straight to the Biscuit Bowl, get inside, and go to sleep. Enough thinking about ghosts and other creatures of the night. I'd be sorry in the morning if I didn't get some rest.

I started whistling. Hadn't I heard somewhere that it kept ghosts away? Maybe it only boosted a person's confidence to hear the sound. I started planning my meals for the next few days in my head as I walked. That was a sure way to feel better.

I was so close to reaching the door to the food truck. There were only a few steps between me and the door handle. I started walking faster, like those women I'd seen in horror movies, glancing back over my shoulder in case someone was coming up from behind.

I heard a sound—the breaking of a twig on the pavement—and faced forward.

There was the ghost of Old Slac.

He was every inch the same as pictures I'd seen of Chief

Slacabamorinico. Tall. Skeletal. A feathered headdress and buckskins. His eyes were glowing as he lifted one arm and pointed at me. "Zoe Elizabeth Chase!"

I almost dropped to the pavement in fear. *He knows my name. That can't be good.*

"What do you want?" I demanded in a quavering voice.

Three other people, tall and broad shouldered, probably men, came out of the darkness around him. They wore black robes and masks, and they stared at me, too.

Great! Now they're a band instead of a solo act.

"Zoe Chase," one of them said in a deep voice. "Have you betrayed the secrets of the Mistics of Time?"

"What?" *So they were with the Mistics.* "I haven't betrayed anything. I don't know any of your secrets. I'm not even a member."

"But your father is a member, and so is your uncle. Have you betrayed them?"

"I think you should go home now." I was starting to be more angry than scared. "It's getting late."

"Yea or nay?" Old Slac demanded.

"Nay." I stood my ground with my chin held high. "I haven't betrayed my father or my uncle. What's this about, anyway?"

I was sure one of them was Commissioner Sloane. He was trying to scare me into saying something I'd regret later.

The four members of the Mistics whispered amongst one another before coming to a decision.

"Remember your vow to keep our society secret," one of them said. "Your life may depend on it!"

They slowly backed away into the shadows they'd come from.

"Seriously?" I called out.

Only the old owl answered my question.

What was that all about?

- - - - - - -

I started the engine and turned on the high beams to make sure I was alone. I honked the horn a few times, just to let them know I was wise to their games.

Someone knocked hard on the window next to me, and I nearly jumped out of my skin.

I closed my eyes and hoped Old Slac couldn't get in.

"Zoe?"

"Go away!"

"Zoe! Open the door. What's wrong?"

I knew that voice. It wasn't Old Slac. It was Miguel. He'd said he was going to stay out there with me that night after he got home from his meeting and changed clothes.

I opened my eyes. Miguel's handsome, concerned face was on the other side of the window. I rolled down the glass. "Old Slac and members of the Mistics of Time."

"What?" He glanced around.

"Right in front of the Biscuit Bowl." I dared a peek in that direction.

There was nothing there. Miguel walked to the front of the Airstream. He shrugged as he looked around and then came to the passenger side of the vehicle. I opened the door, moving Crème Brûlée quickly out of the way.

"Hurry! Get in."

He opened the door and got in, locking it after him. "I didn't see anything out there. Are you okay?"

"I saw them, Miguel. They were right there in the moonlight, pointing at me and asking if I'd betrayed them. I'm never going to another secret society ball again!"

"Let's calm down for a minute. Take a deep breath. Where did you see the ghost of Old Slac?"

"Right there in front of the Biscuit Bowl." I pointed and

finally had enough courage to look at the spot again. "He's not there. Where did he go?"

"I didn't see him. I think you imagined him. Between the stress of getting ready for the food truck rally and finding a dead man at the masquerade—anything is possible, Zoe."

His voice was so kind and understanding.

It really made me mad.

I jumped out of the truck again, slamming the door closed, forgetting the relative safety I'd been so eager for just a few moments before. But there was no denying that the only thing in the headlights' beam was the pavement and the portable toilet.

Miguel followed me. "Nothing's here."

"Something was here. Maybe not a ghost, but someone who wanted me to think it was a ghost."

"Zoe—"

"I know what I saw. It's not like I could make up something like that. He was standing right here."

"Why don't you go back to your father's apartment and get a good night's sleep? I'll stay here with the food truck. That's what I should've done to begin with. You shouldn't be out here at night by yourself."

"I'm not falling apart, Miguel. I can handle this. You know something is going on—we all do. Someone wants to make sure I don't look into Jordan's death."

"I'm not saying you can't handle it."

"I'm not giving up trying to figure out what happened to Jordan." I said it the first time in a normal voice. I shouted it a second time for my own satisfaction.

Several food truck drivers who were also spending the night with their rigs looked out of doors and windows to yell at me to shut up. The few that had dogs with them got especially angry, since their dogs started barking.

"Sorry. That's it," I yelled back. "I'm finished. Go back to sleep. Early morning tomorrow."

I crept back to the front seat of the food truck with Miguel. As soon as I got behind the wheel, I took out my cell phone and called Patti Latoure.

"Zoe?" she answered. "Do you know what time it is?"

"Yes, Patti, I'm sorry. But things keep happening to me, and I think they're part of Jordan Phillips's death."

"What kind of things?"

"Crazy things." I told her about Old Slac and the Mistics. "I think they're trying to scare me off."

"I don't know what to tell you, Zoe. I got my butt severely chewed by Commissioner Sloane. And he was right. This is Dan Frolick's case. I'm not supposed to spend time on someone else's cases. You need to tell Frolick everything you've told me. I'm sure he'll be a big help."

In the background, I heard Patti's husband wanting to know who was calling her in the middle of the night. She told him it was nothing and that he should go back to sleep.

"Patti, I think Frolick is in on it. He hasn't spoken up about being there with me in the garden where I found Jordan's body. How can I trust him?"

"I don't know. You just have to. Good night, Zoe."

The phone went dead, leaving my screen with only a picture I'd taken of Patti eating a biscuit bowl in front of police headquarters.

"She doesn't want to hear it?" Miguel guessed.

"Worse. She wants me to talk to Frolick." I put my phone away and stared out the front window. Crème Brûlée was snoring on the seat between us. He didn't care what was going on.

"I can't forget what I saw," I told Miguel. "I know they're lying to protect their secret society. They don't care if they find Jordan's killer as long as they're safe."

He put his arm around me. "You don't know that. Maybe the police are covering up where they found Phillips for another reason. At least give them some time to work it out."

"Maybe you're right." I closed my eyes as I leaned my head against him. Crème Brûlée sleepily batted at us with his paw and then turned over. "Maybe if I act like it's over for me, they'll leave us alone."

He kissed me slowly. "At least for a few days. Let's see what happens."

TWENTY

So I worked the food truck rally for the next five days. Morning and night blurred together as the nonstop celebrations and parades brought in thousands of customers.

I baked biscuits. Uncle Saul and Ollie helped me make tons of sweet and savory foods to fill them. Chef Art donated some throws for us to give away with each meal after my plastic cups were gone. Miguel barely got the Coke barrel filled with ice and drinks before he had to fill it up again.

The weather was good—sunny and warm during the day, cool at night. We took turns staying with the Biscuit Bowl at night. There were a few break-ins at some of the other food trucks where no one was attending them. Probably most of it was crazy, excited teenagers, but losing food was difficult to make up.

My father was back on his feet quickly. He came to visit me early one morning with a pretty young woman on his arm. I actually sighed with relief to see that whatever insanity had gripped my parents at the house was over.

Nothing else happened out of the ordinary. No visits from people dressed like Death or the ghost of Old Slac. I didn't hear anything else about Jordan's death on the news. I also didn't hear anything from his grandfather or Chef Art.

We were sitting outside at a picnic table sharing breakfast one week after Jordan had been killed. Uncle Saul had made some beignets and coffee—the beignets at the restaurant were nothing compared to his. He'd also brought some orange juice and a newspaper. We'd been checking for any news of Jordan each day.

Delia was asleep in the food truck with Crème Brûlée. Ollie was sleeping with his head cradled on his arms on the picnic table. Miguel was gone after spending the night at the truck with me. He had to meet with some clients.

Some of the other foodies were up and getting ready for the new day. There was a rhythm to the tides of people who showed up. The breakfast crowd went from around seven thirty to ten thirty with the largest number of people at nine A.M. The lunch crowd came in around ten thirty and lasted until three P.M. with the busiest time from noon until two P.M. Dinner lasted from six until midnight.

That gave me time in the afternoon to make food and freeze it for the next day. I baked biscuits twice a day, but in huge quantities. It made me wince to hand out the last biscuit bowls. They weren't as good as they could be, but we hadn't had any complaints.

"What day is it?" Ollie moaned without lifting his head.

"It's Saturday," Uncle Saul told him. "Drink some coffee and orange juice. You'll feel better."

Ollie sniffed. "Is that beignets I smell?"

"And eat one of these." Uncle Saul laughed as he put the pastry near Ollie's arm.

"I never knew making food could be so hard." Ollie yawned and lifted his head. "I feel like I'm on a never-ending road trip."

"It's halfway over," Uncle Saul said. "We've had most of the big krewes' parades."

"What about the Order of Inca?" Ollie asked. "There's still the Order of Athena, Neptune's Daughters, and the Crewe of Columbus."

"Eat," I said. "You'll feel better. I'm going to get Delia."

There had been no friction between Ollie and Delia in the kitchen. I was so thankful but felt like I couldn't say anything until it was over. It was a sure way to jinx our good luck so far.

Delia was already awake when I reached the food truck. "I'm going to run home and take a shower, Zoe. You want to come with me? Do you need anything?"

"I'm fine, thanks. I've been showering at the diner in the afternoon while the biscuits are baking. It gives me a little break from here, too."

I put Crème Brûlée's harness on and lifted him carefully. I kissed him and explained that he needed to get some exercise in the grass. He'd been such a little trooper, too. I promised him salmon when it was over. He licked my nose without biting it. I took him back to the food truck and fed him.

Delia was gone. Uncle Saul and Ollie were still sitting at the table with the weirdest expressions on their faces.

"What?" I smiled and grabbed a beignet. "What's up with you two?"

"You should tell her." Ollie shook his head. "She's gonna find out one way or another."

"Didn't I say we weren't doing that?" Uncle Saul hissed.

"Does the Biscuit Bowl have a flat tire or something?" I looked at my food truck. Everything seemed okay from the outside. "Tell me."

Uncle Saul slid his copy of the *Mobile Times* across the table top. "You aren't going to like this, Zoe. Try to be calm."

I read the article on the front page. The byline was Bennett Phillips. It was a short piece about the medical examiner declaring that Jordan's death was a suicide.

"What?" I pulled my cell phone from the pocket of my jeans. "How can they say that?"

"It's what the man said," Uncle Saul reminded me. "And just because you saw Jordan and he'd been shot doesn't mean he didn't shoot himself."

"No. I don't believe it. There was no note."

"Finish reading the article," Ollie suggested. "The police found one at his apartment."

I finished punching in Bennett's number. There was no answer—it went right to voice mail. I tried Tucker's number. It did the same.

"That poor family. Now they have to live with the idea that Jordan killed himself, which we all know isn't true."

"We don't know that," Uncle Saul persuaded. "You didn't even know this young man. He may have been suicidal his whole life."

"Why wouldn't Bennett and Tucker have mentioned that when we talked about him? And why would he have killed himself at the masquerade ball? It doesn't make any sense."

"What doesn't make any sense, Miss Chase?" Detective Frolick had sneaked up on us while we'd been talking. "I had a feeling you wouldn't agree with the ME's verdict. That's why I decided to pay you a visit. Consider it a courtesy call from the commissioner to your family."

"You and I both know someone killed Jordan." I stared him down. "Don't bother denying it."

"I admit that's the way it looked when we found him."

"At the masquerade ball—or in the alley?"

He grabbed my elbow. "Let's take a walk, shall we?"

Uncle Saul and Ollie were on their feet next to us faster than I would've imagined possible. They both stood a head taller than Frolick, and Ollie was wearing his mean look.

"She's not going anywhere alone with you," Uncle Saul said. "Anything you have to say to her you can say in front of us, too. We know the whole story. Don't bother trying to cover it up."

Detective Frolick removed his hand from my arm. "Take it easy, gents. No harm, no foul. I just thought it would be better talking about this sensitive subject in private."

Ollie flung open the back door to the Biscuit Bowl. "In here. This is about as private as you get with her today."

Frolick shrugged, holding up his hands as though he was surrendering, and we all went into the kitchen. Ollie closed the back door behind us.

"Nice place." He looked around. "I always wondered what the inside of one of these things looked like."

"Get to the point," Uncle Saul said before I could. "Okay—but this is for your consumption only. I guess your father is good friends with the commissioner so it's okay to tell you this." He stared at Ollie and Uncle Saul. "You couldn't tell in the garden what had happened to the Phillips's kid. Hell, I couldn't tell, either—not for sure. Then his girl-friend found the note he left. It clarified a lot of things."

"Like what?" I crossed my arms over my chest.

"The ME found gunshot residue on Jordan's right hand and the wound. That meant he was holding the gun when it went off. The GSR was on the wound because the gun was close to it."

"So whoever killed him made it look that way. Or he was struggling with someone," I argued. "Jordan doesn't strike me as the kind of person to kill himself."

"We all do crazy things when we're in love," Frolick said. "We know his girlfriend had broken up with him. We've seen hundreds of texts on her phone from him, begging her to come back to him and threatening to kill himself if she didn't."

I thought about Tiffany. Was he talking about her or Lisa Rakin?

Frolick didn't know that I knew about Tiffany. To say something would give it away.

Lisa, on the other hand, had only been dating Jordan a short time. How much could she have known about him? And didn't Tucker say that Jordan was too involved in his work to give any woman much attention—thus the short relationships?

When I didn't say anything, Frolick frowned and scratched his neck. "I'm gonna tell you something that only a few people know—Phillips was engaged to the commissioner's daughter. She's the one who found the note for us. She's cooperated completely during this terrible tragedy. We now believe that Phillips was at the masquerade to do her harm. The gun he was shot with was his own. We think that he meant to kill her, and maybe the commissioner, but he lost his nerve."

I'm afraid my mouth dropped open by the time he'd finished. It explained everything so perfectly. How could anyone hear it and still have doubts?

But I did.

"It's the truth, Miss Chase. If you don't believe me, you're welcome to come back to police headquarters and look at the file. We didn't release the information about where Phillips was found to the media, but our files reflect what actually happened."

"He's right, Zoe," Uncle Saul said. "It makes sense. Telling everyone where Jordan was found wasn't necessary. The media had to piece it together."

"And it would've been an embarrassment to the commissioner and his daughter, not to mention the Mistics of Time, for anyone to know Phillips's true motive and where he was found." Frolick watched me intently, waiting for me to acknowledge that what he said was true.

"What about my father and everything that's happened to me?"

"I don't know what's happened to you, Miss Chase, but I'll be glad to take a report on any incidents. As for your father, there's no reason to think his injuries were due to anything but a drunken street brawl. I'm sure I don't have to tell you how many of those happen during carnival."

He was right. Uncle Saul was right. It all made sense. There was no point in butting my head against a wall trying to make something out of nothing more than a tragic incident. Jordan's death still bothered me, but I had to admit that any death where I'd found the dead person was bound to personally affect me.

I managed to smile at Detective Frolick and shake his hand. "Thanks for telling me. It was a terrible thing. It seemed like Jordan had so much to live for."

"We just don't know what's going on in someone else's life. Maybe if Phillips had been able to move on after his breakup with the commissioner's daughter . . ." He spread his hands and shrugged. "But who knows? If you have any other questions, please let me know. Thanks for your concern."

Ollie let him out of the food truck. I sat on the counter thinking about all of it. The one thing that didn't seem to make sense was that Jordan *had* moved on after Tiffany—with Lisa—or at least it seemed that way.

I ran my thoughts past Ollie and Uncle Saul.

"Maybe his family didn't know who he was dating," Ollie said. "After all, he was a grown man. Maybe he lied to them."

"Or even made up this other girl so they wouldn't know

he was obsessed with the commissioner's daughter," Uncle Saul suggested.

"I suppose that's possible." I glanced at my watch. It was time for me to bake biscuits. "I'll take Ollie back to the diner with me if you can handle the food truck for a couple hours."

Uncle Saul nodded. "Please. And make sure he takes a shower and changes clothes."

Ollie sniffed himself. "I don't smell that bad."

I laughed. "We'll be back as soon as we can. Thanks."

"It's gonna be good to get home to the swamp and do nothing for a while after this." Uncle Saul smiled. "Hurry back. I'll hold down the fort."

Cole came to pick us up a few minutes later. The city was mostly asleep, recovering from the exciting night before. The streets were covered in throws and leftover food. I didn't envy the cleanup crew who came out every day and made things look like new again.

"I saw the article about that poor boy from the newspaper this morning," Cole said as we drove quickly down the empty streets toward the diner. "That was a terrible way to die. He never hardly had a chance to live. I feel for his parents."

"Me, too." We had arrived at the diner. Cole wouldn't take any money. He was always so stubborn about it. "I have to pay you. What will happen if you go out of business because people stop paying you?"

He laughed. "If I go out of business because you stop paying me, I must deserve it. Make me some food, Zoe. Your money's no good with me."

I thanked him and added another plate or two to what I owed him. I'd have to find some other way to say thank you as well.

Ollie turned to walk to the shelter. "I'll be back in a bit. I'm glad the shelter director has let me have a few nights off to help with the Biscuit Bowl. That was decent of him."

"And I don't know what I'd do without you. Tell him I'll be glad to make him some food for his trouble."

"Nah." Ollie shook his head. "He's not *that* great!"

I let myself into the diner and mixed up the biscuit dough as I thought about Jordan.

Now that I knew that Tiffany had been dating Jordan, it was also apparent that she was at the masquerade ball with her father. If Jordan had meant to hurt her, he would've made sure of it. I suppose that also answered my question about why he was there dressed as Death.

I put in the first tray of biscuits, showered, and changed clothes.

All the while I kept reminding myself that I didn't know Jordan Phillips at all. I had no idea what he was like, if he was suicidal, how he felt about Tiffany. Everything I knew about him was secondhand knowledge—mostly from the people who'd loved him.

It was only because I'd found him and felt sorry for him that my mind kept insisting that his suicide couldn't be true.

I smacked myself in the head as I dried my hair and tried to get it into some order. The curls were running rampant. I didn't want to use gel on them because it wore off in the heat of the kitchen. Instead I used a colorful scarf to tie them back from my face. They didn't like it and promised revenge when I least expected it. I fluffed them back and added some lip gloss.

"You have to get a grip," I impatiently told my image in the mirror. "Quit daydreaming about his death and face the facts. Detective Frolick probably knew Jordan better than you! The cover-up thing was because of where it happened and who was involved. You might not like it, but you understand it. That doesn't make it murder!"

Ollie was back by then in clean jeans and a Mardi Gras T-shirt from 1995.

The talk I'd had with myself had done me good. I felt calmer and more rational about the whole thing. It was good to be free of the responsibility I felt I'd owed Jordan for finding him.

Ollie pilfered the pantry and the freezer as we talked about what we could make for the biscuit bowls today. "What about sauerkraut and sausage in a biscuit bowl?" he asked.

"I know I have some sauerkraut, but in a biscuit bowl? Really?"

"You gotta be open to new ideas, young'un." He held up a can of sauerkraut and grinned at me. "How about it?"

My stomach twisted at the idea. It was a little too revolutionary. "How about sausage gravy? We could cut up the sausages and pan fry them to mix with thick milk gravy. It would go a long way."

"That's true," he admitted. "We can jazz it up with some peppers, too. Doesn't mean it has to be bland."

"I can live with that." I laughed at his crazy face. "You're something else!"

"Always have been." He looked at more frozen bags. "Hey! Plums! That sounds good. What could we do with plums?"

"Plum pudding?"

He hit himself in the head with his open hand. "Plum clafouti! Why didn't I think of it? My French grandmother used to make it all the time when I was growing up. All we need is some almonds, milk, amaretto—where's the amaretto?"

"I don't have any." I moved two trays of biscuits. "Would brandy do?"

"Don't be silly!" he scowled. "You could add brandy to it, too, but you have to have amaretto!"

"Ollie—"

"The liquor store around the corner is open. I have ten dollars. I'll be right back."

"I can give you money for it, but—"

He took my chin in his fingers and grinned. "Plum clafouti could be what makes your name, little girl! Just wait and see!"

"All right." I gave in with a smile. "But let me pay for it." I grabbed my bag from under the counter.

"You have visitors." Ollie pointed to the parking lot.

"Not Mr. Carruthers!" I whispered, hoping I was wrong.

"Tucker and some young chick. I hope he isn't here to announce his engagement!"

TWENTY-ONE

Tucker was pale with deep, dark circles under his eyes. I could see the misery in his face. I went to him and threw my arms around him. "I'm so sorry."

He sniffed a few times and wiped tears impatiently from his eyes. "It doesn't matter what they say. My grandson didn't kill himself. The whole idea that he would is ludicrous."

I gazed at the slight woman to his right. Her limpid blue eyes were fastened on me like I could save her from the storm. "You must be Lisa."

"I am." She shook my hand. Her eyes were very red and puffy. "And you're Zoe?"

"Oh. I'm sorry. Of course. I'm Zoe Chase."

"I brought Lisa here because she can refute everything the police are saying about Jordan." Tucker frowned as he spoke. "They didn't even talk to her."

"Excuse me." I tried to gather my thoughts that had been

so calm and rational. "I have to cook while we talk. I hope that's okay."

I started cooking the sausage. There was a lot of it—good thing. I added some onions to it and decided to wait and let Ollie add the spices when he got back from the liquor store. He'd left as Tucker had come in with Lisa.

I took my time even though it seemed rude to keep them waiting for a response. What could I say? Why had they brought this to me? It wasn't like I'd been able to help with the other information they'd given me.

When I'd waited as long as I could, I turned back to them. "I know this is a terrible loss for both of you and it must seem very unfair. I didn't know Jordan, but he seemed like a wonderful young man. I just don't see what I can do to help you."

Tucker looked around. "Isn't your mother here yet? She said she'd meet us here."

Oh. That's it.

My mother's car pulled up outside. At least I understood why they were there.

- - - - - - -

Chef Art arrived soon after my mother. The four of them sat at one of the lumpy booths and drank up an entire pot of coffee while I got food ready for the Biscuit Bowl.

Ollie was back with the amaretto. The plums were simmering in the pot.

Chef Art had known exactly what Ollie was talking about when he said plum clafouti. He kissed his fingers to the idea and called it a masterful stroke.

I was glad he'd heard of the dish, anyway. The almonds were defrosting, and custard was in the double boiler on the stove.

I knew Tucker and Lisa were grieving. My mother? I

wasn't sure why she was involved except that she admired Chef Art. Maybe she saw some way to help her political ambitions with them. Chef Art was there for his friend.

I just couldn't figure out why they hadn't met at a real café so they could've had a waitress bring them coffee and serve them breakfast. I didn't mind them being there, exactly. It made me feel like my diner was a real place to eat.

But on the other hand, I had so much to do and only so much time to do it.

Ollie was getting the sausage gravy ready, no doubt spicing it up more than I ever would. He loved hot food and frequently accused me of being scared of spices, which wasn't true at all.

He glanced at the group huddled over the table. "I don't understand why your mother is here again, Zoe."

"Me, either." I packed the last tray of biscuits into a warming bag like they use to deliver pizza. The bag kept the biscuits fresh and warm until lunchtime. "They're going at it, though, aren't they?"

"Why aren't you over there, too? I thought you wanted to help."

"I did until I heard all Detective Frolick's information." I glanced at the booth. Lisa was crying again. "I feel bad for Tucker and Lisa, but they have all that proof. What more can anyone do?"

"I don't believe the cops, anyway." He stirred a little more cayenne into the sausage gravy. "Probably just covering their own butts."

"I've got the biscuits ready. How's the savory coming?" I thought changing the subject was the best way to go.

"We're ready here. I need a few more minutes with the custard and then the clafouti will be ready, too."

"I guess that's it." I glanced at the table again. "I hate to kick them out, but they really need to go someplace else."

I took a deep breath and told my nonpaying customers that I had to leave. They looked surprised that I was trying to get them to go, too.

"Just leave the keys, Zoe," my mother said. "I'll lock up before we go."

I wasn't comfortable with that. My mother tended to underestimate the importance of the diner to my business. It didn't matter at her house if she didn't lock up because Martha took care of things. My mother had plenty of people to take care of things for her.

I only had myself.

"I'm sorry. I'm going to have to ask you to leave. There must be somewhere else you could talk that would be better than this."

She looked around. "This is the best place. No one would think to look for me in this old place."

That was it. "Really? You need to go. Ollie and I are taking the food to the Biscuit Bowl. I need you to leave now."

There was a lot of grumbling—mostly from my mother. Chef Art understood. Lisa and Tucker were too devastated to really care.

Chef Art was the last to go. He gave me a hundred-dollar bill. "Thanks for putting up with us. How's the food truck rally going?"

"It's been really busy, but I figured out how to keep the food longer and plan better."

"My food truck will be in the parade today. It's a shame I couldn't have managed to get yours in, too, Zoe. I'll talk to you later. Sorry for the inconvenience this morning."

Chef Art's food truck was a full-size RV with his face painted on both sides. It had all the comforts of home, including a double gas oven. He really didn't use it as a food truck, but he sometimes took it out for demonstrations and to create a spectacle in parades.

Someday I wanted one just like it—except not with my picture painted on it.

"That was nice of him to give you money," Ollie said when we were alone again. "So you don't think there's anything to what Lisa and Tucker were saying about Jordan not killing himself over his fiancé?"

I put the hundred-dollar bill in my pocket. I'd use it to pay Ollie and Delia. I'd wrapped five plates of food for Cole. I'd have to figure out later what I'd give Miguel and Uncle Saul for their help.

"I don't know. I can't think about it anymore. Let me call Cole for a ride and get this table cleaned off before we go."

I took the plates and cups off the table and put them in the big stainless steel sink behind the counter. I wiped the tabletop down and then noticed a cell phone on the lumpy seat. I thought it probably belonged to one of my visitors, but when I turned it on, I realized it was Jordan's. I put it in my pocket. I'd have to give it back to Tucker as soon as I could.

Cole was there to pick up us a few minutes later. The first thing I did was give him a hot egg-and-cheese biscuit. Then I piled five plates of food on the front seat beside him.

"Just to say thank you." I smiled and hugged him.

"You didn't have to do all that," he complained. "That's enough to feed me and my wife for the rest of the week." He took a bite of the hot biscuit and rolled his eyes. "But I'm mighty glad you did. I love your biscuits."

"You bring your wife and grandkids over to the Biscuit Bowl anytime. Your money is no good with me there, either, but I'll feed you all up until you can't walk to your car."

He laughed at that.

Ollie had already finished filling the trunk with food. He looked up at the dark sky and shook his head. "Looks like a storm is brewing. I hope this food doesn't go to waste."

He had barely spoken when it started raining. I knew none

of the carnival celebrations would cease because of the weather. We'd keep going at the Biscuit Bowl, too, as long as we had food.

It was pouring by the time we reached the food truck rally. Great sheets of cold rain blew in from the Gulf accompanied by high winds that threatened to blow all the carnival decorations into the streets.

The parades were still halting traffic. People waved from the sides of the streets in their rain gear and dived for throws as the floats went by. Bands still marched, and royalty from the various krewes, some masked to hide their identities, still waved from convertibles as they drove by.

Somewhere out there my father was waving and smiling as King Felix. I could hear the music, and sometimes applause, as ornate parade art passed inspection by the crowds.

But the crowds ignored the food trucks for the most part— probably sheltering in cafés and restaurants. If the day cleared, we'd be busy again, but the morning was nothing.

I called Delia and told her to enjoy the free time. Uncle Saul went to see one of his friends. Ollie stayed at the Biscuit Bowl with me, occasionally calling out orders as an intrepid customer braved the weather.

I mostly played with Crème Brûlée and looked through Jordan's phone.

I couldn't help myself, though I knew it was wrong. I was curious. Jordan was dead, but he still deserved his privacy. Once I'd opened the phone again—supposedly to call Tucker and let him know I had it—I couldn't close it.

It was like being inside another person's mind. All of his thoughts and dreams were cataloged here. His stories and ideas for stories, his calendar with notes, all of it was interesting. He didn't use full names on anything, but it didn't take long to figure out that L meant Lisa, G was Tucker, and E was his father, the editor. I could follow along on his good and bad days. Sometimes E would throw out a story and L would be late for an appointment.

It struck me as the morning passed that Tucker was right about Jordan. His calendar was marked and annotated into the new year. He had so many things going on in his life, so much he wanted to do. It was hard to believe he had time to think about Tiffany. I couldn't find a single text or email to her. How much could he have cared if they never talked? He never mentioned her in his personal diary, though he mentioned Lisa.

I finally called Tucker. We talked for a while. He'd left Jordan's phone at the diner on purpose for me to find.

"I thought if you really had a chance to look through it, Miss Chase, you'd come to the same conclusion I did."

"I know. You're right—and that was sneaky. Why do you care what I think about it?"

"I just feel like you and Jordan are linked in some way. You found him and were the first to raise suspicions about his death. It's like you were meant to figure this out."

I didn't agree with his assessment of the situation. I suppose I didn't want to. I'd found Jordan, but I didn't know what else I could do to help. The medical examiner and Detective Frolick had said Jordan killed himself. Commissioner Sloane wanted to keep him, and his daughter, out of the picture. It seemed like a done deal.

"I'm sorry, Tucker. I'll get the phone back to you as soon as I can. I wish there was something more I could do."

"You did your best. I appreciate it. Bennett feels the same as you, unfortunately. Lisa and I plan to go and lodge a protest at the police department. We'll see what happens then."

"Be careful. I know you want to make this right for Jordan, but he wouldn't want something to happen to you."

"Thanks. We'll watch our step. I'll drop by the food truck rally later today, if that's all right with you, and pick up Jordan's phone."

"That's fine. I'll see you then."

I hit end call on the phone and thoughtfully put it back in my pocket. The rain still drummed on the metal roof. The parking lot outside the open customer window was still empty.

"Was that Tucker Phillips again?" Ollie asked.

"Yes. He thinks I have a connection to Jordan because I found him after he was killed. What do you say to a thing like that?"

"I'd say you have two choices—ignore him or believe what he says. My old granny migrated to Mobile after growing up in New Orleans. I used to love being at her house. It was filled with dried lizards, skulls, and things I couldn't identify."

"I'm sorry. What does that have to do with me and Tucker?"

"Nothing except she used to say the same thing. Souls who were there when you were born, or when you died, had meaning in your life. Maybe he's right about you and Jordan."

Before I could answer that I wasn't with Jordan when he died, there was a sharp rap at the door and Tiffany ran into the kitchen.

"This weather is ruining our food truck rally." She shook her poncho like a dog. "We've had some spot outages on electricity and some problems with gas lines. Are you all okay in here? Do you need anything?"

"We're fine as far as I know. Thanks, anyway."

"Have you had any customers today?"

"A few," Ollie answered. "It won't rain all day. My bunions don't hurt. That's always a sure sign that the weather is going to clear."

Tiffany grimaced at the mention of his bunions and took a quick look at her plastic-covered clipboard. "Yes, well, let me know if you have any problems. We lost another food truck this morning. We can't stand to lose any more or it won't be much of a rally."

"Thanks for letting us know." I smiled at her even though she was a little bossy and perky for me. She had the hard job of keeping a bunch of independent foodies together for two weeks. I had it in my heart to feel sorry for her.

She fussed with her pink poncho for a moment.

"I'm sorry about Jordan," I said quickly. "I know about the two of you. He seemed like a nice person."

Her wet face paled, and she bit her lip. "I really can't believe he's gone, you know? When my father said he'd been shot, I thought—"

"You didn't think he'd killed himself?"

"No," she admitted. "I still don't. But I hadn't seen him since December. He was always working. He didn't have time for me."

"What about Lisa?"

"Lisa?" She looked puzzled. "I don't know her."

"She was his new girlfriend." I was skeptical. What woman doesn't know who her old boyfriend is dating?

"Oh. I didn't know." She held up her clipboard as though it was a shield. "I have to go. Good luck today."

"She's kind of cute," Ollie said when she was gone. "I wonder if she's seeing anyone."

"I don't know. Maybe you should ask her out."

He shuddered. "Still recovering from my breakup with Delia. She was the first woman I've been interested in for years."

I smiled at him, knowing some of his background. Ollie's wife had tried to kill him. Miguel said she had PTSD and was out of her head at the time. Ollie's career with the Marines had ended that day. I understood why he was reluctant to try other relationships.

There was another knock on the back door. Ollie answered it reluctantly. "Someone needs to tell people that we have the side window open."

It was one Mr. Carruthers. "Miss Chase."

Why was he here? "Yes. What can I do for you?"

"I only wanted to stop by and apologize for giving you a hard time." He managed a small smile. "I'm new at this and I really need this job. Perhaps I was trying too hard to make sure you were up to code."

"That's okay." I could certainly understand wanting to make things work out right. "Would you like a biscuit or something?"

"No. I have to get back to work. Good luck with your food truck."

"Thanks."

"That was odd," Ollie said as we watched Mr. Carruthers walk away.

"Maybe he was feeling guilty."

"Yeah. I don't buy it."

"I don't know what else he could hope to gain."

"We'll see."

One of the other food truck drivers walked by. "You all should come out and take a look at this." He pointed toward the sky.

Ollie and I both shrugged and followed him into the parking lot. There was a double rainbow over Mobile Bay. We stood and stared at the arches in the sky as everyone proclaimed the rainbows to be a good sign. It had stopped raining and the sun was shining again.

"Can I call it or what?" Ollie drawled. "Well, not me, but my bunions."

There was one older man. I guessed he was from one of the food trucks, but I wasn't sure. He stared at the sky, crossing himself a dozen times as he took in the rainbows.

"No good luck from those things," he said. "It just means the gods are walking the earth. When did anything good ever come from that?"

TWENTY-TWO

I wasn't sure what the double rainbows meant to anyone else, but to us they meant customers. Groups of people in ponchos, not trusting the weather, started walking through the parking lot. Some of them stopped at the Biscuit Bowl. They were hungry, too, ordering several biscuit bowls each.

We'd forgotten to put ice into the big cooler outside, so our Cokes were cool rather than cold. Most people didn't seem to care. A few people gave Ollie a disgusted look and walked off when he told them there was no ice.

I called Uncle Saul, not knowing how much longer Miguel might be busy. He said he'd bring more ice as soon as he could.

"Your father convinced me to ride on the Mistics of Time float this morning. I'm soaking wet, and I think I'm getting a head cold." He sneezed several times. "I'm gonna go back to the apartment and change before I come over."

"Don't plan on working if you don't feel well. We can handle it."

But by the time Uncle Saul got there with the ice, it was all Ollie and I could do to keep up with the orders. There was a long line of customers waiting in the parking lot. Uncle Saul filled the ice barrel and then stepped into the kitchen.

"Where's Delia?" he asked. "I believe you could use a hand."

"She's on her way but got stuck behind a parade. She'll get here as soon as she can. We'll be fine until then. Go back to the apartment and get some rest."

He grinned, put on some plastic gloves, and then grabbed some paper products for the order Ollie was barking out. "Don't be silly. I might have a stuffy nose, but I can still help. I just won't touch the food."

I didn't argue with him. I couldn't even remember what the last three orders had been that Ollie had yelled out. "You're going to have to write them down," I told Ollie. "I can't keep up with what you're saying." He grabbed a pencil and paper, but his handwriting was so bad I couldn't read it. "Print, please."

He growled and began printing the orders. Sometimes he reminded me of Crème Brûlée, except for the biting and licking.

We were moving more smoothly when Delia arrived. That extra pair of hands made a big difference. We split up into our usual jobs, but Uncle Saul helped with plates, forks, and napkins instead of making food.

It was three P.M. before I glanced up and there were no people at the window. Ollie had slumped on the counter. Delia was up front with Crème Brûlée, her head on the steering wheel. Uncle Saul was sneezing and coughing. I hugged him and told him to go back to the apartment.

"You need me, Zoe." His voice was getting raspy. "I'm not really sick."

"You sound sick to me. Go have a long nap. I'll call Cole. He can drop you off and then take me to the diner to make biscuits. We'll probably be slow again for a couple hours."

"Okay. Fine," he agreed. "People just use you up around here. I've tried to help and what do I get?"

"I'll make you some hot garlic soup while I'm at the diner. That should pick you right up." I gave him a hug and a kiss. "And I appreciate all your help. You know that! I just don't want you to get worse."

"I guess that's fine. But you'll call if you get busy again, right?"

"I will."

Miguel showed up in a blue Biscuit Bowl T-shirt and jeans. He was done working for the day and wanted to help out. I told him about my plan to drop Uncle Saul at the apartment and go on to the diner. He offered the use of his car.

"Thank you so much." I kissed him quickly and smiled. "I'm going to have to think of something special I can do for you."

He grinned. "I'm sure I can think of something."

Ollie and Uncle Saul both laughed at that. I could feel my cheeks turning pink. I supposed that's what happened when you said possibly suggestive things to your boyfriend in front of relatives and co-workers.

We were all set to go. Delia was staying at the Biscuit Bowl to handle any light traffic. My phone rang, and I answered it, but there was no one there. I put it away and it rang again.

I realized then that it was Jordan's phone that was ringing in my pocket. It gave me a creepy feeling. "Hello?"

"Jordan? I-is that you?"

I lowered my voice and coughed, trying to imitate Uncle Saul. "I have a cold. What's up?"

"It's Dylan. I read that you were dead, man. I mean I guess you're not, right? Listen, this thing is getting too intense. I have to move on. Maybe get out of town or something."

"Wait." I coughed again and tried to gather my thoughts. This was obviously a friend of Jordan's who might have information about him and what he was working on. I had to be careful. "We should meet. I can't talk about this on the phone, you know?"

"I hear you. I didn't know this would blow up. Honestly. I didn't understand what I'd heard until later. I'm sorry I dragged you into this. We should meet and then we should both get out of town. This thing with the police commissioner is crazy, man."

"Yeah. Really crazy."

"Let's meet at the Mardi Gras museum. You can buy me a drink after at Clawfoot. You owe me, man."

"Sure. I know. I'll be there."

"Midnight. I'm out of here after that. I already quit the paper. I think someone has been following me. I'll try to be careful not to lead him to you. See you then."

That was it. The phone went dead. I tried to figure out what the call had meant.

"What's wrong?" Miguel asked.

I explained about how I'd come to have Jordan's phone. "That was someone from the newspaper. He was talking about something crazy with the police commissioner and that Jordan owed him a favor. I want to meet with him."

"We should call the police," Miguel said.

"I don't think you should involve the police," Ollie added. "They've made it pretty clear that they're done with this case."

Uncle Saul nudged him with his elbow. "Are you saying Zoe should talk to some man she's never met? He might be a killer! How is she equipped to handle something like that?"

"I guess that's true." Ollie stared hard at me. "I could give her a quick course in self-defense and death moves."

"I don't think I need death moves," I retorted. "But I think I should meet him—Clawfoot is that bar near the *Mobile Times* building, right? He works for the newspaper, like Jordan did. He might have something important to say. He said he's leaving town."

"At least give Patti a call." Miguel was always a fan of doing things the "right" way. "I think she'll help. She'll know what we should do."

"I don't think I should call her. Not yet," I disagreed. "The police aren't interested, and it might be nothing. If I do it myself—no complications. If he doesn't really have anything to say, I don't have to feel bad for dragging anyone out at midnight."

"Midnight? That's dramatic, don't you think?" Delia asked. "Why not when it's sunny out?"

"I don't think he wants anyone to see him," I replied. "He sounds scared."

"I should go, too," Ollie offered. "Maybe Miguel could stay here. Or Delia. Neither one of them can look mean like I can. I could protect you."

"I can stay," Delia said. "But, Zoe, I think Miguel is right. This person could be a crazy killer. You can't tell by talking to someone on the phone for two minutes."

"I might not get another chance to talk to one of Jordan's friends."

She put her hand on my shoulder. "You aren't responsible for this young man's death. I know you found him, but that doesn't mean you have to do anything more. I don't want to find you dead."

I hugged her. "Thanks. Will you stay until six? There shouldn't be many people. Call if it gets busy."

"Sure. But think about this, Zoe," she said. "And get back here as soon as you can. I don't want to face a ravenous crowd of drenched parade watchers alone."

I thanked her for being such a big help and left with Miguel and Ollie. Miguel had found an app for his phone that showed which streets were blocked off for the big parades. We avoided those areas, but it still took an extra twenty minutes to drop Uncle Saul off at Daddy's apartment on the way to the diner.

He protested between sneezes all the way. "You're gonna need me tonight, Zoe girl. Things could change suddenly and you might get hurt."

"I'll be fine. I'm going to make biscuits and get the food ready for dinner. I won't meet with Dylan until later. I'll have Ollie and Miguel looking out for me."

He seemed pacified by that idea and went inside the apartment building after I promised that I would call when I heard anything else.

Miguel still wasn't happy about it. "You're determined to be part of this, aren't you?"

"Not at all. Tucker and Jordan's girlfriend were both at the diner this morning. I didn't offer to help. Same thing when I called Tucker after he left the phone for me to find."

"Why is Tucker Phillips—a millionaire and a man who has many friends in this city—turning to you for help? Have you thought about that?"

"I agree with Miguel," Ollie said. "I don't trust that man."

"He thinks Jordan and I are tied together because I found his body. It's a philosophy thing."

"Maybe so, but it's a bad philosophy thing, Zoe. *He* should hire a private detective, not try to get you to figure this out for him."

"It's going to be fine now that we know a little more," I

assured him with a bright smile. "Dylan is Jordan's friend, a co-worker. He might know what Jordan was working on when he died. He might be able to give us insight into Jordan."

"Or he might be the one who killed Jordan."

"No denying that, young'un," Ollie chimed in after being quiet for so long that I almost forgot he was in the backseat. "This could be a good thing, or it could be a trap."

We pulled into the diner parking lot and I got out of the Mercedes.

"It's not a trap, Ollie. You should've heard his voice. He was terrified." I had to dig around in my bag to find my keys. "This is something I was meant to do or I wouldn't have found him. You should understand that, Miguel."

I could tell he didn't understand at all. I opened the diner and started mixing biscuits, all the while thinking about the meeting with Jordan's friend. Would he be willing to talk to me when he saw I wasn't Jordan?

Ollie was humming as he searched through my freezers. "We need something exciting for dinner tonight. Something to spice things up and make people think food truck food is the best!"

Miguel made coffee. "Is there something I can do to help?"

"I might need some things from the store."

"Why don't I ever get to go to the store?" Ollie asked.

"You don't have a car," I answered with a smile. "Anything exciting in the freezer?"

"You've got a huge amount of mushrooms in here. What about some mushroom chowder?"

"Mushroom chowder?"

"Like clam chowder, but with some of these fat mushrooms. You've got plenty of potatoes, too."

"Sounds good. Do I have everything else for it?"

"Looks like you're out of fresh onion, celery, carrots, and garlic. Want to use powdered?"

"No, thanks." I glanced at Miguel. "Would you mind?"

"Not if you'll forget about talking to Jordan's friend tonight."

I thought he was kidding at first, but he was serious.

"Miguel, I have to find out what Dylan knows."

"I'll go, too," Ollie volunteered. "I'll go to the store, too, if you want."

"Do you have a driver's license?" Miguel asked.

"No. You know I lost it with that bus thing. But I can drive everything from a motorcycle to a tank."

"So you drove the Biscuit Bowl back here from Uncle Saul's place with no license?" I asked.

Ollie shrugged and took out the mushrooms.

"I'll go," Miguel said. "I'm not much of a cook like you two, and our time is limited before we have to head back to the food truck rally."

"I'll make a list." I hoped he'd give up on the idea of convincing me not to meet with Dylan.

"I'm not kidding about this, Zoe." Miguel was steely eyed. "This thing with Jordan has been one problem after another. It's dangerous. If you like, I'll tell Tucker he should quit bothering you with it."

"I can handle Tucker. And I'll think about Dylan while we cook," I promised. "Can we talk about it when you get back?"

"All right. But it has to be a serious conversation! You're taking this too lightly."

"It will. I promise." I kissed him and made up a quick list.

When he was gone, Ollie started peeling and chopping potatoes for the mushroom chowder. "I thought we were gonna get to mix it up, Zoe. What happens about Jordan now?"

"We go to see Dylan." I put a tray of biscuits into the oven and tried to decide what to make for the sweet biscuit bowl filling. "I think Miguel will feel better if he goes, too, don't you?"

"I think he was already planning to go even though I can take care of one punk reporter by myself. I think you'll need more to convince him than that, young'un."

I took a deep breath. "How about I'm going to meet with Dylan—with or without him."

Ollie punched one fist into the palm of his other hand. "Now that's what I'm talking about. When do we go?"

TWENTY-THREE

I talked Miguel around when he returned with his car stuffed full of fresh produce.

"With all three of us, it can't be too bad, right?" I suggested.

"It could be a disaster," Miguel said. "But I can see you're determined to go through with it. I think there's less of a chance for trouble with me and Ollie there, too. I wish Saul felt better. We can't have too many backups as far as I'm concerned."

Miguel was talking to me as I finished baking biscuits. I was only listening with half an ear as I mentally calculated if there were enough sweet and savory fillings for the rest of the day. I thought I was doing a better job deciding how much food we needed after a week, but it was scary each time. I knew it was a lesson in cooking for crowds that I wouldn't forget.

My sweet filling was finally cool. I was making a coconut

custard with a dash of brandy that Ollie had suggested. It was really good. He'd wanted to add mint, too, but I thought that was too much.

"Zoe? Are you listening to me?" Miguel asked. "Your life could depend on making this man think there are more of us than he's going to see at the meeting."

"I hope not—but I was listening."

"You're going to have to tell him right away that you have people in the car waiting for you and something at home that will ruin his life if you don't get back safely."

"Like one of those letters you give your lawyer to give to the newspaper if you die," Ollie agreed. "I've seen those in the movies."

"Is that what you're talking about?" I asked Miguel.

"Something like that," he agreed. "Ollie and I will be right there with you. But if we could make Dylan think there was more than just the three of us, he might think twice about trying anything stupid."

"I can do that."

Ollie tasted the garlic soup I had been simmering for Uncle Saul. "This stuff is great! Too bad it's too thin to go into a biscuit bowl. Maybe we could thicken it up."

"Maybe later." I transferred the soup to a covered dish. "Right now everything is ready. Let's get back to the Biscuit Bowl. I don't like leaving Delia there by herself too long."

We piled everything into the car and then made a brief stop at Daddy's apartment. I left the soup with Marvin, the security guard, who promised to take it right up to Uncle Saul.

There was nowhere to park when we got back to the food truck rally. It had become the staging area for a 5K race with about two hundred runners all limbering up in the street. Everyone was dressed in green, gold, and purple. Some wore masks or had feather boas on their shoulders. There were even some runners with fool's hats on, their bells ringing when they moved their heads.

"We can't get through," I said. We had so much food, plus drinks and ice, that had to go to the Biscuit Bowl. "I don't know how we're going to get it there."

An older man with a golf cart came to our rescue. We loaded up his little green gator cart three times. The front of the cart was painted with a gator's face and teeth. The back had a short, stubby tail that swished from side to side when the cart was moving.

"I just like gators." Frank Curlee grinned when I asked him why he'd painted his cart to be a gator.

I told him about Uncle Saul's albino gator, and he vowed to watch for my uncle's arrival at the rally. "I'd love to have a conversation with him! I had three gators that I kept in my swimming pool for a while. The city said I couldn't keep 'em there anymore. This little cart, and my memories, are all I got left of them."

It was hard to imagine why anyone wanted to keep alligators. I knew I wouldn't want to. I was always afraid with Crème Brûlée when we visited Uncle Saul's cabin. Alabaster had snapped at him several times. I was pretty sure he'd make a nice snack for her.

I thanked Frank for his help and gave him a coconut custard biscuit bowl. I scribbled Uncle Saul's phone number down. "I'm sure he'd like to talk to you, too. There's nothing he likes to talk about more than food and his gator."

He bit down hard on the biscuit bowl and smiled like a gator—a toothless one. "This is very good! Why haven't I had this before? You're a culinary genius filling these little biscuit bowls, Zoe!"

"We're right over there in the parking lot." I laughed. "You can't miss us. We have the big biscuit on top. Usually,

I'm parked in front of police headquarters five days a week. Sometimes I take the Biscuit Bowl out for special events like this one."

"Police?" He shuddered. "Why in the world would you park there?"

He and Uncle Saul would get along just fine.

"Business is good over there," I explained. "I have to park somewhere people are going in and out during the day."

"And whose kin did you say you were?"

"Chase," I repeated. "My uncle is Saul Chase, and my father is Ted Chase."

"I know those Chase brothers. I knew their daddy well. He was a good man. Those boys of his were always fussing and feuding. Never saw two brothers who loved each other more, though. You take care, little girl. Keep makin' these biscuit bowls!"

"Thanks. I will!"

Miguel took Delia home while Ollie and I unloaded the food. We were going to be shorthanded with Uncle Saul out sick, but Delia needed the break. It hadn't been all that busy while I'd been gone, but I knew it was tiring just sitting there waiting, too. I didn't expect anyone to be there twenty-four hours a day.

"So what are you gonna say to this man tonight?" Ollie asked as he spooned the thick chowder into the warming trays. "Got any ideas?"

"I don't know. I'm hoping he'll want to do the talking. He's a reporter. He should like to talk, right?" I filled the refrigerated trays with the coconut cream filling. "What do you think I should say to him?"

"Miguel is right—you should play it cool. Don't let him know that you don't know what he knows."

"What?" I laughed. "How else will I get him to tell me what he knows?"

He waggled his brows, making the tattoo on his head move. "You could use your feminine wiles. He's a man. You're a woman. I mean, he's gonna know right away that you're not Jordan, isn't he? You need another way to approach him. Showing him that you're a woman and making promises you won't keep is the standard way."

I felt bad that Ollie's experience with women had led him to that conclusion.

"I suppose he'll know right away that I'm not Jordan and that I'm a woman. I'm hoping to convince him that I was Jordan's friend, too. We can talk about Jordan, mourn him some. I don't think I have to seduce him to get him to talk."

"But why would he spill the beans to you? You're gonna have to convince him—especially if he's afraid for his life."

"Because he wants to unburden himself? And he wants to talk about Jordan with someone else he thinks knew him, too."

"Better rethink that. He doesn't want to be unburdened. He wants someone to worm the truth out of him. A sexy, seductive lady, like yourself."

"You must be talking about someone else!"

He put his hands on my arms. "Zoe, you are one of the sexiest women I've ever known! You're cute and petite. And you're just sexy. *Hot!*"

"Thanks." My face felt a little flushed. "I wouldn't know where to start using my, er, sex appeal, though."

"I'll show you."

He put one hand on his hip and held the other hand in the air as he sauntered through the limited space in the kitchen with his butt swaying.

I barely contained my laughter.

"Why, Dylan"—he raised the pitch of his voice—"you should tell me everything you know about Jordan. I really want to help him . . . and *you*. Give me a chance to make you feel better."

Ollie bent forward slightly and pushed out his chest.

That was too much. I laughed. I couldn't help it. "Is that how I'm supposed to sound?"

"Well you have more"—he waved to my bosom—"but you get the idea."

"I don't think I'd be very good at that, but thanks for the suggestion."

"Don't give up so easy. Girls do it naturally," Ollie barked in the tone I'd heard him use on the other men in the shelter when they wouldn't listen to him. "Try it, Zoe. You can do it."

"All right." I turned around and rolled up my T-shirt under my breasts, tying it tight behind my back. I pushed my black curly hair free of its restraint and turned around with my lips puckered. "Don't you want to tell me all your secrets, *Ollie*?"

I fluttered my lashes and thrust out my breasts.

Ollie stared at me for a moment before he got up from the counter. "That was good. That was very good. I think he'll talk to you if you approach him that way. I would. I mean—I have to go and stock the cooler. Keep practicing. You'll be great."

TWENTY-FOUR

The Mobile Carnival Museum highlighted the history of Mardi Gras in Mobile, its true birthplace. It was mainly for tourists, but schoolchildren visited here, too. There probably wasn't a child in the city who couldn't talk to you about designing costumes and constructing floats.

There were also videos of parades and past coronations. The photos in the gallery went back to 1886. Everything anyone needed to know about carnival was located here.

There were two tour buses outside the museum—probably a special event, since I knew the museum had closed much earlier. I could see all the floral decorations through the windows. Women danced by in masks and silk gowns, as did men wearing fancy French costumes from the 1700s. I could hear a small quartet of musicians playing inside. Tables were elaborately decorated with fine china, silver, and leftovers from their champagne supper.

I wondered how this would all go down with a museum full of people. I hoped it wouldn't spook Dylan.

There was light drizzle in the streets after the food truck rally had closed down. It didn't hamper celebrations on the way from the municipal parking lot to the museum. People danced in the rain even when there was no music. Three men played guitars on one corner with a hat to catch coins. Horse-drawn carriages were making the rounds with lovers kissing inside them.

I wished I was doing any of that with Miguel instead of being exhausted and waiting for a man I didn't know to give me information about his dead friend. I started to call the whole thing off several times on the way there, but it had been so hard to talk Miguel into believing it was something that I should do. I couldn't just back out.

Ollie's advice about seducing the information from Dylan wasn't right for me. I would have felt stupid enough if it was only me and Jordan's friend. Ollie and Miguel would be right there, too. I stuck to my belief that Dylan would want someone to talk to about Jordan like a friend. If it didn't happen that way, I didn't think it would happen at all.

"Just remember," Miguel said as we waited outside the museum, "we're right here with you. Tell him there are other people, too. Don't let him intimidate you."

"Okay."

"You can still call this off," he reminded me.

"I'm fine."

Ollie hugged me. "Remember to talk sexy, like we practiced today. You'll be great. I almost"—he gulped—"well he won't have a chance."

"*What?*" Miguel asked with panic in his voice.

"Kidding!" I said, though Ollie didn't like that I sounded as though I might back out. "Quiet! Someone's coming."

My heart was pounding and my breathing was shallow

as the figure walked toward me. I knew Ollie and Miguel were behind me, but they were in the shadows of the trees and the museum building.

It was someone dressed as Folly, Death's partner during the Mardi Gras revels. He was wearing gold and red, his costume a little like the Renaissance fools that hammed it up for kings and queens.

He was slight, thin, and didn't appear to be much of a threat. His gold mask covered his face. All I could make out were the eyes and mouth behind it.

"You're not Jordan," he said in a muffled voice. "Are you with the police? Is he really dead?"

"Yes. I'm Zoe Chase. I found him—dressed as Death. He'd been shot. Do you have any idea who would want to hurt him?"

"They said in the paper that he killed himself," Dylan reminded me. "I knew it wasn't true. That's why I was hoping—" He started to turn away.

I grabbed his arm. "You know what Jordan was working on, Dylan. You were helping him, weren't you?"

"I was. I didn't know what was going on when I told him about the story. I overheard someone at the office talking about a threat to the commissioner. I didn't even know if it was real. I was just looking for someone to take me seriously. I wanted to write about the good stuff, not gardening, you know? I'm sorry I did it now. I didn't mean for Jordan to get hurt."

"What did you give him, Dylan?"

At that moment the party inside the museum began to let out. At least a hundred people spilled into the street with cars coming to pick them up at the curb. The smell of alcohol was strong, mingling with perfume and cigar smoke.

The rush of people separated us. Dylan backed away as the golden light from inside spilled out into the darkness.

"Dylan!" I called out. "Please talk to me."

"Meet me at Clawfoot," he answered. "Twenty minutes. I'll get what I have from my apartment and show you. I'm leaving Mobile. Maybe you can do something with it."

"Twenty minutes," I agreed. "I'll be there!"

"What happened?" Miguel asked when I hurried back away from the crowd still spewing out.

"He panicked when everyone came out of the party, but I think he's going to help. He said to meet him at Clawfoot. I'll buy him a few drinks. He said he has information he can give me. This might be it."

Miguel grumbled, and Ollie shook his head as we got back in the car.

"It's a wild-goose chase, Zoe," Miguel said. "He doesn't have anything or he would've given it to the police."

"I agree with Miguel this time," Ollie muttered. "If he really had something, he would've spoken up before now."

"He read in the paper that Jordan had killed himself," I reminded them. "He wasn't even sure if it was true. I think he just needs someone to talk to, maybe even confess to."

"All right." Miguel put the Mercedes into the heavy traffic at the museum. "Let's see what he has. At least he didn't sound dangerous."

"I think he's just a scared young man," I said. "He's afraid of the police. It has something to do with what he gave Jordan. He wanted to work with him on the story—whatever it was. We're close now. Dylan has the answers. I'm sure of it."

We drove across town to Clawfoot. I had no idea where it got its name. I'd thought it was a newspaper term. But there was a large mummified animal foot with claws near the door on the inside. Clawfoot.

I waited alone at a table in the noisy, crowded bar while Miguel and Ollie sat close by. I was afraid if we sat together at the table that Dylan might be scared away.

My foot tapped impatiently on the old wood floor as dozens of parade-goers in costume and makeup came in for a drink. I had to fend off several men who wanted to buy me a drink or sit with me. Most of them were too drunk to do more than mumble their request.

Not very attractive.

It was two A.M. before we finally gave up. I was worried about Crème Brûlée out in the food truck alone. I knew he couldn't get out or hurt himself, but it still made me nervous. I needed to check on him and maintain some kind of presence at the Biscuit Bowl as we had since we'd started the rally. It was an awkward situation.

I had to face that Dylan wasn't coming to meet me. He was scared and had probably left town when Jordan didn't show up at the museum. I wished I knew his last name so I could find him.

Miguel and I dropped Ollie off at the shelter and then headed back to the food truck. Crème Brûlée was sleeping peacefully in the front seat where I'd left him. He probably hadn't even noticed I was gone. I took him for a short walk and then climbed wearily into the truck with him and Miguel.

Miguel took my hand. "You did what you could, Zoe. That's all you could do."

"I know. I just feel like I botched it, you know? I wasn't prepared."

"You should have seduced him?" He smiled.

I laughed at that. "You should've seen Ollie telling me how to do it. I wish I would've recorded it. I could've had a million hits on YouTube."

"I wish I'd seen that, too," he agreed. "Good night, Zoe."

But I couldn't go to sleep. I was so tired I could barely see straight, but my mind kept working over everything Dylan and I had said to each other—admittedly not much.

Then it hit me—he wrote the garden columns for the paper! All I had to do was look that up and I could find him.

I found the *Mobile Times* website on my cell phone. Miguel was asleep. The light didn't seem to bother him. There it was—Garden Column by Dylan Medlin, staff reporter.

It was easy to find his address in the white pages online. I could find him, talk to him. Convince him to give me the information he said he had.

I didn't want to wake Miguel, but it was too far to walk. What if Dylan left town before morning?

I thought about taking Miguel's car keys and sneaking out. Really, I had no idea how sound a sleeper he was. I'd seen him put his keys with his wallet on the dash as he was settling down for what was left of the night. If I could reach them, I could sneak out and find Dylan.

Crème Brûlée was snoring. He rolled restlessly on his side. I reached across him and felt around on the dash for the keys. My hand hit the wallet, and I knew I was going in the right direction.

"Looking for something?" Miguel's voice was husky with sleep.

"I had an idea about Dylan. Sorry I woke you. Can I borrow your car?"

He glanced at the clock on the dash. "Zoe, it's almost four A.M. You have to be up in another two hours to make biscuits."

"I know. And I'm sorry. I'll be back before you know it."

He sighed. "I'll go with you."

"You don't trust me to drive your car?"

"I do. I just don't want you to be out there alone."

"Thanks." I kissed his cheek.

We were both already dressed—I longed for a shower, but that would have to wait until morning. We crept out of the sleeping food truck rally. This time I brought Crème

Brûlée with me. I put him in his car seat in back and read Dylan's address to Miguel.

There were still people out celebrating. Drums were beating in the night, and fireworks lit up the sky. We passed what looked like a bikini beauty pageant on one corner and a dog show on another.

"This town doesn't sleep during carnival," I said. "You were right."

"People barely work. I've had five appointments cancel in the last week."

"Sometimes I forget what a big deal it is until I'm in the middle of it again." I grinned as I saw the lights on the bay. "I really love this place."

"Me, too." He squeezed my hand. "I love you, too, Zoe."

I swallowed hard. I wasn't expecting this. We'd never talked about love. Here it was as big as the blue lights that had just sparkled across the sky. We had a good relationship. We enjoyed each other's company. But love   that took me by surprise. I'd hoped that one day he'd be ready to love again. I didn't plan to rush him.

My response was easy, though. "I love you, too, Miguel." I kissed his lean, shadowed cheek.

We kissed at the next stoplight until it had turned green and then red again. I was smiling like a crazy person as I looked into his eyes.

"Now let's find Dylan," he said. "I'm looking forward to some scrambled eggs for breakfast this morning. I'm cooking!"

- - - - - - -

It wasn't hard finding Dylan's small apartment. It was close to the newspaper. I could imagine that he walked to work each day. The neighborhood was quiet, which was surprising—no music or other festivities. Maybe it was just that it was so early—or late.

I yawned as we parked the car. I was so tired. I knew I'd be falling over tomorrow.

"None of that," Miguel said. "We might need more than one pot of coffee this morning."

"It says 1A," I read from my cell phone. "That's three over there. At least it's on the ground floor."

"I see it."

We walked up to the door. There was a tiny dying azalea in a pot on a garden chair with a red ribbon tied around it. He *really* didn't like gardening.

Miguel quietly knocked. "No point in waking the whole building." But the door swung open when his hand hit it. "Should we go in?"

"We've come this far."

He took out a handkerchief and pushed the door open the rest of the way. "Call him so he knows it's you and he's not afraid."

"Dylan?" I walked into a very plain living room that barely had any signs of personality. It could have been a motel room. "Are you here? It's Zoe Chase, Jordan's friend."

"Maybe he's already gone." Miguel looked around. He pushed open the bedroom door and quickly stepped back, grabbing my arm as I would have walked in beside him. "No! Don't go in there, Zoe."

I caught a glimpse of a chair kicked over beside an unmade bed and caught my breath.

Still in his Folly costume, Dylan was hanging from the ceiling.

TWENTY-FIVE

It was time to call Patti Latoure.

The ambulance arrived in five minutes and pronounced Dylan dead. Patti was there twenty minutes later with five officers and a crime scene team.

"What are you two doing here?" she asked me and Miguel.

"It's a long story," he said.

"I've got time."

I explained as well as I could. It wasn't easy, since I felt like I'd been kicked in the stomach. I didn't know Dylan, but I had just met him last night. I couldn't even see his face. He was still wearing the mask he'd had on at the museum.

"Two suicides over this thing, Patti? Really?" My head ached and my eyes were burning.

"We don't know what this is yet, Zoe. Go on back to the Biscuit Bowl and cook something. Come in later and give us your statements. I should know more by then."

"All right." I was thinking about the information Dylan

had claimed to have. "I don't know what to look for, but there may be information here that has something to do with Jordan Phillips's death, too."

"I'll look around. And don't talk to anyone about it, okay?"

Miguel nodded, and we walked back out to the Mercedes.

"I should have come to look for him right away."

"You couldn't have known." He opened the car doors and we got inside.

Daylight was peeking over the horizon. Another day of carnival was on the way. Yet I had never felt less like celebrating. I didn't even want to cook anything.

Miguel drove back to the diner and made breakfast for us both. I could barely do more than push the eggs around on my plate. Crème Brûlée ate and went into the office to sleep again. I didn't even want to play with him.

Ollie showed up a few minutes later, right after Uncle Saul and Cole had arrived. Miguel told them what had happened. We didn't have much time to dwell on it—the Biscuit Bowl needed food.

For once I didn't even notice what was made for the savory and the sweet biscuit bowls. I felt like a zombie going through the motions, trying to keep moving when I felt like falling on the floor and crying.

Whoever had done this to Jordan and Dylan—I was convinced even more now that Jordan had been murdered—was a monster. Someone had to catch him before it was all over and the killer was free of any responsibility.

We headed for the Biscuit Bowl when the food was ready and the car and taxi were loaded.

It was no easy task. People were crammed together in the parking lot and not happy about it. The lines to the various trucks were filled with hundreds of customers. It was a food truck owner's dream but a customer nightmare.

"Why is it like this?" I asked as we grabbed what we

could and headed through the food trucks. "It's not even eight A.M. yet."

"It's the food eating contest," Delia reminded me as she met us right outside the Biscuit Bowl. "They've already been at it for an hour. I gave them what we had to add to the contest."

"I completely forgot! How did you know?"

She held out a sheet of paper with a reminder about the contest. "I came in early in case you needed help. No one was here so I just got it going."

I hugged her. 'Thank you so much."

"It's okay," she said when I started to cry on her shoulder. "Zoe, what's wrong?"

"She's gonna have to tell you later when we come up for air," Ollie said. "We need her hands, not her mouth."

I put on an apron and scooted past Miguel and Delia to reach the fryer. I was in my element and tried hard to concentrate on what I was doing and not on what had happened. Ollie was calling out orders again. I had to remind him to print them on paper.

We could see the contestants sitting at picnic tables. They were putting as much food as they could into their mouths as their times were called out. Men and women were stuffing in hot dogs, biscuit bowls, and kabobs as they went against the clock for a new winner in each round.

"We're almost out of paper plates," Miguel said.

"Just give them napkins for now," I answered. "How are you doing, Delia?"

"We have plenty of sweet filling, but we're out of icing," she advised.

"Use the powdered sugar. There's a shaker of it right above your head."

"Thanks, Zoe."

The remainder of the morning went the same way. I updated Delia on things that had happened. I glanced out the customer window. There was still a long line outside. Miguel was refilling the Coke bucket. Ollie was trying to cash a hundred-dollar bill despite the sign on the window that said we didn't take bills that size.

"Give it back," I told him. "We can't take bigger than a twenty."

"We'll lose the sale," Ollie said.

"I don't care. No hundreds."

"Yes, ma'am."

Miguel came back. "That's the last of the Cokes, and the ice is almost gone."

I glanced up at the clock. "We should be reaching a slow-down point soon. We can't worry about it right now. If we run out, we run out."

That was ten thirty. The crowds lingered until after lunch. The food held up until the contest was over and the customers had thinned out. I felt successful but so tired I wanted to fall on the floor and sleep.

Delia went home, dragging herself out the back door. Miguel, Ollie, and Uncle Saul helped finish cleaning up.

Uncle Saul was still sniffling but said he'd stay at the Biscuit Bowl until we could get back with the dinner menu. He didn't feel much like cooking. "Zoe, honey, I'm sorry it turned out this way. I wish you could've helped Jordan and Dylan. But sometimes there's just nothing you can do."

I was working on a shopping list for Miguel. The words kept fading in and out on the page as I wrote. "I think I handled it wrong."

"You aren't trained for that type of work, like I said before," Uncle Saul continued. "You have to take that into consideration before you beat yourself up. You hear me?"

"I do." I looked up and smiled. "This couldn't have happened at a worse time, either, with all this extra work. I'm sorry I signed up for the Mardi Gras rally now. Everyone is so tired. People have died. It's horrible."

Ollie came running inside. "Zoe—Frank the gator man just pointed a local news crew our way. They're coming with cameras and reporters. Now's your chance to shine!"

We went through the kitchen like human tornadoes, looking for flyers and scrounging up a few biscuit bowls to impress the TV news team. I put on some makeup and forced my hair under an old Biscuit Bowl ball cap. I'd be sorry later, but there wasn't time for anything else.

The reporter knocked on the door and then entered with his crew right behind him. "I hear you make the best biscuits in the world, Zoe Chase," he said. "I hope you have one for me to try."

We talked about my biscuit bowls and how I'd come to make them. I wished I had fresh biscuits for the reporter and his crew, but after going through the rush, I was lucky to have any food at all.

"I love this filling!" the reporter said. "What do you call it?"

Ollie stepped in to cover for me. "I call it Stoke's Pie after my Granddaddy Stokes. It's rutabagas and potatoes in a secret sauce and mixed with fried pork."

"Rutabagas?" The reporter frowned and looked at the biscuit bowl again. "Well, it's good, anyway!"

They ate the last sweet biscuit bowls—berries with custard. We talked about my plans for the future and how I came up with my ideas. It really was a moment in the sun—exciting but fleeting. Maybe it was worth being there. I wasn't sure.

As soon as they left the kitchen to interview someone else, I took Crème Brûlée outside for some fresh air. He was feeling playful after being cooped up most of the day in the front seat. He rolled in the grass and wanted me to pet his tummy. He swatted at bugs and a dandelion he'd found growing there. I held him in my arms and snuggled my face against him, hoping he could make me feel better. As I turned to go back to the Biscuit Bowl, Detective Frolick was there, with a deep scowl on his face.

I held Crème Brûlée a little tighter for my own benefit and reminded myself that it could've been the ghost of Old Slac. Even Detective Frolick's frown was better than that.

"Miss Chase." There was exasperation and impatience in his tone.

"Detective. What can I do for you?"

"Why are you still involved in Jordan Phillips's death? I thought we had an understanding." He glanced around as though he was worried about being seen there.

"I'm not. I know you're talking about Dylan's death. I'd give anything not to have seen that—believe me. He called me. I didn't know what was going on."

"And you couldn't pass that on to me instead of trying to do it yourself?"

"I operate a food truck. I didn't want any part in this at all. If you would've just told the truth from the beginning—"

"The truth can be subjective and in this case would've caused difficulties that you don't comprehend."

"Maybe so, but you still only have yourself to blame."

I started to walk past him. He didn't budge.

"Excuse me. I have to get back to the diner so I can cook for dinner."

"Sometimes bad things happen to little girls who like to play games." The words were rough and mean.

"Stay away from me or I'll file a stalking charge against you to add to the rest of your problems." I could hear my voice wavering. I knew he could hear it, too.

He stepped to one side. "The answers you're looking for might not be good for your family, either, Miss Chase. Have you thought about that?"

I calmly took Crème Brûlée back to the truck. Detective Frolick got into his vehicle and left the parking lot, burning rubber.

I let out a pent-up breath and buried my face in Crème Brûlée's fur. "I don't like that man. What is he trying to hide, anyway? Did he kill Jordan? He acts like he did."

Crème Brûlée's answer was a loud snore.

"How can you be tired? You slept all night. I need some comfort. You're supposed to be here for me."

He flipped on his side away from me as though I'd been bothering him.

"Fine. Next time you want a special treat at the store, I'll remember this moment."

The passenger side door opened. I threw my arms around Miguel, and my story about Detective Frolick came out in a nervous rush.

"I don't understand why that man keeps coming to see you," Miguel said. "What does he think you know?"

I held him tight. "I wish I could go back in time and not find Jordan's body."

"I know." He kissed me. "I'm sorry."

"I don't understand what they're covering up."

Uncle Saul stalked up to the cab of the truck. "Better get a move on it. Dinner won't cook itself, and we're completely out of food!"

"Thanks for the kick in the butt." I sighed, not wanting to go. "I'm leaving Crème Brûlée here while I'm gone. He should be fine. I just walked him."

"I can handle that. I'll see you later."

Ollie climbed into the back of the car with all the hot bags on his lap. "So what are we cooking this time?"

"Stoke's Pie?" I asked him with a smile.

"It was the best I could come up with at the time."

"Thanks for that. My mind was a complete blank."

"You're stressed." He shrugged. "You shouldn't have to think."

"I appreciate that, but I have to think now. What are we eating the rest of the day?"

When we reached the diner, we peered through the freezer for possible savory and sweet foods while Miguel took out bags of plates, napkins, and forks to restock the food truck.

Ollie laughed as he took out a large package of bacon. "Black eyed peas and bacon sounds good." He handed me the frozen peas I'd already cooked and seasoned last summer before I froze them.

The door to the diner chimed. Chef Art strode in with a grin on his face. His RV was parked in front. "Good afternoon, lady and gents. If that's coffee I smell, I'll have a cup or two." He planted himself on one of the stools at the counter.

I had just started the biscuit dough. "How's Tucker doing? I looked through Jordan's phone. Can you tell if someone is suicidal from reading what they write on their phone?"

"You never know," Ollie said. "How much bacon do you want in the beans?"

"You can't have too much bacon," Chef Art said. "Question is how hot do you make it?"

Ollie laughed. "Can't be too hot, either."

Chef Art smacked his lips at the prospect. "Zoe Chase, you were wasted at that bank, girl. Your food is to die for."

I grinned. "Would you mind putting your face and those words on every billboard in Mobile?"

"Maybe one day."

I hoped that day would be the opening day of my restaurant. I knew Chef Art liked me and enjoyed my cooking. I didn't want that endorsement for my food truck. There was only so much I could do with the Biscuit Bowl. But later his words could be helpful.

"I'm riding in another parade today." Chef Art delicately

wiped his tiny white beard with a moist towelette. "You're welcome to join me, Zoe. You could drop flyers instead of throws."

"I don't think people would appreciate that when they're expecting candy or beads. We're doing almost more than we can handle right now at the rally. I've given out a thousand flyers with biscuit bowls. I hope people will remember me when carnival is over."

"I'm sure they will. If they don't remember you, they'll remember your food. That's more important, anyway."

The bacon was frying and the peas were heating in the big pot. I chopped a mountain of onions for the bacon and pea savory. When I'd finished with that, I made a huge batch of icing for the sweet biscuit bowls. It was time to figure out what would be inside those bowls and get started making it.

"What about cheese?" I asked.

"Cheese?" Chef Art scowled. "With wine, yes. I'm not sure about in a biscuit bowl for a sweet."

"Ricotta. Sweet cheese with some candied fruit in it," I suggested.

"Add some rum to that and you've got a hit," Ollie said.

Tom, my UPS driver, whistled as he walked through the door wearing his usual brown shirt and shorts. "How's it going, Miss Zoe? I got this big package for you. Maybe something good to eat, huh?"

Tom handed me the large package, and I put it down so I could hand him a warm biscuit bowl.

"That's what I love about delivering to you. See you later."

I put aside the frozen peaches I'd been looking at and opened the box.

There was a loud popping sound, and most of the box blew apart.

TWENTY-SIX

Everything went quiet for a minute. I was stunned, and covered in glitter and sequins, but not hurt.

"What was that?" Chef Art asked.

"Are you okay, Zoe?" Miguel rushed to my side.

"Outside of looking like a party happened on me, I think I'm fine." I needed to take a shower, anyway. I didn't think there was a part of me that wasn't full of glitter.

"Someone could've been hurt with that," Ollie observed.

Chef Art frowned. "In my day we called that a surprise box. It went to people we didn't like during carnival. No one ever suspected until it was too late. My friends and I did it to dozens of people. I wonder who sent this to you, Zoe."

"I think right now they must be standing in line with numbers." I brushed off as many sequins as I could. "I'm going to take a shower now. You all carry on without me."

A surprise box.

It was aptly named, I thought, as I washed off the glitter.

There were rivers of purple, gold, and green going down the drain. I hoped it didn't clog anything.

Was it supposed to be a threat or a prank? I'd never heard of it before. I guess it was old school. I'd have to ask Chef Art after I got dressed—and later, Uncle Saul.

When I got out of the shower, I still had a lot of glitter on me. I would probably have to live with it for a few days. Lucky it was time for carnival. I fit right in.

It was difficult getting dressed in the tiny bathroom. Usually, I dashed to my temporary bedroom, but with a diner full of men on the other side of the wall, that wasn't an option. I struggled into my last pair of clean jeans and a T-shirt. All my Biscuit Bowl T-shirts were dirty. I was going to have to wash clothes soon.

I brushed my wet black curls and then held my head down to fluff them up. They'd have to dry a bit before I could use gel on them. I was tempted to cover them with a colorful scarf, but I knew that would be another problem tomorrow if I did.

I went back out to the kitchen. The surprise box was on the counter. Ollie, Miguel, and Chef Art were all looking inside it.

"Did I miss something?" I asked.

"There was a note at the bottom." Ollie handed it to me. *The next one will be real.*

"What does that even mean?" I looked up at my friends.

"I believe it's a threat, Zoe," Chef Art said. "I never heard of a surprise box with serious intent. It was just supposed to be a prank on someone you didn't care for, you know? Like filling a paper bag with dog poop and leaving it for someone to step on. Just harmless fun."

"*Eww.*" Better glitter than dog poop. "You think someone is saying this could have been a bomb?"

"Maybe it's your friend the commissioner," Ollie said.

"You better get a robot to open your packages in the parking lot from now on."

Chef Art got up from his stool. "That sounds like my cue to leave. I'll see you later, Zoe. Be careful today."

I finished defrosting and reheating my peaches with brandy sauce, but my hands were shaking. What if it had been a bomb? I wouldn't have to worry about crowds today or my future restaurant. It would all be over. The thought made me shudder.

Miguel put his hands on my shoulders. I jumped with a screech. "Sorry. Don't let Chef Art's words bother you. I'm sure no one was trying to kill you."

Ollie made a loud humphing noise. "Someone is always trying to kill someone else. And that person is the last to know."

I agreed with Miguel. "I think this was a stupid prank. There's no return address on the box. I'm sure one of my old friends from school sent it. Maybe even my mother, since she seems to have gone crazy." I finished my sweet ricotta cheese with fruit filling. The biscuits were ready to go.

Ollie got a clean spoon and put some of the spicy black-eyed peas on it. "What do you think?"

"It's good. Really good." And then the heat hit me. "Wow. That's hot. You don't think it's too hot, do you?"

"No such thing," Ollie told me. "Customers like it hot."

Within the next thirty minutes, we managed to get everything ready to go. We piled into Miguel's car and Cole's taxi and started toward the food truck rally. Delia called, frantic because she'd already had to turn two customers away.

"We'll be there as soon as we can," I told her. "Just hope we don't run into any parades."

I thought about the surprise box as we got closer to the food truck rally.

Did someone really just mean it as a prank? It seemed like it, but with everything that had been going on the last few days, I was suspicious. I couldn't imagine Commissioner Sloane, despite his veiled threats, sending me that box. I watch TV. If I'd decided to call the police, his fingerprints and DNA would be all over it. He was smarter than that.

We managed to avoid most of the street traffic except for some small groups of people dancing. This time of year everyone made room and shared the street with dancers and musicians. We saw some elaborately decorated bicycles that looked parade-bound. They yelled and waved as we passed them.

"I'm a little disappointed with carnival this year," I said as we parked the car close to the food truck rally. "It's not the same when you're working."

There was still a three-block walk carrying all the food to reach the Biscuit Bowl. Ollie, Uncle Saul, and Miguel volunteered to bring what looked like a mountain of Cokes and ice after we got everything set up.

Delia was fending off customers who were giving her a hard time. She saw us come in the back door and gave a sigh of relief.

"What kind of crappy food truck is this, anyway?" The man at the window was wearing a costume—Dracula, I thought. He yelled at Delia and pounded his fist on the side of the Biscuit Bowl.

Ollie politely asked Delia to move away from the window. He stuck his mean face out at the complaining vampire. "Cut that out unless you want to end up *under* the truck. Come back or get lost. Your choice."

The vampire quit pounding and backed away.

"Thanks, Ollie." Delia smiled at him. "I thought my customers at the bar were bad. That man needs to go to jail for being so rude."

"Don't worry about it. I'll handle the window."

It was the most they'd said to each other since their breakup. Not that there had been yelling or cursing. It was more a cold ignoring of each other as we worked each day. I hoped it would be better now.

We got all the food stowed away so the hot food stayed hot and the cold food stayed cold. Once we were settled in, Ollie and Miguel set up the Cokes. Uncle Saul took the window—though his mean face had miles to go to equal Ollie's. I wasn't going to argue with his choice of jobs.

"Could I take a break?" Delia asked. "My nerves are frayed."

"Of course." I hugged her. "Thanks for doing this crazy job. Next year we'll just enjoy the carnival."

"Thanks, Zoe. You know I'm here for you. I'll be back in a few minutes."

There was a rap on the back door. It was someone with a clipboard checking in with us.

"Everything going okay back here?" she asked.

"It's been hectic, but we're fine." I stared at her. "Do I know you? Where's Tiffany?"

"She's out sick, I guess." She shrugged. "They called me in this morning to take her place."

"Oh."

"I'm supposed to tell you that a few cruise ships are docking and we might expect an extra ten thousand people the next few days. Are you prepared for that?"

"As prepared as I can be." I swallowed hard. "Thanks."

"No problem." She smiled. "Tiffany had a lot of information in her notes, thank goodness. Otherwise, I don't know what I would've done. This was a big surprise when they called and wanted me to work."

"I'm sure," I sympathized. "What a way to ruin Mardi Gras, huh?"

"Don't I know it?" She rolled her eyes. "Have a good day."

There were no other customers as I put away the paper products and straightened up the kitchen.

"You know, Zoe, about that surprise box—" Uncle Saul began.

I'd filled him in earlier. "Let's not talk about it. If someone really wanted to bomb my diner, there wouldn't be much I could do about it. I'll stick with the things I know I can do." I hugged him to keep my words from sounding too harsh. "Are you going to be okay if Mom and Daddy decide to get back together?"

"That ship sailed a long time ago for me, Zoe girl." He kissed my cheek. "I'm still young. I still have a grand romance coming my way. I don't need Ted's leftovers."

"Good. You need to find someone new." His words had been deep and painful. I was sorry I'd brought up the subject. I'd just been trying to get away from the gloom and doom.

For me, my parents deciding to get back together wouldn't be the end of the world. Maybe it would even be a good thing. But I'd have to see it last for more than a few days to believe it.

I stirred the peas with crumbled bacon and made sure the cheese filling was cool in the mini-fridge. The icing was ready to go. I couldn't imagine putting that much icing on sweet biscuit bowls in one day, but with cruise ship visitors it was possible.

It was dinnertime on the dot when we were set up. I saw the first group of partygoers in crazy costumes as they walked across the parking lot toward us.

"Here we go."

- - - - - - -

The day had been warmer and the crowds were bigger, but otherwise it was a copycat of the day before. I was so glad every day wasn't like this. There was barely time to think much less time to plan and observe my customers.

The food held up, but I ran out of flyers. I'd forgotten to

make more at the diner before I left. Miguel offered to run back to his office and print some. I took him up on it without a pause. He could be back in ten minutes if traffic wasn't bad. We wouldn't miss getting out too many flyers while he was gone.

Delia came back from her break looking wonderfully relaxed and happy. She took over filling the sweet biscuit bowls as Ollie called out and wrote down orders.

I could hear the music as a parade passed close by the parking lot. It sounded noisy and fun. I wished I were standing on the sidewalk watching it go by instead of knee-deep in customers and black-eyed peas.

I was just tired, I told myself, promising a few days off when carnival was over. I hoped all this work would be worth it. The money had been good so far, but I'd also put out a bunch of money. I hadn't had time to balance my records. I wouldn't know about any growing awareness of my food until after the celebrations were finished and life went back to normal.

Thinking about everything that had happened in the last two weeks, I just hoped everything would actually go back to normal again. I was beginning to doubt it.

TWENTY-SEVEN

Ollie was spending the night at the Biscuit Bowl again.

Uncle Saul had wanted to, but he'd forgotten in all the food truck madness that it was Spirit Night. That meant a family obligation for both of us. Neither one of us was looking forward to it, but no one with family missed Spirit Night.

All of the Chase family from the 1700s forward was buried in the same cemetery, Our Lady of Perpetuity. The cemetery was put in during the 1800s, but earlier family members had been disinterred and moved there.

Every year on Spirit Night people visited with their dead loved ones leaving candy, cookies, beads, and other throws. Sometimes you'd see colorful masks on tombstones or pictures. You could leave whatever you wanted to honor the dead.

My mother's family, the Olivers, weren't from Mobile originally. Their dead were scattered from here to Atlanta. *Thank goodness!* It would've been impossible to visit with all of them on Spirit Night.

Daddy had texted me that he'd send a car for me and Uncle Saul. Miguel had dropped us off at the apartment after midnight.

Uncle Saul and I were able to get cleaned up and change clothes before we had to go to the cemetery. Looking your best was an essential part of Spirit Night.

I'd smuggled Crème Brûlée into the apartment for the night so he could get a break from the food truck, too. He'd been walking around the apartment investigating everything as though he'd never seen it before.

"How are you feeling?" I asked Uncle Saul.

"I'm okay." He grinned. "Not a fan of Spirit Night. I'd forgotten that was one of the reasons I don't come home for carnival. How about you?"

"I'm hanging in there. I don't think there's ever been another time in my life that I wished carnival was over. Is it ever going to be Fat Tuesday?"

He laughed at that. "You're still young, Zoe. There'll be plenty of times you'll wish Mardi Gras was over."

"Why? I can't imagine feeling that way if I wasn't working the food truck."

"Even though there are plenty of people in the city for carnival, I used to lose most of my regulars at the Carriage House. Everybody is busy going to parties and staying out too late. It makes it hard for a small business to plan for a normal two weeks."

"Now you tell me." My phone buzzed—it was Daddy downstairs with the car. "They're waiting for us."

"Then I guess we better go. I was crazy to tell your father that I was over my cold. As far as I know, being sick would've been the only thing to save me from Spirit Night."

I took his arm and smiled at him. "Well, at least you have that awesome suit. It could be worse. You could've had to wear black."

He looked down at his burgundy suit and purple tie, adjusting the matching hat on his head. "You're right. I'm looking good tonight. Too bad there are only our relatives and dead people to see it."

I was wearing a bright emerald green dress that ended in a flounced ruffle mid-calf. The rest was formfitting across my curves. I had a matching green hat that I had to pin on my head. I didn't wear the pumps that went with the dress—walking in the cemetery wasn't good for shoes. Instead I wore a pair of ankle-high flowered boots.

"I'd say we make quite a spiffy pair." Uncle Saul opened the door. "As much as I hate Spirit Night, it will be good to get away from that food truck for a while. I never want to see that many black-eyed peas again."

"It's hard for me to believe you wouldn't open another restaurant like the Carriage House again if you had the chance." I pushed the button for the elevator.

"I think those days are behind me, Zoe. I don't know how long I'll live out in the swamp. There's still a part of me who will always feel like Mobile is home. That part would like to live here, but what would I do?"

"You could work with Daddy at the bank."

The elevator doors parted, and we stepped into the lobby.

"I don't think I could ever be *that* homesick," he confided. "I said no to that when I was eighteen. I've never regretted it."

We walked out into the cool night air. Music was playing across the city. Fireworks were creating brilliant pinwheels in the dark sky. It wasn't strictly legal to shoot fireworks during carnival. That never seemed to stop anyone.

Small impromptu parades of three or more people carrying banners and throws marched up and down the streets. The closer we got to Fat Tuesday, the later people stayed out.

Daddy's driver, Maurice, opened the back door to the white limo. I could see Great-Aunt Tildy and Granny Ginny waving and smiling from the interior. Cousins Baxter and Dori were also in there. Daddy was in front with the driver.

"Here we go," Uncle Saul said.

- - - - - - -

We drove to the cemetery with everyone crowded together, talking at one time. The Chase clan was a noisy, boisterous group when we got together during the year. It didn't happen often, but when it did, you had to fight to get a word in.

When I was a child and Grandma Chase, Daddy's mother, was still alive, I used to sit and listen to everyone talk. I never said a word—until one day she poked me and told me I'd better start talking.

Grandma Chase was a formidable woman, in girth and intellect. She was the only woman I'd ever seen my mother back down from.

Grandma Oliver was a short, dainty woman who'd died before I was born. I'd seen her pictures. She looked a lot like me, minus the curly hair.

Everyone in the limo, except for me and Uncle Saul, had brought something to put on the graves. Great-Aunt Tildy had brought a beautiful scarf to put on Grandma Chase's cross headstone. Grandma Chase had loved scarves. I still had a dozen she'd given me.

Uncle Saul mentioned that he didn't have anything to leave for Spirit Night. He was immediately inundated with beads, cookies, and colored bottles that Cousin Dori made for a living and sold on eBay.

I didn't say anything. Let them think I had something.

The cemetery was far from empty when we arrived. Other families were observing Spirit Night, too. Already, graves were littered with trinkets, and four-course meals, left behind for the dead.

We piled out of the limo when we reached the Chase

family plots. Right in the middle was a huge stone mausoleum where my great-great-grandfather, General Isaiah Chase, was buried. He was an important man during the Civil War. He'd died after his leg was blown off by the Union Army, but he still managed to save dozens of soldiers.

While Daddy's family was wonderfully proud of that heritage, I'd always been a little uncomfortable with it. I didn't care so much that the Confederacy lost as what they were fighting for. Grandma Chase had old photos of her great-grandfather's plantation showing the slaves at work.

A wreath was placed on the door to the mausoleum by Great-Aunt Tildy. Everyone bowed their heads and said a little prayer for the General. The rest of the time it was a free-for-all with everyone walking around the Chase graves putting items on the tombstones or on the graves themselves.

The event reminded me of the *Addams Family* movie when they played "Wake the Dead." I was glad none of the Chases got up to answer the call.

I lingered a moment at Grandma Chase's grave, already tied with a scarf and hanging with beads. I missed her. She'd been a bright spot in my life. I felt like I'd learned more from her than from my bickering parents. I wished she could've seen me with the Biscuit Bowl. I knew she would've been proud.

I glanced up as the night breeze rustled the trees around the graves. I felt a chill go down my spine. Not surprising since I was standing in a cemetery in the middle of the night.

There was a dim light moving through the trees. It looked like someone who'd lost their way and had taken out a flashlight. The light kept moving until it was close to where my family was now taking out champagne and plastic glasses to salute the Chase dead. After that would come shrimp and beignets. Spirit Night could go on until dawn.

I kept watching the light, hoping it wasn't someone who

wanted to ask us where his family plot was located. This was the only part of the cemetery that I knew. Maybe Uncle Saul or Great-Aunt Tildy might be able to give directions.

I was getting that weird feeling that comes into the pit of your stomach right before the Frankenstein monster attacks in the movies. I kept staring—even though common sense dictated that I should move away, preferably out of the cemetery.

"Who's that?" Uncle Saul brought me a glass of champagne.

"I think it's someone lost in the cemetery." At least I was hoping that's what it was.

The old magnolias parted slightly, and the Spanish moss swayed with the movement.

I caught my breath. "It's Old Slac again. Run!"

TWENTY-EIGHT

Cousin Baxter was at least six-foot-six and weighed two hundred something pounds. He came up behind us as I was preparing to run. "What's that?"

The light shining on Old Slac was ghastly. It turned his face an unearthly shade of green and made his turkey feathers stand out. His dark eyes stared at us with cold conviction as he pointed at me and Uncle Saul.

"It's the ghost of Old Slac," I whispered, starting to slowly back toward the car. "Seeing him is a death warning."

Cousin Baxter played football for the Crimson Tide. He was in his third year at the University of Alabama where he was studying insects. I wasn't sure what career he had in mind, but he'd always loved insects—especially if he had a chance to put one on me.

The one thing celebrated about Baxter was his prowess at tackling anything that got in his way. I'd always admired that about him. He wasn't brilliant in school, but he sure could throw down.

As I kept backing away, Baxter spit out the gum he'd been chewing and growled. "No old ghost is gonna crash Chase family Spirit Night. Look out Old Slac. I'm coming at you!"

Uncle Saul grabbed my arm as I reached to stop Baxter from attacking Old Slac.

Baxter ran full tilt into the ghost. He was hunched down, head first, like when he tackled the opposition on the football field. He grunted loudly as he tackled and then fell to the ground. The surprising thing was that Old Slac fell under him.

Uncle Saul ran toward them and I followed. Daddy saw us and asked what we were doing. I felt like I was in an episode of *Scooby-Doo*. Whoever was under Baxter (who'd inherited his girth from Grandma Chase) was trapped but still kicking his arms and legs trying to get free.

The ghost of Old Slac was painted with some kind of phosphorescent color, which was why he'd appeared green. A supersized flashlight rolled out of his reach. I felt sure if he could have, he would've smacked Baxter in the head and run.

He didn't know Baxter. Once he got them down, they stayed down.

Uncle Saul moved closer despite my plea not to go there. Daddy grabbed me and held me tight as we stayed about three feet from the ghost and Baxter.

"Let's see who we have here." Uncle Saul reached down, and Old Slac's scary face came off in his hand.

"Bennett?" I couldn't believe it. "What in the world are you doing?"

Uncle Saul and Baxter got Bennett Phillips to his feet and pushed him toward the limo in the cemetery. I was glad they were able to do something, because Daddy was still terrified. He clung to me like a frightened child as he walked back.

The cemetery lights weren't good, but they were better

than the darkness in the trees. The Chase family gathered around to stare at the intruder. Baxter occasionally bared his teeth at him.

"It would be a good idea to tell us why you're here and dressed like that," Uncle Saul said. "Baxter isn't known for his patience."

Bennett struggled a little more, but there was no way he was leaving until Baxter said he could go. "I'm here because I have to be here. Let me go. I'm just a small cog."

"I think you might be responsible for the attack on my brother," Uncle Saul said.

"What about that newspaper reporter getting killed?" Baxter asked. "He has a murderer's face, if you ask me."

"I didn't kill my own son," Bennett denied. "And I didn't attack Ted with a knife, either."

Daddy was finally able to overcome his terror and stepped up to the limo. "Bennett? Is that really you? Why would you pretend to be the ghost of Old Slac?"

"To scare you." He struggled again. "Get this big oaf off me."

"Is he calling me an oaf?" Baxter demanded.

"Yes." I was struggling to understand why Bennett would be involved with this. "Why would you want to scare us off? You asked for my help solving his murder. What happened to change that?"

"I'm not saying anything else. Call the police. I'll call my lawyer. The only thing I've done is get into the carnival spirit. I haven't hurt anyone."

Uncle Saul wasn't happy with that answer. "Who are you working for? Who sent you?"

"I'm not working for anyone. I'm doing a favor. You'd best drop it here if you know what's good for you."

"Was that a threat?" Baxter clutched Bennett around the neck with his large fingers. "First you insult me and then you threaten my family. I should take you in the woods, old man, and feed you to the gators."

It was easy to see that Bennett was more afraid of whoever had sent him than he was of us. Baxter continued holding Bennett while Daddy, Uncle Saul, and I moved away from the group of curious family members who had no idea what was going on.

"I think calling the police is a waste of time," Uncle Saul said.

I agreed with him. "But what else can we do?"

Daddy shrugged. "He hasn't done anything that we can prove except standing around looking scary. At this time of year most people would think it's part of the fun."

"So we just let him go?"

"I think so." Uncle Saul nodded.

"Okay." Daddy shrugged. "But maybe we should let Baxter rough him up a bit more to make a point."

Uncle Saul laughed. "I never realized how bloodthirsty you are, Ted."

"We don't know for sure that he didn't attack Daddy with a knife," I added. "He might've killed Jordan. It seems to me that he deserves a lump or two."

Uncle Saul put his arm around my shoulders. "Let's just harass him a few more times and see if anything pops."

"I know where an empty warehouse is over by the docks." Daddy rubbed his hands together. "We could take him there and get some answers from him."

Uncle Saul chuckled. "I don't think we should go quite that far, Ted. We can't prove he did anything."

Daddy frowned. "Easy for you to say. You weren't almost killed!"

"Then I suggest we take advantage of this opportunity and get some information from him here," Uncle Saul suggested. "Baxter will get bored soon."

My uncle and my father stepped up like two Mafia brothers standing over their captive prey.

"Does this have something to do with Jordan's death?" Uncle Saul started in questioning Bennett again.

Bennett put his hands on his face. "Leave me alone. Or kill me. I don't care which."

"Where can I send the bill for the suit you ruined when you attacked me?" Daddy wanted to know. "And don't think I'm not cancelling my subscription to your newspaper. Our friendship is over."

Uncle Saul and I exchanged humorous glances behind Daddy's back.

"Did Commissioner Sloane put you up to this?" I asked. "Is he the one you owe a favor?"

Bennett started crying. In a moment, he was breathing hard as his loud sobbing filled the cemetery. "I didn't want to do any of this. I only wanted to find Jordan's killer. I'm caught in the middle like you all. It's just a big game. My son's life meant nothing."

I felt sorry for him. He was in a bad place. He probably was sorry he'd been involved in whatever was going on. That didn't make him less responsible. Everyone is always sorry after they get caught.

He suddenly started making choking sounds and was having trouble breathing. He grabbed his left arm and held it to him.

"He's having a heart attack," Baxter said. "Call 911 and stand back. I just finished CPR classes at school. I can handle this."

I called emergency services as Baxter and Uncle Saul performed CPR. Daddy went to stand with the rest of the family.

The cemetery was outside the city, but the ambulance reached us in only a few minutes. They checked Bennett before putting him on a stretcher and racing for the hospital. Baxter had been right. He'd had a heart attack.

Probably too much stress, I thought. Whoever or whatever had made him dress like the ghost of Old Slac had been too much for him. I hoped he'd survive and could answer some questions later. He might not have all the answers, but I was betting he had more than we did.

"I think that's enough excitement for Spirit Night," Uncle Saul told everyone. "Let's get going. It feels like rain."

Of course Great-Aunt Tildy, Granny Ginny, Cousin Dori, and Cousin Baxter all had dozens of questions as the limo returned them to their homes. I suspected even great-great-grandfather Isaiah Chase had some questions he wanted to ask, too.

I had questions, but I knew there were no answers. Not yet, anyway. I would've settled for some kind of fruity cocktail drink with a lot of rum in it. At least that would've smoothed out the rough edges.

"I don't think Bennett was the one who hurt me," Daddy said when it was just me, him, and Uncle Saul going back to his apartment. "I've known him since we were kids. He just doesn't have it in him."

"I think he's afraid of someone and is letting that person push him around," Uncle Saul said. "I feel sure it's Chadwick Sloane. We just have to find a way to prove it."

"Don't look at me," Daddy said. "I think I've been through enough. I'm sorry about Jordan's death, but I'm not doing or saying anything else that would get the commissioner riled up against me. I suggest you do the same, Zoe. Saul, you always go your own way. You do what you want."

We were all quiet after that until we'd reached Daddy's apartment and got out. I could hear someone playing a slow, sad trumpet not too far away and could smell hush puppies frying.

Carnival wasn't over yet—like this whole question of what had happened to Jordan. I wasn't sure if we were really any closer to understanding it. Bennett's arrival as the ghost of Old Slac had completely thrown off anything I thought I knew.

We said good night to the doorman and the young man at the desk in the lobby. I was exhausted as we went up in the elevator to the apartment.

I could see Daddy was tired, too. His face was pasty-looking and his lips were colorless. I asked him if he was okay. He told me it was time for him to take a pain pill for his injuries.

Uncle Saul seemed to be himself as we unlocked the door and went into the apartment. He went to pour himself a drink.

"Save one of those for me," I said. "I'll be back after I help Daddy into bed and check on Crème Brûlée."

He held up an empty glass and the almost full bottle of whiskey. "I got you covered."

Daddy was fumbling around in his dark bedroom. I tried to help him with his jacket and tie. I couldn't see a thing with the blinds drawn. I went to turn on the bedside lamp, but someone beat me to it.

"Surprise!"

It was my mother. In Daddy's bed. Wearing a sexy black nightie.

Eww.

TWENTY-NINE

Seriously?

"Zoe! What are *you* doing here?" she demanded after she'd pulled the sheet up to cover her.

"We just got back from family Spirit Night. What are *you* doing here?"

"I knew all the Chase family was at the cemetery," she said. "I'm here to help Ted change the bandage on his chest."

"Really?" he asked as he sat on the bed.

"Dressed like that?" I couldn't even look at her. Who knew she even possessed a sexy garment of any kind?

"I can dress however I want to," she sharply replied. "I'll take care of your father now. You go on to your biscuit truck or wherever."

Uncle Saul rapped once at the door and then stuck his head in. "What's going on in here, Zoe?" His gaze fell on my mother. "Anabelle? Why are you here?"

"Why are any of us here, Saul?" my mother asked in

snarky voice. "All of you just get out." Daddy started to leave, too. "Not you, Ted. You're supposed to stay. What's wrong with you people?"

"Nothing a few drinks won't help." I left the room.

Uncle Saul trailed behind me. "Well, that was something." He poured himself another drink and poured one for me, too.

I steered away from the uncomfortable chair and put my feet up on the sofa. "I didn't want to make a big deal out of it before, you know?"

"I understand. I'm sure it will pass. Don't worry about it."

I didn't want him to worry about it, either, so I started talking about food for the next day—later that day, now. "I really like the fricassee. I think it goes well with the biscuit bowl, don't you? And the sweets have been good. No complaints there, right?"

He smiled. "I'm fine, Zoe. Don't worry about me. I made peace with your mother's choice a long time ago. I don't feel anything when I see them together. You don't have to change the subject to save my feelings."

I got up and hugged him. "I wish you'd find the right person for you. You deserve someone special."

He rubbed my arm as he hugged me. "Thank you. You know, it's not over yet. I'm sure I'm going to find the right person. Don't you worry about me."

The bedroom door slammed and my mother joined us. She poured herself a drink and sat in the uncomfortable chair. She was still wearing her black nightie, but it was covered by Daddy's robe that I'd bought him for Christmas. Her very blond hair was mussed, but her makeup wasn't even smeared.

"Someone tell me what happened at the cemetery tonight." She looked at Uncle Saul first and then at me. "Why is Ted shaking and afraid of his own shadow?"

Uncle Saul shrugged. "Zoe?"

I blurted what had happened with Bennett and Baxter. She took it all in as she finished her drink.

"I thought this would be over by now," she said. "What are you doing to get rid of the problem?"

"What exactly would you like us to do, Bella?"

"Whatever. Figure out who killed that young man. Zoe is good at that kind of thing."

"As you wish." He inclined his head.

She finished her drink and said good night, going back in the bedroom as though it was an everyday occurrence.

Before I could say anything about it, Uncle Saul also wished me a good night and went into the other guest room.

I ran into my room and closed the door before I took off my green dress and snuggled on the bed with Crème Brûlée. "There is some crazy stuff going on," I whispered to him. "I'm glad you're normal, anyway."

He nibbled my chin and then licked it. I fell asleep right away and dreamed of large chocolate cakes.

- - - - - - -

I was up early the next morning. I got dressed and fed Crème Brûlée right away. We tiptoed out of the apartment before it could get any more awkward. Cole showed up when I called for a taxi.

"Morning, Miss Zoe."

I wondered how he could always be so cheerful. "Good morning, Cole. I need to go to the diner."

"Course you do. Gotta bake them biscuits, right? It might be dark out, but it's the start of a new day for you."

"That's true. Those crazy, starving partygoers wait for no one."

The streets were empty, rain swept, as Uncle Saul had predicted last night. Cole dropped me off and went to pick up another fare. I went inside with Crème Brûlée and switched on the lights before I called Ollie at the Biscuit Bowl to see how things were going.

"They were going just fine until you woke me up," he complained. "What's cookin' today?"

He yawned loudly and I yawned, too. "You know, I never remember hoping carnival would be over quickly before."

"That's the price you pay for seeing the man behind the curtain—like in *The Wizard of Oz*, you know? Normally we just take it all for granted. Then one day, it changes. *Poof!*"

"That might be too profound for me this morning." I told him about catching Bennett dressed like Old Slac last night. "I'm ready for this to be over."

"Don't talk like that. I'm starving. And if I'm hungry, think about all those other poor slobs out there looking for food. Get some biscuits over here, girl. What's inside them today?"

I searched through the freezer as I spoke to him. Crème Brûlée had crept into the office and gone back to sleep. I kept expecting Mr. Carruthers to barge in even though I'd locked the front door. I hoped that was over, too.

"Looks like I've got some frozen apples and I've got a big bag of frozen shrimp, the tiny ones."

"That doesn't sound good even to me," he declared. "Maybe you could make the apples by themselves with a lot of cinnamon and sweet icing. The shrimp need to be separate."

"Oh you." I smiled. "You know I wasn't making apples with shrimp. But I've got a butt load of grits to make with the shrimp. I think that might do us for most of the day. I'll need supplies before dinner."

"You'll need biscuit bowls by then, too. And don't forget the Cokes. I drank the last one during the night."

"I won't forget. Thanks, Ollie."

"Hurry on over. I'm getting desperate for company."

I thanked him again for staying the night. I knew he'd had to make special arrangements since he was supposed to be at the shelter each night. He always came through when I needed him.

Coffee was on and the shrimp were cooking when Miguel called to find out where I was. I had the apples defrosting and found a large container of cinnamon candies that I planned to put one of into each biscuit bowl as we served them.

"My day is clear, so whatever you need me to do," he said, "I can be there in a few minutes."

"Sounds great. I'm making some omelets with bacon and cheese."

"I'll be right there."

Delia came in a few minutes later. She was dressed in jeans and a red Biscuit Bowl T-shirt. "I got this matching hat. What do you think? I know it doesn't say Biscuit Bowl, but it's red like the shirt."

I looked at the visor and smiled. "It looks wonderful. I wish I had one, too."

She produced another visor out of her bag. "I thought you might say that." She sniffed the food cooking. "Anything I can do?"

I tried on my visor. It looked kind of cute, holding back the curls. "Thanks!"

I had her chop some shallots, and I cut the last of the celery. I was trying to think of something else to make for dinner that night. For once my brain was stumped for another kind of food.

"Maybe you should make some dumplings," Delia said as she chopped. "I loved those little dumplings you made with the chicken a while back. It's good weather for that, don't you think?"

"Good idea." I put the ingredients for chicken and dumplings on my shopping list. I hoped Miguel wouldn't get tired of shopping before Mardi Gras.

I gave Delia the first omelet and threw on a second one for Miguel as he pulled up. I had some chopped red and green peppers by then that I added to the shrimp. I liked to slow cook my grits, so it was just coming to a boil.

We were eating and discussing plans for the day as the sun was peeking over the horizon. Chef Art's brown BMW pulled into the parking lot. I saw him and Tucker get out and start toward the diner as I was pulling out two trays of biscuits.

"Don't look now, but I think we have company." Miguel nodded toward the two men.

"What now?" Delia asked. "Why don't these people leave you in peace?"

The door chimed before I could answer. I only had two more trays of biscuits before it was time to go to the food truck rally and get set up. I had an idea of why my company was there after last night.

"Good morning, Zoe. Miss Delia. Miguel." Chef Art inclined his head in an old-fashioned manner before he removed the straw hat that he'd added to his usual ensemble.

We all said good morning, and he sat down at the counter. "My goodness, something smells delicious. Another day at the Biscuit Bowl, eh?"

I noticed that Tucker stood off to the side by himself, his head bent as though he were studying the old tile floor. It had to be hard for him to deal with what his son had done. I wondered what he'd say.

"I just came from the hospital," he finally said. "Bennett is in the ICU after his heart attack last night. For once words don't seem adequate."

"There was no way for you to know what was going on, Tucker." I told him. "I don't know what caused Bennett to go crazy that way, but no one was hurt. Daddy and Uncle Saul don't believe he had anything to do with the knife attack."

"Thank goodness for that. I don't know what's got into Bennett," Tucker said. "He wasn't conscious this morning. He left me a voice mail on my phone last night, but it didn't explain what happened at the cemetery. Just a bunch of gibberish."

"And, of course, Tucker filled me in," Chef Art said. "It's a tragedy when a man of Bennett's stature in the community loses it. He was under a lot of pressure. I understand that. I wish he'd spoken to me."

"What did he say to you all last night?" Tucker asked.

Everyone looked at me. The timer went off for the biscuits in the oven. I rescued them first and then explained everything.

"What kind of favor could he owe someone that would make him dress up to scare you and your father, Zoe?" Tucker shook his head. "You know, once when Bennett was in college, he had a problem with gambling. I was sure that part of his life was over twenty years ago. Maybe I was wrong."

"Unless Commissioner Sloane had something to do with Bennett gambling, I don't think that's it," I told him. "I'm sure this all relates back to what happened to Jordan. Bennett is involved somehow and can't find a way out."

Tucker was livid, his normally pink face turning bright red. "I don't like to call a lady mistaken, Zoe, but to think that my son would hurt Jordan in any way is wrong. He loved that boy."

"That's not what I'm saying. I'm sorry you misunderstood me. I don't think Bennett wanted Jordan to get hurt. He's trapped in the middle. I hope he recovers so he can explain."

"But in the meantime," Chef Art cleared his throat, "my friend Tucker wanted to express how deeply sorry he is that this has happened to your family, Zoe."

"That's true." Tucker nodded. "That's why I came by today. My son certainly hasn't been himself. I'm taking over the day-to-day running of the *Mobile Times*, and the gloves are coming off as far as the investigation into Jordan's death. If Commissioner Sloane and his daughter are involved, I'm going after them one hundred percent."

I couldn't doubt the serious intent in his voice. I wished we understood better what demons Bennett had been facing that had driven him to dress up as Old Slac. Not knowing put us at a disadvantage.

The timer went off on the last two trays of biscuits. I put them in the warming bags as Miguel held them open. The huge pot of shrimp and grits had been divided into smaller covered trays that would be easier to transport. The apples were ready to go.

"I have to get over to the food truck rally," I told Tucker and Chef Art. "I'm so sorry about Bennett. I hope he can explain himself better to you before this goes any further."

Tucker came up and firmly shook my hand. "If I have any notion of who he might be protecting, believe me, you'll be the first to know. I appreciate everything you've tried to do for my grandson. It's a debt I know I can never repay."

I saw the tears in his eyes. Chef Art pushed him out the door before he got too emotional.

I looked at Miguel and Delia. "I guess it's time to go."

"It couldn't be too soon for me." Delia grabbed a few bags of hot biscuits. "Those two are starting to creep me out."

"I'll get the shrimp and grits," Miguel offered.

I passed by the side window as I went to grab Crème Brûlée and put him in his car seat. Was that Mr. Carruthers's old car I caught out of the corner of my eye leaving the parking lot?

THIRTY

I walked outside, but there was no sign of Mr. Carruthers except possibly two empty disposable coffee cups. The parking lot was littered with gum wrappers and partially eaten candy bars, not to mention soda and beer cans. Two empty coffee cups didn't necessarily mean anything.

We brought everything out to Miguel's car. Delia and I barely squeezed in with the supplies, and Miguel drove us to the food truck rally for another day.

Ollie was exhausted and grumpy after being up most of the night. "There were some bratty teenagers hanging out and shooting off firecrackers every few minutes. Funny how that kind of thing is cool when you're a kid. Last night it was just irritating."

"Go back to the shelter and get some sleep," I told him. "You look ragged. We can keep the Biscuit Bowl running today. Take a break."

"But what if you need me? It's a long walk from the shelter."

"I'll send Cole or someone to get you if we need help." I looked up into his haggard face. "Please, Ollie. We'll be fine. Let Miguel take you back and get some sleep."

His broad shoulders sagged. "Okay. I can do that. Will you save me some grits?"

I told him I would and then shooed him out the door. I knew he'd just hang around if he could. Miguel left to take him to the shelter a few minutes later.

Delia and I distributed the food where it belonged.

"Ollie has the biggest heart of any man I've ever known." She put forks, plates, and napkins together and stacked them. "Of course he has the biggest everything of any man I've ever known."

I laughed at that. "I'm sure that's true. I've never met anyone like him. If he cares about you, there isn't anything he wouldn't do for you."

Delia shook her head. "I wish it could be enough, Zoe. I really do. I know he's wonderful—why doesn't he want more for himself? Why doesn't he expect anything more than to live in the shelter?"

"You know his past. He's wounded. Maybe not physically, but emotionally. Someday he might be different."

She sighed. "It scares me. You know my past. My father was a lot like Ollie—not as big, but good-hearted. Everyone took advantage of him. He didn't care. He was happy to help. But when it came time to help his own family, he wasn't able to give any more. Then he started drinking. I can't be with a man like that."

I hugged her. "I understand, Delia. I do. I didn't mean anything by it. If you and Ollie can't work it out, you can't work it out. I know that from my parents."

Customers started coming early. I figured the first dozen or so had been out all night. They had that partied-out look about them. I gave them each a sweet and savory biscuit bowl, and they drank some Cokes. A few of them fell asleep on a picnic table, and the police reminded them that they had to go home.

Miguel got back in time for the rush. The three of us pitched in together, but we missed the fourth person. I called Uncle Saul, but there was no answer. I really didn't want to bother Ollie. We'd just have to get through without either of them. I reminded myself that there were people running food trucks around me by themselves.

It was two P.M. when the lunch rush was finally over. Miguel, Delia, and I straightened up the kitchen. Wrappers and broken forks tended to litter the tile floor while we were busy. After that we refilled the Coke holder.

Miguel and I took Crème Brûlée out to a small area with some trees and grass at the other side of the parking lot.

Miguel said he was going to get Cokes and more ice so we wouldn't have to leave Delia with nothing while I went back to the diner to bake biscuits. We'd sold a lot more drinks than I'd anticipated. It made sense, really. People were thirsty. They couldn't drink Sazeracs all the time.

I picked up Crème Brûlée, since he would never walk across the parking lot to the other side on his leash. I found a small bench where I could sit down while he nosed around in the dirt and old leaves until he found the spot he was looking for.

I saw the new woman with the clipboard who was taking Tiffany's place. I realized that it had been a few days since I'd seen Tiffany. Maybe she was down with a cold as Uncle Saul had been.

Of course my suspicious mind came up with all kinds of

scenarios—probably none of which were even remotely true. If anything, didn't I believe that Tiffany could be involved with Jordan's death? No one would kidnap her to keep her quiet.

Another one of the food truck operators, this one from Harry's Hot Dogs, was walking his boxer in the same area. Crème Brûlée looked up at the big dog and hissed. The boxer barked at him and backed away.

Harry, as I had come to think of him, smiled. He was a clean-cut young man with spiked brown hair. "My dog's a chicken when it comes to cats. He won't take one on for anything."

"Bad experience with claws?" I asked.

"You could say that." He shuddered. "My ex-girlfriend had a cat. They didn't get along."

"I know how that can be. I'm Zoe Chase. I run the Biscuit Bowl over there."

He shook my hand. "I'm Harry Deaver. I run Harry's Hot Dogs. This place is weird at night, isn't it? I thought it would be quiet, but there's that tall, skinny guy who always seems to be watching your food truck. Isn't he a health inspector? Does he have it in for you or something?"

It had to be Mr. Carruthers. I knew he'd been watching me, despite the warnings he got at the diner. What did he want with me? How far was he willing to go to catch me doing something wrong? Miguel was right about him—I might have to take out a restraining order to get him to leave me alone.

"And that big Native American dude, the one with the big feathered headdress. I've seen him skulking around out here, too." Harry smiled as he sat on the bench next to me. "I'm not from around these parts. But back in Texas, when we see people stalking other people, we shoot first and ask questions later. Are those two bothering you, Zoe?"

Old Slac? Had he shown up more than once? What was Bennett doing out here?

"No. The one with the feathers is Old Slac. He's a mythical figure during carnival."

His blue eyes were very sincere, and he appeared completely concerned for my well-being. His arm snaked around the back of the bench as he moved closer. "Mythical, huh? Why don't you tell me about it?"

"There's nothing much to tell."

"I saw that nice PR lady with the pretty green eyes and freckles get into a car with the tall, skinny man a few nights ago. She's been gone ever since. Do you know what happened to her?"

THIRTY-ONE

Was that what had happened to Tiffany? Was Mr. Carruthers part of everything that had been going on with Jordan? Was that why he was following me around?

Before I could ask Harry any other questions about what he'd seen, his dog gave out a loud howl and Crème Brûlée returned a sharp hiss. There must have been more than noise exchanged between them. The next thing I knew Harry's dog was running through the trees with his leash dangling behind him.

"Get back here, Balzac!" Harry chased after him.

Miguel lifted Crème Brûlée and stroked his soft fur. "Good job," he said. "You did exactly what I told you to do if some other man talked to Zoe. Good cat."

I smirked and took Crème Brûlée from him, smoothing down the cat's ruffled fur. He was still upset from his encounter with Balzac. "Yeah, right. He goes his own way. Unless you promised him salmon, he wouldn't go through all that because you asked him."

We started back toward the Biscuit Bowl. "Really—who was that you were talking to?" Miguel asked.

"He owns the hot dog place. He isn't from Mobile and was asking me about our strange customs during carnival."

"He seemed to be doing it on a very personal level. Or were you talking so quietly that he had to put his arm around you to hear what you were saying?"

"You're not jealous of Harry the hot dog man, are you?" I smiled in what I hoped was a flirtatious manner. I was too tired to know for sure, and I probably smelled like fried biscuits. "He had some interesting things to tell me."

"I'm sure he did."

I gave up torturing Miguel and told him about Harry's observations. "Tiffany has been missing for the past few days. That could coincide with her getting into a car with Mr. Carruthers."

"Although saying it was a tall, thin man could be anyone."

We stepped into the Biscuit Bowl for me to take a quick inventory of any other supplies we needed.

"That's true, but we know he's been hanging around. He could have something to do with Jordan's death."

"I thought we were finished with that since we know it was a suicide."

"We were until we discovered that Bennett Phillips has been posing as the ghost of Old Slac to scare us away."

"Did he say that when he was having a heart attack?"

"No. But he apologized and said he didn't have any choice."

"I wouldn't want to go up against you in court, Zoe. I have no idea what you're talking about."

"I'll explain on the way back to the diner. Is Delia still sleeping in your car?"

"She moved to the front of the Biscuit Bowl. Is she staying while you're gone?"

"Let me put Crème Brûlée up there and find out." I kissed him quickly. "I was just teasing about Harry, you know. He's got nothing I'm interested in."

He kissed me back and smiled. "You didn't see me running after him, did you?"

Delia said she'd stay with the food truck as long as she could nap until someone came up to buy something. I told her that was fine. Crème Brûlée snuggled up against her and was snoring after his exciting but exhausting time with Balzac.

Uncle Saul called and said he would be there for dinner. I thought that would be a good time for Delia to go home. I hadn't heard from Ollie. I hoped he was sleeping.

Miguel and I talked about Tiffany on the way to the diner. We got stalled at the end of one of the big krewe's parades. It was the Order of Athena. Most of the people in the parade were on horseback. The horses were beautifully groomed with ribbons in their manes and tails. The riders were dressed appropriately to be members of the order with scanty white tunics and flowers in their hair.

Miguel found it hard to believe that Tiffany was really missing and not just out enjoying carnival. "Let me look her up on my phone. Maybe we can run by her place," I suggested. "If she's at home because she's partied too much, we can wish her well. If not, we can decide what to do then."

"I'm not sure what that would accomplish," he complained. "And we're on a schedule. I still have to shop and you have to cook what I buy."

I found Tiffany's home address on the Internet. "Her apartment is really close by. If we turn right on the next street, we'll be there in two minutes."

"All right. Two minutes there, and you go up and wish her well if she's home. Then we're going to the diner, right?"

"Right."

Tiffany's apartment was in a nice older building that was covered with ivy. The red bricks had been painted white a long time ago so that the red peeked through in some spots. The doorways were arched, and azaleas lined the sidewalk going up to the front door.

"How are you going to get inside?" Miguel asked after parking by the curb.

"Maybe I won't have to. If she has one of those intercoms, she can answer and tell me she's fine." I kissed his cheek. "Wish me luck."

I walked up to the building, enjoying the riotous shades of azaleas. There seemed to be every hue from white to red and purple. The bushes were old and full of flowers like the ones at my mother's house.

There were two separate intercoms for the apartments. I rang the buzzer beside *T. Bryant*. There was no answer. I tried again, waving to Miguel. Still no answer.

I realized that it didn't mean anything. Maybe she was too sick to answer the buzzer. Maybe she wasn't sick at all and wasn't home.

I wanted to make sure, so I rang the buzzer again.

This time, she answered. "Hello?" Her voice was shaky and sounded as though she'd been crying.

"Tiffany? It's Zoe Chase. Just checking on you. I was worried when you didn't show up for work again. Are you okay?"

"I'm fine, Zoe. You should leave now. I'm sure you have things to do."

"I have plenty of time. Is there anything I can get for you?"

"No. I'm not going in today. I'll see you later."

It wasn't a very satisfying conversation. She sounded upset and tearful. Something was wrong—although it could just be that she was still upset about Jordan. He may have broken up with her, but that didn't mean she didn't care about him. She hadn't shown it immediately after his death. Some people were slower to grieve.

But I couldn't make her let me in, either, and I'd promised Miguel I'd only be a minute. I was going to have to put my feelings aside.

I went back to the car thinking about Tiffany. Who'd have guessed after our rocky start that we'd almost be friends?

"She answered," I told Miguel as I got in the car. "She sounds upset but definitely hasn't been kidnapped, at least as far as I can tell. Maybe I should've been pushier about her inviting me upstairs. I don't know."

I finally looked at Miguel when he didn't reply. He was sitting very stiffly with his hands on the steering wheel. His brown eyes glanced toward the backseat without moving his head.

"What's wrong?" I asked him.

"I think I might be the fly in the ointment." Mr. Carruthers sat forward with a small gun in his hand. "Fasten your seat belt, Miss Chase. We're going for a ride."

THIRTY-TWO

Miguel started the engine and pulled away from the curb. Mr. Carruthers had his head between the seats with the gun prominently displayed.

"Where are we going?" Miguel asked him.

"I thought we'd take a short trip to police headquarters. You two just sit back and take it easy. There's no reason for anyone to get hurt."

I turned to face him. "Really? You're a cop? Why were you pretending to be a food inspector?"

"I was following orders to keep an eye on you. No one wants you to be involved in this investigation," he said. "Regrettably, it's too late. For your sake I hope the commissioner is right and you aren't all part of the plot."

"Plot?" I glanced at Miguel. "What plot? Are you talking about covering up Jordan's murder?"

"I'm not talking about Jordan Phillips at all," he replied.

"And don't pretend like you don't know the whole picture. I think you're more involved than you're letting on."

"And this from a man posing as a bad health inspector? You must be joking."

"With this face, Miss Chase, I usually don't joke."

"I'm Miss Chase's lawyer," Miguel said. "I'd like to hear the details of why you're doing this. It seems like a rogue action to me. We know you did something with Tiffany Bryant."

Mr. Carruthers had a laugh like a braying donkey. "You're involved with this, too, Mr. Alexander. You probably need a lawyer yourself. As for Miss Bryant, it was my duty to get her to safety."

"Be careful, Miguel," I warned. "I think he might be crazy. Maybe he killed Jordan."

"Those are some wild accusations," Mr. Carruthers said. "We'll figure out what's going on and why you two seem to be at the heart of it. I've been thinking that you didn't just find Phillips's body, Miss Chase. Maybe you and your father murdered him."

"I was wrong, Miguel. He's completely crazy. Maybe you should ram the car into a brick wall. We'll be protected by the air bags. He'll go through the window."

Miguel looked at me like I was crazy. "Zoe, now might not be the best time to say something like that."

"When else will I say it? It's too late after he kills us. You know he's not working with the police. He's probably the killer."

"I have ID." Mr. Carruthers fussed with his jacket and pants trying to fish his ID from a pocket.

The small gun went slack in his hand as he grew upset because he couldn't find his ID. I gathered my courage and grabbed the gun from him, turning it around so the barrel was facing him.

—

Miguel pulled to the side of the road with a loud screech of the tires. "Zoe! What the hell are you doing?"

"Saving our lives." I gulped hard, but not as hard as my heart was pounding. "What should we do now?"

Miguel glanced back at Mr. Carruthers. "Call the police."

"I *am* the police," Mr. Carruthers hissed.

"You were just the food inspector," I reminded him. "How can we believe what you say now?"

He finally managed to get his badge out and flashed it at us. "There you go. Now give me my gun back before I charge both of you with assault on an officer and kidnapping."

"Is that real?" I asked Miguel, who was examining the ID.

"It looks real to me, Zoe."

"You better believe it's real." Mr. Carruthers nodded and reached for his gun.

"Not so fast." I took out my cell phone and called Patti Latoure. "Let's get someone else's opinion. After all, you lied to me and held a gun on us. I think that might be kidnapping. And what did you do to Tiffany?"

"You're going to regret this," he warned. "I've been making sure Miss Bryant is safe on the commissioner's direct orders."

"I don't believe you." I hoped Patti would pick up. "I'm not handing this gun back to you until we're sure who you are."

"Detective Patti Latoure."

"Patti, we're over here on First Street near where the commissioner's daughter lives. A man who's been posing as a food inspector got in Miguel's car and was holding a gun on us. He says he's a police officer, but you can understand why I don't believe him."

"Stay right where you are, Zoe. I'll find you. And don't give the man his gun back until you hear from me."

When she'd hung up, I smiled at Mr. Carruthers. "I guess

now we'll find out the truth. I hope for your sake that you really are a police officer."

"You'd better hope I'm not," he threatened. "Because if I am, you're both going to jail. And I am. A police officer, that is. So you're in big trouble."

"We'll see."

It didn't take long for Patti to reach us. She came down the street with her siren on and lights flashing. She parked her car in front of Miguel's Mercedes and jumped out with a gun in her hand.

"Are you okay, Zoe? Miguel?" she asked right away after taking the gun from me. "Get out and tell me what happened."

"I can tell you what happened," Mr. Carruthers said from the backseat. "These two held a gun on me and threatened me. Cuff both of them, Detective."

Patti gave him a snarky look. "Pipe down back there. I don't even recognize you. I'll hear what you have to say after what they've told me."

Miguel handed her the badge Mr. Carruthers had given him. "It looks real, but with everything that's been going on, we're not sure if we can trust it."

Patti took the badge and perused it. "Officer Carruthers." She glanced in the car again. "You're undercover?"

"That's right. Now arrest them, if you please."

"Not so fast. Let's hear it, Zoe. What happened?"

I told her about Harry the hot dog man seeing Tiffany leave the food truck rally with Mr. Carruthers. "She's been gone since then. I thought I should check on her. I knew there was something weird about Mr. Carruthers. He didn't know how to do a health inspection. He was at my place at four A.M. Then he showed up at my food truck and again didn't know what he was doing. Even after I'd passed inspection he was hanging out at the diner and at the food truck rally. Harry said he was watching the Biscuit Bowl."

Miguel shrugged when she looked at him. "I offered to help her get a restraining order against him since his behavior was so odd. Zoe went to check on Tiffany, and while she was gone, Carruthers put a gun in my face and got in the backseat to wait for her."

Patti looked at the badge again. "I'm going to call this in. It looks real enough, but there are some good forgeries out there. His behavior sounds strange to me, too. And I think I know almost everyone at the department, but I don't recognize him."

"Let me out of here," Mr. Carruthers demanded. "You are in so much trouble—all of you. You don't know me, Detective, because I report directly to the commissioner."

"That may be true, but it will only take a moment to verify. I'll be right back."

Miguel and I stood at the front of the car and watched her call in the information.

"Can he really arrest us if he's a police officer?" I asked quietly.

He shrugged. "Theoretically, it's possible. But I think we have a good case to support our actions. We'll see what happens."

Patti came back a few minutes later and opened the back door for Mr. Carruthers—apparently *Officer* Carruthers. "I'm sorry about the misunderstanding, Officer. But even if you're undercover, your actions are irregular."

Officer Carruthers climbed out of the backseat. Patti handed him his ID and gun. "If you won't arrest them, Detective, I will."

"What are you arresting them for?" she asked.

"Kidnapping, assault on an officer, assault with a deadly weapon. Possible involvement in the death of Jordan Phillips. And a few charges I haven't fully formalized as yet."

Patti smiled, but it was only a polite gesture. "From what

they told me downtown, you're new, Officer. I don't know why they've had you out on an undercover assignment already, but you've botched it. We're all going to headquarters to hash this out. No one is arresting anyone until after that. Do you want to ride with me?"

"I have my own vehicle parked around back." Officer Carruthers gave us all a dirty look and then stalked off to his car.

"Patti, maybe you should check on Tiffany," I suggested. "She sounded like she was crying, and she wouldn't let me in. I don't know if Carruthers did something to her or what."

"Okay, Zoe. Let's do that. Officer Carruthers is legit. I don't understand why he's out here yet, but I'm sure he'll meet us at headquarters, if nothing else so he can rub our noses in it."

We went back up to the apartment door. I stepped aside so Patti could ring the bell. Tiffany answered, and Patti told her who she was.

"Are you all right, Miss Bryant? Do you need assistance?"

Tiffany sniffled. "No. I'm fine. Are you the new duty officer?"

Patti looked at me and then answered, "I'm not here to take over your security, Miss Bryant, but I'd feel a lot better if you'd buzz me in."

The buzzer sounded, and I pushed open the inside door. Miguel had waited by the car, but I wanted to go upstairs with Patti.

"I'm not taking you up there, Zoe. I don't know what's going on yet, and I don't want to make it any worse if what I think is happening is really happening. Just wait by the car with Miguel, please."

"All right."

"She didn't want your help, did she?" Miguel asked when I went to stand by him.

"Nope. I think Officer Carruthers is the real deal and

we're about to get our butts whipped, as Grandma Chase used to say. I'm sorry. I didn't know."

He put his arm around me. "If that's the case, we'll handle it. It's definitely not routine."

A few minutes later, Patti came back downstairs with a thunderous frown on her face. "I don't know how you manage it, Zoe, but you've done it again."

THIRTY-THREE

We waited impatiently at police headquarters as Patti and Officer Carruthers disappeared into an office with two other men in suits. I kept glancing at the big clock on the wall as time went slowly toward dinner at the Biscuit Bowl.

What was I going to do? If there was no food by six, I'd have to close the food truck. The new PR woman wasn't as strict as Tiffany, but there was no way to fake having food.

I got on the phone with Uncle Saul and told him my dilemma.

"Don't worry about a thing. I'll get Ollie, and we'll take care of it."

"We need ice and Cokes, too," I reminded him. "I'm so sorry to put this on you. I'm afraid Miguel is stuck here, too. I'm sure Ollie won't mind cooking, but don't let him over spice the food. You're probably better at making biscuits. You know my recipe."

He laughed. "I should. I was the first one you tested it

on, and I think the basic recipe came from Grandma Chase, right?"

"Yes. I've added my own ingredients, but you know about those."

"Don't worry. Everything will be fine. We'll have the Biscuit Bowl up and running by six. You just get out of whatever mess you're in with the police."

"Thank you. I'm so glad you're here."

I pressed end call on the phone and looked at the clock again. It was four thirty. I hoped there was enough time to get everything set up. If not, I only had myself to blame.

We waited until a little after five before another officer came to get us. He led us through a maze of desks and cubicles until we reached a large conference room.

"Looks like whatever is going on has been settled between Patti and Carruthers," Miguel observed. "They're both in there."

"What does a lawyer do who needs a lawyer?"

"He has a good friend who's also a lawyer." He squeezed my hand. "Don't worry. We'll be fine."

The officer opened the door for us into the conference room and told us to take a seat. Patti nodded as we sat by her. Officer Carruthers stared at us as though we were wanted criminals.

I was surprised when Commissioner Sloane entered the room with another man and woman. They all sat at the big table. The officer who'd shown us into the room closed the door and stood in front of it.

"Well, this is a fine mess we're in." Commissioner Sloane cleared his throat and frowned at me. "I believe you're responsible for this, Miss Chase. What part of *stay out of it* didn't you understand? Because of you, my daughter's safety may be jeopardized."

Miguel held my hand under the table, but he didn't sit idly

by as the commissioner talked trash about me. "I'm sorry, Commissioner Sloane, but I fail to see how Miss Chase has endangered anyone's life. Perhaps you'd like to explain."

The commissioner rolled his eyes. "Great! Who let a lawyer into the conversation?"

"Apologies, sir," Patti said. "But if Zoe knows what's going on, so do all of her friends and family."

I started to object. What was wrong with sharing things with friends and family, anyway? Miguel squeezed my hand again and almost imperceptibly shook his head.

"So all my machinations have been for nothing." Commissioner Sloane let his hands fall on the table with a thud.

"Maybe you should explain," Miguel suggested.

"I was hoping to get away from this until we found the killer." Commissioner Sloane shook his head. "I guess this is it."

He went on to explain that they'd received a death threat against him and Tiffany before the masquerade ball. "We believe Jordan Phillips heard about this threat somehow and was following up on it. That's all the information we currently have. The investigation has led us to believe that Phillips was killed in pursuit of the story. After that event, the killer seemed to give up, perhaps fearing he'd be caught."

That explained a lot for me. I knew Jordan wasn't suicidal. What a relief this would be for his grandfather and his father.

"I've been keeping the whole thing under wraps," the commissioner went on. "I was hoping the killer would try again. I wanted him to use me as a target, but then we received a death threat against Tiffany. I wanted everything to stay quiet as far as the media is concerned, so I used a retired officer to keep an eye on her."

He nodded toward Officer Carruthers, who smiled like the Cheshire cat. "Exactly," he said.

"But if he was guarding Tiffany," I asked, "why was he posing as an obnoxious health inspector?"

"Because we thought you, Miss Chase, or someone with you could be the killer. We've kept a close eye on you since the masquerade."

"Did that include using Bennett Phillips to pose as the ghost of Old Slac?" I wondered.

Commissioner Sloane's vision went from the woman on his right to the man on his left. Both of them shook their heads and went back to searching through documents in front of them.

"No. I can only assume Mr. Phillips also believed you were part of understanding what happened to Jordan, Miss Chase," the commissioner explained.

"And what about my father being attacked at the bar? Was that part of this, too?"

Again, the looks passed between the three people at the other end of the table. This time, the woman whispered something to Commissioner Sloane.

"I've been advised that the police have investigated the attack on you father. There seems to be no correlation between the events. As you know, we sometimes encounter late-night brawls during carnival."

I didn't agree with him, but I didn't say so. I needed to keep the subject in focus—what was going to happen to me and Miguel?

"What now?" Miguel asked him.

Commissioner Sloane shrugged. "We have to replace Officer Carruthers and find somewhere else for my daughter to stay until this is over. I hope I can rely on your discretion not to share this information with family and friends. Right now, a second threat against me is the best way for us to have the killer reveal himself."

"What about your belief that Miss Chase is somehow involved in Jordan's death?" Miguel asked.

The woman seated beside the commissioner glanced up. "We have no evidence that shows any participation on Miss Chase's part in this terrible tragedy."

Now that my name was cleared and it didn't look as though they were going to arrest me and Miguel, I had another question. "What about Dylan Medlin?"

"Who?" Commissioner Sloane asked.

The woman beside him whispered something, and he nodded.

"Oh yes. The other reporter at the *Mobile Times* who died. Is that right?"

"Yes. Was he killed as part of the conspiracy? Because when I spoke with him before his death, he claimed to know who the person was that was threatening you and Tiffany. I tried to get Detective Latoure quickly enough, but we found him dead in his apartment."

Commissioner Sloane's frown deepened. He looked at his advisors again. Both of them shrugged. "Come on now. This food truck driver knows more about this than we do?"

"If I may," Patti intervened, "I was with Zoe after she found Mr. Medlin's body at his apartment. I didn't have a chance to question him. The information he gave her was sketchy. I filed a report on the incident. I guess it didn't make it to your desk, sir."

"What exactly did he tell you, Miss Chase?"

"Dylan said he'd overheard a conversation at the newspaper office that made him think someone was going to try to kill you. He told Jordan because Dylan wasn't allowed to do anything but the garden feature for the paper. He thought if he shared a byline with Jordan it would help his career. But he didn't go into any other details." Commissioner Sloane drummed his fingers on the highly polished wood table. "I can't believe no one thought this was relevant. Why didn't I receive this report?"

The man at his side got up and left the room—maybe to find the report. I couldn't be sure.

"We'll look into this, Miss Chase." Commissioner Sloane focused on Patti. "Was this other reporter also shot, Detective Latoure?"

"No, sir. He appeared to have hanged himself. His body is at the morgue now awaiting autopsy."

"Get me those results," he barked at the woman who sat beside him. "Do I have to do everything myself? Maybe I should hire Miss Chase to get results."

I knew that was rhetorical. He didn't really want to hire me, and I certainly didn't want to work for him.

"Needless to say, Miss Chase, you have to stay away from this—no matter what else happens. I hope that's understood. I don't want to hear from Officer Carruthers's replacement that you've been snooping around again."

"I don't really feel like I've been snooping," I countered. "All I've been trying to do is keep my food truck going. Bits and pieces keep coming to me."

He nodded. "I know all about Chef Art and Tucker Phillips. I'm sure if you tell them you can't be involved with this any further, they'll understand."

"I believe a little gratitude is in order as well," Miguel said. "Miss Chase has brought several important matters to the police in this investigation. I wouldn't say she's been snooping so much as doing your job."

Commissioner Sloane accepted the criticism. "I do appreciate your help, Miss Chase. All the citizens of this city should be as well-informed as you."

"Thanks." I was ready to leave.

The commissioner and his assistant left first, followed by Officer Carruthers as he tried to get the commissioner's attention.

Patti smiled at me. "That worked out okay. You were lucky. So was I. Don't get involved again."

"I won't," I promised. "And I won't tell anyone what was said here, although you hurt my feelings the way you said I'm a gossip or something."

"I'm sorry. Don't be upset. I was really just telling him the way it is. You're not required to keep your mouth shut around your friends. Don't worry about it."

Miguel shook her hand and thanked her.

"I hope to grab a promotion out of this," she confided. "Maybe with going over Dylan's stuff again, I can find more information. See you two later."

As Miguel and I were walking back to the car, I wondered, "Why did they think I might be involved in Jordan's murder? Was it just because I found his body?"

"I'm sure it was a combination of that and your name popping up all the time in the investigation. I have a feeling Officer Carruthers kept them up-to-date on everything you did."

"You're probably right." I looked at the clock on the dash of the Mercedes. There was only forty-five minutes until the Biscuit Bowl had to be ready to serve dinner. I called Uncle Saul and told him we were leaving police headquarters.

"Good deal," he said. "You two stop and get the ice and Cokes. Ollie and I will meet you at the Biscuit Bowl. Everything okay?"

"Yes. Everything's fine. I'll explain it all when I see you."

When I was off the phone, Miguel frowned. "But you aren't going to tell him everything, right? You promised Commissioner Sloane you'd keep it quiet."

"Who are Uncle Saul, Ollie, and Delia going to tell? I

won't say anything to Chef Art or Tucker. That's what I was talking about."

"I don't think that's what he meant, Zoe."

"That's how I interpreted it, Miguel. *You* know. They should know, too."

He sighed but didn't say anything else about it. We went to the store to get Cokes and ice. We almost made it to the municipal parking lot without getting behind any of the celebrations until we hit a small unplanned parade.

The people in the parade—not more than twenty of them—carried banners from the Mobile Garden Club. Some were dressed like trees with flowering limbs. Some carried azalea branches and were covered with flowers. There were several wagons pulling children who carried small flowers they used as throws for people on the street.

"That's really pretty," I remarked as we waited for them to pass. "It makes a lot more sense than some of the parades."

"How are you doing on flyers?" Miguel asked.

"I'm not sure. I'll take a look when we get there. Thanks for reminding me."

We found a place to park near the food trucks and got everything out of the trunk. Uncle Saul and Ollie had put the food away. Delia was absent, but Uncle Saul said she would be back soon.

"What's for supper?" I asked before I went to check on her.

Ollie got a devilish expression on his face. "I took the last of the chicken out of the freezer and made Brunswick stew. Try some."

He put some of the stew on a spoon and stuck it in my mouth. It felt as though there was a four-alarm fire in my tongue. "Uncle Saul—you were supposed to keep Ollie away from the hot stuff."

The two men exchanged glances, and both of them grinned.

"I was the one who put the spices in," he said. "I can't

believe you think that's too spicy, Zoe girl. You're getting bland."

I took exception to that remark, but I waited for a better time to argue the point. "What about the sweet?"

"We made a big batch of blueberry trifle with the blueberries we found in the freezer," Ollie said. "And no spices in that."

The two men did a high five. I realized that I couldn't complain. They'd saved me from being kicked out of the rally. I was grateful. "Thanks so much."

"I hope you have something sufficiently lurid in exchange to tell us." Uncle Saul rubbed his hands together.

"It's pretty good." I glanced out the customer window and saw Miguel setting up the cooler outside. "I might have to wait until Miguel leaves to tell you. You'll understand why when you hear it. I'm going to check on Crème Brûlée. I know he can be a handful."

I found my cat and Delia by one of the park benches. He was rolling on his back hissing at her and slapping at her with his paws.

"You silly cat," she said. "You may not have another chance to get out until midnight. You need some exercise."

Crème Brûlée didn't care.

"Thanks for trying to help with him." I took the leash from her.

"I'm glad to see you. This cat is so stubborn."

"I know. I've spoiled him." I picked him up. She laughed. "I guess Ollie and Saul are set up. It's almost supper time."

"Yep. We're good here if you want to take off. Tomorrow is Lundi Gras. It's almost over. Have you heard from your sister?"

"She's doing fine now that she has Mama to wait on her. Thanks for asking. I think I'll go home. But call me if you need me."

"Thanks, Delia. See you later."

I scolded Crème Brûlée on the way over to the little patch of woods. I wondered if I'd see Harry there with Balzac. It would be better if that didn't happen. I could already see customers starting to wander into the parking lot. Some were in elaborate costumes, dressed like Marie Antoinette and other beautiful women from history. The men were in pink satin coats with knee breeches and powdered white wigs. All of them wore masks. No doubt they were from one of the krewes or secret societies.

I put Crème Brûlée down in the leaves and pine needles. He started sniffing around right away. That was always a good sign.

I looked up as someone else approached us. It was Tucker minus Chef Art for a change. He didn't know what had transpired at the police station today, so he wouldn't know to ask me about it. I felt safe.

Not that I would've told him, anyway. I'd promised, after all.

"Evening, Zoe." He gazed around the parking lot, which was starting to get busy. "Just checking on you, making sure everything is okay."

"I'm fine, thanks. How is Bennett doing?"

"He's improving. He might be in therapy for a while. He's having trouble walking and talking. The doctors aren't sure yet if it's permanent."

"I'm sorry. I hope he gets better soon." I smiled at his blue suit. "I guess you were working at the newspaper today."

"Yes. I've been out of it for so long. It's been a learning curve going back. Bennett has always done a good job. I had high hopes that Jordan would do the same or better."

"I know."

"The newspaper game has changed, anyway. I don't know how long the paper will manage to stay open. It's amazing to me that folks like Commissioner Sloane can do such a poor job running this city and people don't want to read about it."

"I guess they'd rather hear about it on TV."

He looked down at Crème Brûlée. "I hear you had a meeting with the commissioner at police headquarters today. What was that all about? Did he mention Jordan?"

THIRTY-FOUR

How does he know?

I guessed it was part of running a newspaper. Someone probably saw me go in there, or he had someone on the police payroll. I wasn't fluent in how newspapers got their information, but it was like Dylan overhearing a threat against the commissioner.

"They accused me of messing up their work and told me to stay out of it," I said. It was the truth but not the whole truth. I hoped he'd be happy with it.

He wasn't.

"I've heard that the commissioner's daughter—the one who dated Jordan—has been hidden away somewhere. Anything about that?"

"No." I picked up Crème Brûlée. "I have to get back to the Biscuit Bowl. It's about time to feed the masses again. I'm sorry I can't help you more."

"That's okay. I hear things. I'll pick it up as I go along. See you later, Zoe." He scratched behind Crème Brûlée's ears. "Have a good one."

I didn't like lying to Tucker. The commissioner should've been honest with him and Bennett about Jordan's death. The police had lied from the beginning. It wasn't right, even though I could understand why they felt they had to do it.

Ollie was at the window taking orders after I got Crème Brûlée set up in front and had petted his belly a little. Miguel was getting plates and forks ready for the rush. Uncle Saul was frying biscuit bowls.

I walked into the kitchen and smiled at them. "You guys are the best. I couldn't have done this without you. It's so wonderful to have you on my side."

"Never mind all that," Ollie said. "Dish about what happened at police headquarters before we get too busy to talk."

"And it better make working with Ollie worthwhile," Uncle Saul said with a grin and a wink.

To make them happy, I told them exactly what had been said after finding out that Mr. Carruthers was guarding Tiffany and that he was a retired police officer and not a health inspector.

"That was sneaky," Uncle Saul said. "What are they doing with the girl now?"

"Moving her somewhere else," I replied. "They didn't share that information with me."

"Don't forget the part about you swearing you wouldn't tell anyone else about what happened," Miguel reminded me.

"I didn't say that. And I wasn't talking about the people in this kitchen." I filled two biscuit bowls with Brunswick stew. They were hot from the fryer. "I saw Tucker while I was walking Crème Brûlée and didn't tell him anything. That was keeping my word to Commissioner Sloane."

Ollie grinned. "I'll bet that was hard to do."

"I hated it. He and Bennett deserve the truth. It's wrong to keep them in the dark this way."

"They'll tell them the truth when it's over and the killer is caught," Miguel said. "That's their job."

I didn't like that answer, and I was considering telling Bennett and Tucker the truth when I saw them next. I didn't really care that I'd promised not to. I didn't trust the commissioner to tell them what had happened to Jordan despite his promise. It seemed to me that he'd done a lot of covering up, maybe for the Mistics of Time. Maybe just for himself.

I didn't have much time to think about it after that. We were so busy that it was all we could do to keep up. I thought the crowds were getting bigger as we approached the end of carnival. People were hungrier, louder, and drunker. I was glad Ollie was at the window.

We had several cases of bad manners that night. One of them included a young man spraying the side of the Biscuit Bowl with a can of Coke after he'd shaken it. He was lucky he didn't hit Ollie with it. I don't think I could have stopped Ollie from going after him.

A marching band dressed in red and gold uniforms entertained us for over an hour. They danced and encouraged others to dance with them. The parking lot was full of people dancing and singing.

"Now that's what I call carnival." Ollie grinned as we all watched from the service window. "Care for a turn, Miss Zoe?"

Because of the crowds dancing, customers had stopped eating to watch. I took his hand and we went out the back door. The music was still playing as we danced under the stars.

"You're a good dancer," I yelled over the music and singing.

"You better believe it. I've got it going on."

He twirled me, and I laughed breathlessly. Ollie did a deep dip, and I looked into his wonderful brown eyes.

"I think this is where I cut in," Miguel said. "You're needed at the window, big guy."

Of course that meant we were all needed. Customers had decided to start eating again. Miguel and I danced for a few minutes before heading back. He took my hand in his as we finally stopped. "Do you think Ollie has a thing for you?"

"Ollie?" I looked at the service window where he was taking an order and yelling it back at Uncle Saul. "No. Why do you ask?"

"No reason really." He shrugged. "Just thinking."

The rush was on again. Hundreds of people had danced and sang their way into being hungry and thirsty. I deep-fried so many biscuit bowls that they were actually starting to look unappetizing to me.

I was horrified to even think of it.

The night stretched on past midnight, and I began to worry about the food. We were almost out of biscuit bowls, and the white icing was gone. The berries kind of looked naked in the biscuit without it.

"Almost out of stew," Uncle Saul called out. "Want me to run and get Chinese takeout? We could fill up the biscuit bowls with it."

"We won't have any biscuit bowls to fill," I told him. "They've almost eaten us out of food."

"Want me to shut down the window?" Ollie asked.

"No. Let's stay until we're out. Then we'll go."

The berries ran out first. The stew was next, followed by handing out the last biscuit bowl. There were still three people in line at the window. I told Ollie to give each of them a rain check for free biscuit bowls the next day.

The waiting customers seemed pleased with that. Behind

them was only the empty parking lot. Fireworks lit up the sky, and music filled the night.

Ollie closed the window. "That's it."

"I hope Fat Monday isn't worse." Uncle Saul rubbed his hands across his face. "I'm sorry, honey, but I'm beginning to hate the smell of fried biscuits."

I laughed. "Me, too. It must be time to go home. We'll see what happens tomorrow."

Miguel took Uncle Saul and Ollie home after we'd finished cleaning. He was coming back to spend the night with me. I was forcing myself to come up with a shopping list even though the mention of food was making me gag.

"What about eggs?" I asked Crème Brûlée as he played with his ball in the front of the food truck. "I could get a lot of eggs and sausage. Ollie could throw in some peppers. I might be able to make that last all day."

He meowed loudly and lumbered to his feet, pushing his head against the door.

"You have to go out, right? I guess I shouldn't be surprised." I rubbed his head. "But you've been a very good boy all this time. I tell everyone else thanks for helping out, but I don't tell you, do I?"

He purred for a moment and then started making less pleasant sounds. I knew he really had to go. I put on his harness and leash and picked him up to take him into the wooded area.

Behind us was the sound of the other food truck owners cleaning and getting ready for the next day. Morning would come quickly. Miguel and I would be lucky if we slept for a few hours before getting up and getting ready for Fat Monday.

There was that old owl calling from a tree. I couldn't see him in the dark, but I could hear him now that the music and people had left the parking lot. It seemed odd that he should be out there in the heart of the city. But nature seemed to know no bounds on sharing her wild creatures. There had been more than one report of a skunk in Mobile. I was glad it was an owl with me instead of a smelly skunk.

Crème Brûlée started playing with some leaves that blew across the pavement. There was a gentle breeze that was moving the clouds around in the sky. It was such a peaceful night. I grabbed my cat and hugged him to me, burying my face in his soft fur.

I turned around and looked up. I had one brief glimpse of Tucker standing in front of me, and then something hard hit me in the back of the head and I slumped to the ground.

THIRTY-FIVE

I woke up in the backseat of a car.

It was still dark outside. My head hurt and my stomach was queasy.

I felt around, but Crème Brûlée wasn't with me. I panicked and sat up quickly. It was a regrettable decision. I almost passed out again. I felt the back of my head. There was a big goose egg there. I winced when I touched it.

"Tucker?" I whispered. There was no dash light, but I could see there were two people in the car with me.

"Welcome back, Zoe," he said with a smile in his voice. "How's the head?"

"It hurts. What happened? Where's Crème Brûlée?"

"Bennett finally worked up enough courage to actually accomplish something. Your cat is still in the woods, I imagine. Unless he's wandered off by now."

"I'm so sorry, Zoe." Bennett's voice was tearful. "I didn't want it to come to this, believe me."

I put my hand to my throbbing head. "Come to what? Where are you taking me? My cat better be there when I get back."

Tucker chuckled. "I don't think you're in any position to make demands. Sit back and enjoy the ride."

"What do you want?" I couldn't imagine why the two of them had done this.

"We want to know where the commissioner's daughter is being kept," Tucker said. "It's hard to kill someone when you don't know where they are."

I couldn't be hearing right. It had to be leftover confusion from being whacked in the head. "Why do you want to kill Tiffany? Have you lost your mind?"

"I've tried to reason with him," Bennett said. "He made me get out of the hospital against my doctor's orders. He's lost it, Zoe. He killed Jordan."

"That was a mistake." Tucker's voice was thick with emotion. "You know I didn't mean to kill him. I thought he was Chadwick Sloane. The commissioner and I were supposed to meet that night in the garden. He was supposed to be dressed as Death. Instead, it was Jordan."

Tucker's voice cracked when he said his grandson's name. Bennett sobbed.

"What were you trying to do that night?" I was horrified at what I heard.

"Sloane has been involved in some shady dealings the last few years," Tucker said. "He was willing to make a trade for the proof I had of what he'd done. I was going to be a million dollars richer."

"But you weren't supposed to kill anyone," Bennett said. "You were just supposed to get the money to cover my gambling debts. That was it, Dad. It was never supposed to end in murder."

"He grabbed the gun, son. I didn't know it was Jordan.

I'd only brought the gun in case Sloane tried something stupid. It was a terrible mistake."

"So why make it worse by killing Dylan?" I wished I had a Coke and some Tylenol. "I'm assuming you killed him."

"Dylan was stupid," Tucker snarled. "He overheard Bennett and me talking but didn't realize who we were. He was responsible for Jordan being at the ball—for getting him to look into the 'story.' Since the police wanted to call Jordan's death a suicide, I decided to do the same with Dylan."

"And Tiffany?" I tried to focus, watching the street to figure out where we were going. "Why kill Tiffany?"

"I'm taking away the one person Chadwick Sloane loves," Tucker said coldly. "Just like he took away the one person I loved."

"What about me, Dad?" Bennett questioned. "Have you ever loved me?"

"You were always a disappointment," Tucker said. "Gambling. Womanizing. I've had to bail you out so many times. This was going to be the last time. You were supposed to retire after I paid your debts, and Jordan would have taken over the paper. He could've put us back on top again. Now he's dead. I think we have to kill Tiffany just to make things even."

My brain was reeling, but I recognized the familiar road to the docks. I could only guess what Tucker had in store for me after I'd told him what Commissioner Sloane had said. I couldn't tell him where they'd moved Tiffany since I had no idea.

I guessed my suicide would have something to do with drowning.

What could I say or do to make him change his mind? No one would even realize that Crème Brûlée was missing if Tucker killed me. He'd be out there on the streets with no one to help him. I couldn't let that happen. He hadn't done anything wrong.

Maybe I could keep them talking and appeal to Bennett, who seemed to be an unwilling participant in the events.

"Why did you decide to dress up like the ghost of Old Slac?" I asked Bennett.

"I was trying to warn you and your father away from all this. I didn't want anything to happen to Ted. I knew Dad was going to go after anyone who got involved. Why didn't you pay attention, Zoe? You wouldn't be here now if you had."

"Was it you who attacked my father with a knife?"

"Are you kidding?" Tucker laughed. "I had to do it myself. I thought your father would be a problem, Zoe. I didn't realize how much worse you'd be than him."

"You don't have to be so nasty to her, Dad!"

"Shut up, Bennett." Tucker parked near the docks where cargo was unloaded from ships on the bay. The lights weren't as good here as they were near the area where they let off the cruise ship passengers. "You had no business getting in my way. You've always been soft and stupid. I wish Jordan had been my son. How he came from a loser like you is beyond me."

"Thank you for trying, anyway, Bennett." Was it possible to play the two men off each other? "At least my dad is safe. I appreciate that."

Tucker turned off the engine and got out of the car. I could see the outline of the gun in his hand as he opened the back door. "Get out, Zoe."

"Can one of you please call Miguel and tell him to look for Crème Brûlée?" I asked as I got out. "You don't have any reason to hurt him."

"That doesn't sound unreasonable," Bennett said as he got out. "I don't see why we can't do that."

Tucker shook his head. "We're not alerting someone that we've got you, Zoe. I've killed two people. Do you think I care what happens to your cat?"

He motioned with the gun, and I moved away from the car. Bennett was standing close to me. I took a step nearer to him.

"Tell me where Tiffany is." Tucker leveled the gun at my head.

"Can we let her go if she tells us?" Bennett asked. "She'll keep quiet."

"She won't keep quiet," Tucker said. "Tell us, Zoe. Where is Tiffany?"

"You're going to kill me, anyway. You won't help my cat. Why should I tell you anything?" I was scared, but I knew I had to stall. I couldn't just tell him that I didn't know. I put my arm through Bennett's and clung to him, whispering, "Help me, Bennett. Don't let him kill me."

"Really, Dad," Bennett began. "Have her tell you where to find the girl and then let her go. That gives her motive to tell you. You could go kill her and then come back. Zoe would be right here with me."

"Don't be stupid." Tucker's voice was full of exasperation. "Get away from her before you get hurt. Quit fooling around, Zoe, and tell us where to find Tiffany."

"What's in it for me?" I asked daringly.

"I won't shoot you in the kneecaps before I kill you," Tucker promised.

"You won't get away with more than one or two shots out here without someone showing up or calling the police," I argued. "At least let me tell Miguel to look for Crème Brûlée. Then I'll tell you what I know."

"I could call him to make sure she doesn't say anything she shouldn't," Bennett pleaded. "We could at least do this one thing for her."

Tucker pointed the gun at his son. "I told you to shut up. We wouldn't be here—Jordan would still be alive—if it wasn't for you. I wish I'd killed *you* that night instead of him."

Bennett started crying again. "You don't mean that. I've made some mistakes, but I've always done what you told me to. You don't want me to die. I'm your only son."

"Then for once in your life have a backbone. Get her to tell us where Tiffany is."

Bennett stared at me. "I'm so sorry about this, Zoe. I wish I could help. I don't know what to do."

"That's okay." I put my hand on his and maneuvered myself between him and the car. "I know you've done the best you could. Your father is crazy."

"Now look what you've done," Tucker said. "Get her out from behind you. Do you want to see this finished or not?"

"I do want to see it finished, Dad." Bennett took a step toward his father. "Give me the gun. Let's turn ourselves in to the police. No one else needs to die."

"Useless!" Tucker pistol-whipped his son.

Bennett dropped to his knees with a groan, leaving me exposed again.

"Tell me what I need to know. There are worse things than dying." Tucker stepped toward me. I thought it was over.

As he approached, walking close to his son, Bennett grabbed him. "Run, Zoe. Get help."

The two men fell to the ground wrestling for control of the gun. I knew I should run away, but I stood there watching in fascinated terror. I willed my legs to move or my hand to take out my cell phone. Nothing happened. I couldn't look away from them.

A shot rang out followed by another a few seconds later. I couldn't tell in the dim light what had happened. Had Bennett shot his father? Or was it the other way around?

Tucker and Bennett fell back on the pitted blacktop. Neither one moved.

I ran to Bennett. He took my hand and tried to speak. His eyes closed, and his head turned to the side. He had saved my life by rebelling against his father. I cried, knowing I couldn't help him in return. At least he was free of the demons that had ruined his life.

I grabbed the gun from Tucker. His eyes were open but would never see again. There was a large spreading stain covering his chest.

At that moment it was like a spell had been broken. I grabbed my cell phone from the pocket of my jeans. They hadn't even thought to take it from me. I called 911 and then Miguel.

"Where are you, Zoe? I've had security out looking for you."

"Never mind," I said. "Look for Crème Brûlée. I left him in that little patch of trees down from the Biscuit Bowl. If you don't see him right away, find Harry the hot dog vendor. He knows where I've been walking him."

"Zoe—what happened? Are you okay?"

"Please, Miguel." I was crying by this time. "Find Crème Brûlée. Please."

THIRTY-SIX

I sat in the police car while the paramedics and police officers did their job. I held my cell phone, hoping to hear from Miguel. There was still no word.

Patti Latoure showed up, this time accompanied by Detective Frolick. I'd already given the officers an idea of what had happened. I told the story again to the detectives.

"Let me call someone for you, Zoe," Patti said. "We can talk again tomorrow."

"I'm glad you aren't hurt, Miss Chase," Detective Frolick said.

"Thanks." I looked at my cell phone again. Still no word from Miguel.

I spoke privately to Patti about the things Tucker had said he had against Commissioner Sloane and told her that he'd said the commissioner would pay him to keep those things quiet. She said she'd look into those allegations, though I had no real hope it would go any further than me telling her here at the docks.

I finally called Cole. He wasn't on duty so there was no answer. I couldn't call Miguel for a ride. I had no choice but to call my mother.

Ten minutes later, my mother and father were both in the parking lot near the docks. My mother took the opportunity to grill the police about what had happened and why I was involved. I left the police car to sit in the Lexus with Daddy.

"Are you hurt, Zoe?" he asked. "Do you need a doctor?"

"No. I'm not hurt." But I was freezing inside, like I might never be warm again. "They were going to kill the commissioner's daughter. They left Crème Brûlée in the woods by the food truck."

My mother got in the car. I was surprised that she'd been driving again. "I'll take you back to the house, Zoe. You need somewhere to rest up and get over this. I'm sure this has been a shock to your system."

"Take me to the Biscuit Bowl. It's parked at the municipal parking lot. I need to help look for Crème Brûlée."

Daddy nodded, and my mother drove out of the parking lot.

"Did either of them survive?" Daddy asked her. "Tucker or Bennett?"

"No. The police said they killed each other." She glanced in the rearview mirror at me. "Zoe is the only one who knows what happened. They'll need her to give a detailed statement as soon as possible."

I knew my parents wanted to hear what had happened before I told the police. But my mind was focused on Crème Brûlée. We got to the food truck rally, and I jumped out of the car.

"Thanks for the ride. I'll call you soon."

Miguel had organized all the food truck drivers and

security officers into looking for Crème Brûlée. They'd even found large portable spotlights to illuminate the forest area.

But there was no sign of my cat. His harness and leash were on the ground by the bench where we'd been, but Crème Brûlée was gone.

We kept searching until it was light. Even my parents helped. I called the police. Miguel went to his office and printed up flyers that offered a reward. He'd taken a picture of Crème Brûlée from my cell phone and added it to the information about him. It was only thirty minutes before the trees and electric poles around the municipal parking lot were filled with flyers.

The officers who'd responded to my call took my information but didn't seem overly concerned about my missing cat. "They wander sometimes, don't they?" the officer asked. "I'm sure your cat will show up."

Somehow I made it through Lundi Gras and Fat Tuesday with no word about Crème Brûlée. We served dozens of scrambled eggs with sausage and peppers in the savory biscuit bowls on Monday. On Mardi Gras, we served Ollie's chili. The weather was cold and wet. It was the perfect meal for the end of carnival.

I breathed a sigh of relief when it was over and we were packing up the Biscuit Bowl to take it back to the diner. Miguel and I had gone out one more time to search for Crème Brûlée with no success. There was nothing else we could do.

Uncle Saul hugged me and introduced me again to Bonnie Tuttle, the wildlife officer from the Farmington area where they both lived. She looked so different out of uniform and wearing a nice blue skirt and sweater. Her blond hair was cut short, accentuating her high cheekbones and blue eyes.

"I thought Bonnie might be able to help look for Crème Brûlée." Uncle Saul winked at me. "She's the best tracker I know."

Bonnie blushed appealingly. "I'd like to help, Zoe. And I'd about decided that Saul had been gone long enough. It was hard work finding someone to take care of Alabaster, but here I am."

I agreed quickly. Whatever help she could be was great. And I liked the way she looked at Uncle Saul. I had great hope for their relationship.

Everything that had been kept secret since Jordan's death hit the media like a firestorm. The *Mobile Times* went into conservatorship until the board of directors could appoint a new managing editor. The police were widely criticized, and there were even some calls for Commissioner Sloane to step down.

I assumed Tiffany was out of hiding, although she didn't show up at the food truck rally again. I'd given a long statement to the police about Tucker's and Bennett's deaths. I knew it might not be the last statement, since they were relying on me to tie up all the loose ends for them.

I drove back to the diner and went into my makeshift bedroom that was filled with Crème Brûlée's toys and blankets. I cried on the first day of Lent after carnival and prayed that someone would find Crème Brûlée and return him to me.

> **Lost: One large tabby colored cat.**
>
> **His name tag says Crème Brûlée.**
>
> **He disappeared from the food truck rally area in the old municipal parking lot during carnival. Reward for his safe return.**
>
> **Please call Zoe Chase at the Biscuit Bowl.**

RECIPES FROM THE BISCUIT BOWL

Sazerac

Sazerac is a potent, alcohol-based drink that incorporates absinthe, an anise-flavored alcohol that is made from wormwood, green anise (where it gets its color), and sweet fennel. This drink was banned in the U.S. for many years because of fears that it caused hallucinations. American companies began making absinthe again in the 1990s when it was proven that the absinthe hysteria was groundless. Sazerac was a "bad" drink but never completely abandoned during carnival in New Orleans or Mobile. The green color is amazing, and so is the taste.

2 ounces of rye whiskey
½ tsp. maple syrup
3 dashes of Peychaud's Bitters
½ tsp. absinthe

Ice
Twist of lemon

Mix the whiskey, syrup, and bitters with ice in a shaker. The serving glass should be chilled first and then misted or coated with the absinthe. Leave what's left in the glass if you want it stronger or toss away what's left after coating. Strain the first mixture into the glass and add a lemon twist.

Plum Clafouti

Clafouti is a traditional French dessert made by pouring custard over fruit and baking. The fruit is quickly sautéed to create a flavorful syrup that sticks with the custard. You can make this dessert with any ripe fruit such as cherries, apricots, or plums.

1 tbsp. sliced almonds
7 tbsp. granulated sugar
2 tbsp. unsalted butter
3 to 5 medium red or black plums, pitted and quartered
1 tbsp. brandy
1 tbsp. amaretto
⅓ cup all-purpose flour
⅓ tsp. salt
3 large eggs
⅓ cup whole milk
¼ cup heavy cream
1 tsp. pure vanilla extract
Confectioners' sugar for dusting
9-inch pie pan

Preheat oven to 350° F.

Toast almonds in the oven until golden, 3 to 5 minutes. Transfer them to a small bowl to cool. Stir in 1 tbsp. of granulated sugar, and set aside.

Melt butter in a pan until bubbling and then add plums. Cook until they are soft on low heat, turning frequently. Reduce heat and sprinkle 3 tbsp. of granulated sugar over the fruit. Cook until the sugar melts into the fruit juices and becomes a syrup, about 1 to 2 minutes. Turn off the heat and stir in brandy and amaretto.

In a medium bowl, whisk together the flour, salt, and the remaining 3 tbsp. of sugar. Whisk in the eggs until the mixture is smooth. Mix in the milk, cream, and vanilla.

Pour the fruit and syrup into a 9-inch pie pan, spreading the fruit evenly. Pour the custard over the fruit. Bake until puffy with a set center, about 15 minutes. Sprinkle toasted almonds over the top halfway through baking.

Allow to cool 10 to 15 minutes. The center will fall. Dust with confectioners' sugar and serve.

Moon Pies

HOME RECIPE VERSION
These chewy, delicious, handheld sweets are necessary to any party during Mardi Gras.
MAKES ABOUT 1 DOZEN

Graham cracker crust:

Don't let anyone tell you these are just chocolate cookies with marshmallow in between. You have to have the graham cracker cookies inside!

    6 oz. unsalted butter
    ¼ cup light brown sugar, firmly packed
    ¼ cup Steen's cane syrup
    ¼ tsp. vanilla extract
    1½ cups all-purpose flour
    1¼ cups finely ground graham cracker crumbs
    ¾ tsp. kosher salt
    ½ tsp. baking powder
    ½ tsp. baking soda
    ¼ tsp. ground cinnamon
    2 tbsp. whole milk

Cream butter, brown sugar, syrup, and vanilla for 1 minute with an electric mixer. In a separate bowl, combine dry ingredients and mix with a fork. Add dry ingredients to butter mixture and mix on low speed, slowly stirring in milk. Continue mixing until the dough forms a ball. Wrap the dough in plastic and refrigerate for at least 1 hour.

Preheat oven to 325 degrees. Turn out chilled dough onto a flour-dusted surface. Roll until it is about ¼ inch thick. Cut cookies from dough using a 3-inch round cookie cutter. Place cookies on a parchment-lined baking sheet and bake 10 to 12 minutes. Cool.

Marshmallow filling

    2 packages (20 ounces) marshmallows
    ½ tsp. unsalted butter

Add marshmallows to a saucepan on low heat. Allow marshmallows to get soft and lose form. Take off heat and add unsalted butter. Whisk together until smooth.

Lightly coat a spoon with nonstick cooking spray and place about ¼ cup of marshmallow on each cool cookie. Use the remaining cookies as tops. Gently push down until you can see the marshmallow come just to the edge. Allow cookies to chill in refrigerator for at least 15 minutes.

Chocolate Coating

    1 lb. semisweet chocolate
    2 tbsp. vegetable oil or canola oil

Melt chocolate in the microwave. Remove bowl, let it cool slightly. Once the chocolate is warm, slowly whisk in oil. Allow chocolate to cool at room temperature for about 5 minutes.

Dip all of each chilled cookie in the chocolate. Use forks or tongs to gently lift the cookies out of the chocolate and onto waxed paper. Let stand until the chocolate hardens.

J. J. Cook is the national bestselling author of the Biscuit Bowl Food Truck Mysteries (*Death on Eat Street, Fry Another Day*) and the Sweet Pepper Fire Brigade Mysteries (*In Hot Water, Playing with Fire*).